OBSESSION is the third novel about Tarquin and Paul, Masters and slaves, friends and enemies in today's Leather BDSM world. A penetrating look at the dynamics of man-to-man sexual relationships, always evolving and diversifying, it provides a powerful and dramatic conclusion to the trilogy of LEATHER MASTERS and slaves.

Submissive Rufus is pulled between his television career and his turbulent sex life with his Master, Paul. When he runs back to England, it is Tarquin who must follow him and, accompanied by James Villier, his sexual rival and Rufus' agent, he tracks the boy down through his previous experiences as a "rent-boy".

In London, after a sex-filled night with James, Tarquin meets a potential new slave, who is to join the household back in Los Angeles.

But Rufus turns away from his Master, Paul, and now fixates on Tarquin. His obsession gradually becomes a mania that leads to the violent and shattering climax.

"Like all the hottest action movies, OBSESSION raises the temperature with the steamy booted Leathersex that Master Alex Ironrod packed into the first two volumes of his LEATHER MASTERS and slaves trilogy."

Tim Brough

Author of First Hand – an Erotic Guide to Fisting

OBSESSION
Leather Masters and slaves
Part Three

Alex Ironrod

Published by
MLR Press, LLC
3052 Gaines Waterport Rd.
Albion, NY 14411

Visit ManLoveRomance Press, LLC on the Internet:
www.mlrpress.com

Cover Art by Melody Pond
Editing by Mychael Black

Print format: ISBN# 978-1-64122-291-4
eBook format available

Second Edition Issued 2019

This book is
Dedicated to and
in Memory of
JOHN and HANK
Two good friends and
Fellow Leathermen,
long-time supporters of
my writing efforts

and to
MICHAEL
For his constant loving support and
efforts to improve my grammar

and to
my Friends at MLR PRESS,
an amazing team.
Laura for always leading us boldly forward
Kris for endless support of my efforts
Mychael for editing with such patience and skill
Melody for cover designs that match the spirit of my story.
Thank you for helping me to bring this series
to a successful conclusion

--for the moment.

TRADEMARK ACKNOWLEDGEMENT

The author acknowledges the trademark status and trademark owners of the following wordmarks mentioned in this work of fiction:

British Airways: British Airways Plc
Wesco Boots: West Coast Shoe Company
Dehner Boots: The Dehner Company, Inc
Chaps Inn: Chaps Inn
Gear Leather: Gear Leather & Fetish
665 Leather Store 665, Inc
Blackberry: BlackBerry Ltd
Pebbletec: Pebble Technology

IN THE BEGINNING

OBSESSION – LEATHER MASTERS and slaves continues the story of Tarquin Charlton and Paul Everest, together with their friends, their enemies, fellow Masters and slaves/boys. It follows on from **SUBMISSION** and **DOMINATION** as the next part of the series about BDSM love and lust in today's world. As before, the story is told by the two men in alternating chapters.

SUBMISSION was set primarily in Los Angeles and Palm Springs and began a journey of sexual discovery for two men whose lives became increasingly intertwined over two decades.

Tarquin's sexual training began at Yale University, where he learned to become a Top. Moving to Los Angeles as an entertainment lawyer, he started training his own slaves and was accepted into the 'Circle of Six', a powerful but discreet group of Leather Masters who helped one another both professionally and sexually.

Paul arrived in LA a largely innocent student, stumbling through a number of submissive relationships, until he was 'taken up' by Tarquin. The bonds that developed were strict but powerful, and all-encompassing. Paul gradually found himself in love with his Master.

The real problems arose when Tarquin's own human feelings were seriously aroused. According to his rules, Masters did not fall in love with their slaves. Their relationship fractured violently. Paul was left to slowly strike out on his own as a Top.

Two years later, they met by chance and had to decide what they truly meant to one another.

DOMINATION began with Tarquin wrestling with his true

feelings for Paul, to the point that he offered to become Paul's slave. Soon, both realized that such a relationship wouldn't work for them. Following a close friend's advice, they discarded their Leather conventions and became partners and fellow Masters.

Tarquin entered the exciting and expensive new world of show jumping when he took young horseman Grant as his slave. There was danger as well as excitement in the equestrian world for Grant, when he clashed with fellow rider and competitor, David. But, with Tarquin's help, their horsemaster, Tim Bronson, punished his treacherous prize student by bending him to his own queer desires.

Dispatched to England on a work project, Paul met the russet-haired and handsome Rufus, who had ascended the hard way from British 'rent boy' to television star. The two began a turbulent Master-slave adventure that continued back in Los Angeles. Rufus' past sexual history had produced an unstable personality. As a result, Paul felt he had quicksilver running through his hands, when the young actor won the lead in the US version of his British television series, thanks to the help of Tarquin and their friend, James Villier, a film agent and member of the "Circle of Six" who made demands of his own.

Paul felt the strain of caring for a boy who was now being pulled in different directions by his career and his sexual needs. Rufus left for a short visit to London to sort out his affairs there, before returning to LA to start shooting the series.

OBSESSION begins…

CHAPTER ONE - PAUL

I flung his buff body onto the leather seat of the sling. Rufusboy didn't have much choice. He was tightly bound into a thick black straitjacket, arms crossed over his heaving chest, straps running past his shaved genitals to hold the leather in place.

I stood back for a moment. I could feel my heavy steel tit rings shaking on my own torso as I drew a sharp breath. My erect prick thrust out from my naked crotch. Tight leather chaps and tall boots encased my muscled legs and feet. Paul Everest wanted Rufusboy McLachlan, wanted to take him in the worst possible way. I wanted to fuck him hard. We were both panting with excitement. Rufusboy's puckered hole looked ready for lube and my cock.

It had only been a couple of hours since I picked up my wandering boy, Rufusboy, at LAX. I waited eagerly for him to be disgorged into the arrivals hall of the Bradley Terminal with the rest of the passengers that had arrived on the British Airways flight from London. Rufusboy's well-built body was easy to spot. His russet hair was slightly longer than when he'd left Los Angeles a month before.

There was a flurry of attention from the crowd. I cursed silently. When I'd first met Rufusboy in Britain, the previous spring, I had been on assignment for my job as a creative graphics designer in Los Angeles. I had left Tarquin, my partner and previous Master, behind for my first visit abroad. The attraction to Rufusboy has been instantaneous. During a horny weekend in the country, I wasted no time in tying the boy up and having sweet and violent sex. He certainly seemed to have enjoyed the events that weekend.

I hadn't known that Rufusboy was an emerging television star, rising from college "rent-boy" to be a leading actor in a hit British TV series. That fact didn't really interfere with our developing a new relationship as Master and boy in London, where I was working temporarily. His show had already been completed and aired in the UK. The *Spycatcher* series had been picked up for US distribution and the rights sold for an American version.

With the agreement of Tarquin Charlton, my partner and lover, I had been happy to invite Rufusboy to stay with us in our Hancock Park home while he came over to the States for a short vacation and a chance to audition for the leading role in the American series.

Tarquin, a leading entertainment industry attorney and James Villier, one of his closest friends (and sexual rival), a major film and television agent, were able to open doors for Rufusboy. Still he had won the role on his own talents—or so I thought.

Almost immediately, the tentacles of television stardom reached around Rufusboy, pulling him away from my influence. James had hosted a party to celebrate my boy's success. The other men in attendance wanted to hump his ass and dick his other opening, during the resulting orgy that ensued. I was shaken. The wheels of possible fame began to turn with schmoozing and favors. Rufusboy seemed to welcome it all. As I thought back on it later, in Britain Rufusboy had seemed less susceptible to these outside influences. Perhaps the volatile seeds had been planted there, the result appearing more visibly in LA, with the promise of greater TV fame and sexual adventures through an American series.

Yes, I was possessive. I'd devoted time and effort to training Rufusboy to meet my demands, in both London and now in LA. I grew increasingly depressed when my boy prepared to go back to London to close out his British apartment and professional commitments. In the month Rufusboy was away, my mind had not changed. I had been almost celibate; well, apart from making violent love with Tarquin several times and jerking off when I needed to.

Now in my mid-thirties, I knew I was an imposing almost six-foot, well-muscled Master, with a major leather kink. I counted the days before my boy returned. My moods fluctuated, making it not only difficult to concentrate on my growing professional graphics duties, but also making me a poor companion at home.

At LAX there had been a brief hug before Rufusboy pulled away. Okay, I was aware that there was a crowd around. In the car, driving back to Hancock Park, my hand groped the boy's crotch. Once we were off the freeway, I insisted that Rufusboy unbutton his 501s and pull out his large and already throbbing cock and balls. I reached over to massage that choice penis. When I turned off the car in the driveway of our Hancock Park home, I ordered my boy out of the Cadillac and down on his knees to worship his Master's boots, outside the side door. Conveniently, Tarquin had a screening to attend that evening. He had taken his slave, Grant, for company. That left the house vacant for us to get reacquainted.

Once inside, I allowed the returnee to warm up my tumescent penis with his mouth. Rufusboy slobbered eagerly on his Master's dick. But only for five minutes; then, I slapped him across the head, ordering him to pull out and to follow me down into the basement dungeon. Once there, I watched Rufusboy look around in the diffused light at the familiar devices—the bondage bench, St. Andrew's cross, ropes, chains, pulleys and the glimmering leather sling. We undressed. I slid into my 'working' leather chaps and Wesco boots. Rufusboy stood straight and proud, wearing only his boots and a heavy metal cock ring, which did nothing to reduce the pulsing of his prick.

"So, boy, you behaved yourself while you were in London? No returning to your sluttish 'rent boy' habits?"

"No, Sir, I kept myself almost exclusively for you, Sir."

That annoyed me. "What the fuck does that mean, 'almost exclusively?'"

"Sir, my former Master, Sir Norman, you remember him. He's also my British agent. Well, Sir, he requested a farewell session."

"Oh shit, another of his costume parties, I suppose."

"Yes, Sir. I met with him on a couple of evenings and did the 'cops and robbers' scene, Sir."

"If your past stories are anything to go by, you must have fucked each other."

"He wore a rubber, Sir, at my insistence. And so did I."

"Yeah, you just couldn't keep your wick clean for me, could you, boy?"

I knew I was pushing it, but I couldn't help it. My mind was filled with the frustration and fear that I felt about losing him, losing my boy to the world of television and its viewers. My emotions churned my insides, yet inflated my cock.

"Stand here with your hands out—you're going into this straitjacket. Go ahead, slip it on. I'll cinch the fastenings in back. Slide your arms into the sleeves and cross them over, so I can buckle them in the back."

I pushed Rufusboy hard, trying to work off my angry mood. "Spread those legs. Let's get the bottom straps past that bouncing dick and joined up behind. I'm glad to see you kept your equipment and your ass shaved and clean."

"Oh, yes, Sir, I shaved last night, so I'd be smooth for you, Sir." Rufusboy charmingly confirmed.

I wasn't taken in by his facile charm. "Yeah, maybe. Let's get the buckles tightened and the collar fastened 'round your neck. That's better. Fuck, but you do look hot and vulnerable. My cock seems to think so, too. So, let's heave you into the sling and lube you up for action."

"Sir, yes, Sir. Whatever my Master wants."

"I hope I can believe you, boy."

I manhandled him into position in the sling, running ropes under his armpits and hauling him up to reach the chains. He grunted as I spread his legs into the stirrups. I then shoved two well-lubed fingers into the hole I knew so well. He groaned and wriggled to accommodate the third digit that I thrust into him. I stretched and checked the passageway, then pulled out my fingers and lined up my own eager prick, sliding it up and down his asscheeks to smooth out the lubricant I'd applied all over my hard and bare tool. I had decided I was going to breed him, to fuck him bareback.

Rufusboy sighed as my cockhead sank home, spiraling rapidly up that familiar shaft. He sweat in the straitjacket as I ran my hands over the smooth, black leather. He knew my rhythms and his ass muscles began to clench in response to the fuck he was taking. My arms moved over to maneuver the sling's upper chains. I thrust myself forward, filling him completely. Then my prick slid down, as I pushed the sling away from me.

We were both trembling with desire and excitement, were panting and moaning, pulsating and clenching. I was breeding my boy anew, to remind him who his true Master was. He was sliding and slithering as far up the leather seat as the straitjacket and restraints would allow, in preparation to receive my seed.

I was on fire with lust, now able to forget my anxieties, as I pumped hard into his passage. My previous sexual experience with Rufusboy enabled me to slide in and out with increasing force and rapidity. I knew I had a hot boy ready to be reclaimed. I ripped the tit patches off the straitjacket, then reached in to pull long and hard on his nipples, timing my actions to the thrusts of my thumping cock.

His pain at penetration was turning into pleasure as he began to buck beneath me, heaving and panting in the sling. My balls could stand it no longer. I yelled, cursed, poured my cum into Rufusboy's innards, which eagerly awaited my gift. Almost simultaneously, I felt his body spasm. His dick spewed his own cream, over his panting and leathered chest, in great white gobs.

My body slithered over his, as we sweat and grunted together. Gradually, I calmed down and my cock slipped out of the warm hole it had been pleasuring. I looked deeply into his eyes. They held mine momentarily, then looked down in submission. I smiled in satisfaction. The sling stopped swaying and I slowly released him.

"Welcome home, Rufusboy. That felt good!"

"Sir, thank you, Sir. My body needed your seed back in it as a reminder that my Master and I have this special relationship."

"And long may that continue. Now let's get you out of the jacket, cleaned up, and a newly greased plug back in you. Even you must be tired after that long flight and a good fuck."

He staggered behind me as we went up to the master bedroom. I hesitated; this was the room Tarquin and I shared. But my need was too great. I hauled him into the super-sized shower with me and let him lather and wash me. Then, I surprised myself by doing the same for him, enjoying the firm muscles beneath my probing fingers. Rufusboy was still in prime condition. His body was mine, at least for the time being.

We slept, entwined in the king-sized bed, my cock residing against the plug I'd inserted between his buttcheeks. His hands were cuffed in front. I was restless. Rufusboy slept deeply, apparently without a care in the world. I must have fallen into a doze. It was seven-thirty before I awoke in an empty bed. I pulled on sweats and went downstairs, drawn by the smell of coffee and the sound of voices.

"Well, good morning, you lazy bastard. Your boy and I thought you were never coming down." My partner sat grinning at the breakfast table.

"Morning, Tarquin. Morning, Slavegrant. Morning, boy. I'll have some coffee and some cereal. I see someone's uncuffed you"

"Master Tarquin, Sir. Breakfast's all here and ready for you, Sir." Rufusboy was anxious to show his serving abilities.

"He doesn't seem to have forgotten too much during his time in London. I hope he hadn't forgotten how to service you properly," Tarquin remarked as he finished his coffee.

"No, I put him through his paces in the sling last night. Sorry we took up all of the bed."

"That's all right, I had the slave here to keep me warm and you needed the time together. The guest room bed is very comfortable. However, we need to do something about the lighting and the bed restraints in that room. Now, what's on the agenda for today?"

"Sirs, if this boy may interrupt? I have a meeting with Master James later this morning, Sirs." Rufusboy chimed in.

"Ah yes. The agent calls and the boy-client jumps. Do you need me there, or can I be on the end of a phone?" Apparently, my partner seemed glad to have my boy back, too.

"Thank you, Master Tarquin. I appreciate your offer. I believe we'll only be going over the schedule and contract. A phone call should be enough, if we have any problems."

"I'll drive you over there. What time's the meeting?"

"That's not really necessary, Master Paul. I can call for a taxi; also, I should be thinking of getting a car and getting—"

"I said I'd drive." I was determined to control the situation.

"Yes, Sir, as you wish, Sir."

Tarquin looked at me quizzically but said nothing. Rufusboy helped Slavegrant clean up the breakfast things, then changed into 'working actor dress'. I ground my teeth and pulled out my Escalade. Yes, I'd moved up in the world, but my timing was wrong, given the high gas prices. Our drive over was short, but silent. We were both absorbed in our thoughts.

Rufusboy was warmly received at his agent's office and I took a decidedly secondary role. James Villier appeared immediately to usher us into his large office—still the Villier customary dark wood and heavy furnishings—He couldn't keep his hands off Rufusboy, flicking his nipples under his shirt and cupping his package under his designer jeans for that extra moment.

"It's great to have you back, Rufusboy. I'm so pleased to se…see you looking so fit. Did you have a ss…smooth journey over?" James' stutter was working full blast that morning.

"Thank you, Master James. I was well looked after on both flights. Oh, and Sir Norman sends warm regards from London. I promised you'd keep him in the loop on financial and contract details."

"Naturally, I look forward to meeting him when I go back to London sh…shortly. Now, let's get on with the logistics, shall we? Sh…shooting starts next week. I sent you the first two scripts. Any comments or ss…suggestions?"

I zoned out while they discussed details but kept a watch on James' face. His eyes never left my boy's body and they gleamed with lust, desire, or longing. Finally, they brought me back into the conversation.

James wanted to take charge. "I don't see any real problem with Rufusboy ss…staying with you in Hancock Park, for the moment, Paul. He'll need to lease a car right away. We can arrange that. Or I'll try to get the company to send a limo. It's a long ride to the studio; it's way out in Valencia, near Six Flags-Magic Mountain. We really sh…should think about finding him ss…somewhere to live nearer to work."

I interrupted firmly, determined to cut short any plans James might have for Rufusboy's 'welfare.' "He'll stay with me for now."

"Well, I ce…certainly don't want to rock your little boat, Paul. By the way, how is Tarquin? You two st…still getting along so well?"

I refused to let James goad me into a scene. Typical of him, he'd like that, to show his control. I owed it to Tarquin as well as myself, to rein in my temper, which seemed very short that morning. I hustled Rufusboy out of there as soon as I could decently manage, turning down James' offer of lunch.

We went shopping for some suitably smart casual clothes, for Rufusboy. There had never been time during his last visit. We laughed, enjoying ourselves in Paul Smith's store, when an older man came up to my boy, smiling.

"It's Rufus, isn't it? Joe Barnes. Welcome back to LA. Did you have a good time in dear old London?"

"Yes, thank you, Sir, and this is Paul Everest. Have we met before?"

"You naughty boy, I had you at James' party for you last month—and a nice piece of ass you have, too. We must get to know each other much better very soon. So good to meet you, Paul isn't it?"

And he drifted off, but the afternoon was ruined. Rufusboy was clearly embarrassed. He didn't remember too much about James' farewell party. My boy was flattered by the attention. I was just annoyed.

The weekend didn't go much better. Tarquin was particularly attentive, trying to help me.

"You need to give the boy time to himself to look over his script for next week. From now on, he'll have work to do, as well as us."

"I don't know, Tarquin, I'm just bad company at present. I guess I'm not much good to you in bed, either, at the moment, am I? Please don't think I've stopped loving you. You're too important to me. I'm just obsessing about the boy."

"Yes, indeed, but it can only be a very temporary obsession, if that's what it is. Next week you'll be sharing him with the *Spycatcher* cast and crew, and the rest of the television world will be after him soon enough."

"I know. I'm so frustrated that I want to take it out on Rufusboy. I am ready to beat him black and blue and then fuck him until I make him bleed."

"That's not healthy, Paul. Surely you realize that. You certainly can't mark him up--at least not where anything will show while he's working. Remember he's starting on a new career out here."

I knew what he was trying to say. That didn't stop me. On Saturday night I put on my chaps and Wescoes for dinner. Rufusboy, who was trying to achieve a balance between being a guest in the house and my slave in the dungeon, as well as a working actor, took one look and quietly slid out of his clothes. Naked, he served my dinner. I forced a thick leather posture collar round his neck at the table. Tarquin excused himself and closeted himself in his study. I pushed aside the food and grabbed Rufusboy by his red hair.

"Get down in the dungeon, slaveboy, and lube that tight hole of yours well."

"Sir, yes, Sir."

Silently, we went down into the basement. Once downstairs, after the lubing, I pulled a heavy leather hood over his head. There was no opening for his eyes or his mouth. The area surrounding his ears was well padded, with only a nose hole for air, and laced it up as tightly as possible. I lashed his wrists with wet rawhide strips that had been conveniently been soaking in the bucket at the bottom of the stairs. Rufusboy was dragged over to one of the chains dangling from the ceiling and fastened to it. We both knew that soon the rawhide would dry and tighten its grip. I flicked, then grabbed and twisted his nipples for several minutes before applying my harshest pair of alligator clamps, the ones having no protective cap over their teeth. He grunted at the unexpected pain. I slapped his leathered head and pulled down his ball sac, making space to add a thick, metal ball stretcher.

By now, I was breathing heavily. My eyes fueled me by their lecherous gaze at his slowly sweating torso. Rufusboy was a nearly perfect inanimate object, hanging there for me to abuse whenever I desired. He was my slave, awaiting his Master's pleasure. I reached for my single-tail, then stopped. Tarquin's warning echoed in my ears.

"That's not healthy. You certainly can't mark him up; at least not where anything will show, while he's working."

Frustrated and snorting with anger and lust, I threw down the whip and picked up the heaviest flogger I could find. If most of his body was now off-limits, at least his ass was still mine.

"You may become a television star next week, boy, but you're still mine for tonight. Your butthole is all mine and I aim to make you remember that. So, you are going to count out the lashes I give you, slowly but surely."

The hood muffled his voice. His body was already hot to the touch and beginning to tremble slightly. I stood back, flexed my arm and let him have it. My demons possessed me. I exorcised my frustration with twenty harsh blows until his butt was darkly bruised and slightly bloody. It was hardly the behavior of a well-balanced Master. Then I shoved the handle of the flogger up his hole until he yelped in pain.

Now my prick was fully erect and demanding, my chest was streaked with sweat and my voice was rasping and guttural. I slathered some lube on my weapon, pulled out the flogger and rammed his hole full blast, boring in by pulling his naked body onto my cock.

I wanted total possession, to sink my dick in farther than it had ever gone before. I wanted to make him totally mine—at least for this one night. We were both on fire, his body quivering with pain as I yanked on the tit clamps. Rufusboy was sweating with strain as I rampaged up and down his passage. The contraction of his ass muscles around my pole gave me momentary pleasure, and perhaps a false sense of assurance that Rufusboy would still be my own. My arms encircled him tightly. They slithered 'round his torso, finding and rubbing his dick, pulling down on his balls, already stretched well by their metal sheath. I forced him further onto my spike as I snarled and spat at my hooded boy.

My own energies couldn't last long in that heat of expression. I felt my cum surging up from my balls and pouring into my groaning slaveboy. My cream was marking him as mine. In turn, my slave's body thrust and jerked, as he gushed into my waiting hands. I smeared his jism across his sweaty chest, pulled off the hood, removed clamps and ball stretcher and slapped his bruised rump to the accompaniment of Rufusboy's gasps and groans. Loosening up the rawhide bonds to improve his blood circulation, I re-secured the victim of my obsessive desires and he was left to hang there overnight.

The next morning, I relented, released Rufusboy, and tried hard to be a good host and Master for the rest of the weekend. I didn't want my frustrations and my anger at James to spill over any farther onto my boy or Tarquin. So, we tried to keep the world at bay for a couple of days. We rented a car for Rufusboy and had fun helping him to drive on the "wrong side of the road."

That proved unnecessary, as the studio sent a car and driver for the boy early Monday morning. No doubt, James had some involvement in the arrangement. It was over twelve hours before we saw him again and he followed the same schedule for the next few days.

Then Rufusboy invited me to come with him in his own car the next week to watch a day of shooting. I took time off from my office and we set off at 6am. I knew the Los Angeles freeways well and the boy had his map, but it still took us nearly ninety minutes to reach our destination out in Valencia. Rufusboy was very quiet on the way, mumbling lines to himself. It was only when we got to the studio that I began to realize how heavy his workload was going to be. He was indeed the star of the TV series, carrying much of each episode on his shoulders.

Clearly, in just over a week, an easy rapport had been established between the star and his fellow actors and crew. I was introduced all round as his friend and LA host. Jokes floated around with the coffee, before and in-between taping, but the work itself was deadly serious, fast, and efficient.

That was the first time I'd seen Rufusboy, 'the Actor' working. He'd adopted a 'mid-Atlantic' accent that seemed to suit the character he was playing. In his role, he exuded an easy charm and fast responses to action and dialogue. There was no apparent hostility against a British actor coming into the leading role of an American television series. His fellow cast members appeared to admire his professionalism as well his experience in the starring role in the original British series.

Still, the work was long and arduous. Even I was tired by the end of the ten-hour workday. We stopped to get some dinner on the way home at a small restaurant that I'd visited before, just off the freeway.

"Rufusboy, that was an impressive performance. You've put in a long workday. I'm beginning to understand why James suggested you move out here, at least for the work week." The words did not roll off my tongue without me realizing that James may have had a genuine reason for his recommendation, as well as his personal plans.

"I thought you might get a kick out of it, Master Paul. Really, I think I can manage the journey; although, you won't see much of me, Sir."

"No, I think you should ask the production office to help you lease a condo out here. You can get some rest in the evenings. I hadn't realized how much you have to memorize for each day." I was being truthful. I also realized that I was going to have to be alert, if I was to stay ahead of James and his designs for my property.

"Well, Sir, could I still spend the weekends with you and Master Tarquin?" Rufusboy sounded almost anxious.

"Of course, and, hopefully, there'll be time to play, if you're not too tired."

So, the die was cast. It shouldn't have been a surprise that James involved himself in the process, as his agent. He used his clout to get Rufusboy an attractive two-bedroom garden condominium with "one bedroom for a study." The following weekend Tarquin and I drove out with Rufusboy to get him settled in, only to find James and a couple of his boys already there.

"I just ss …stopped by to check the furnishings and to add a few personal touches. These places can look so ss…sterile, don't you think? If I'd known you were all coming, I needn't have bothered, since I'm sure your ss…superb taste, Paul, would ensure a perfect home away from home."

Tarquin, smoothly, stepped in to lighten the growing tension. "Hello, James, and, how are you? Paul and I will be taking the boy out to dinner when we have settled him in. Why don't you join us? By the way, you and I need to get together soon. I've decided to become a kind of unofficial business manager for Rufusboy, to help him keep a firm eye on his financial interests. He doesn't have anyone at the moment."

This was news to Rufusboy and I, and even more so to James, who didn't look too pleased. That, I assumed, was Tarquin's idea. After a reasonably pleasant dinner interlude--we could all be mature when we wanted to be--I took Rufusboy into the bedroom, while the other two retreated to the garden to enjoy their cigars. I hugged him tightly and lipped him hungrily.

"I hate to turn you loose, boy, with all these wolves around you, but I know you've got a shitload of work to get through each week. I can wait for the weekend to give you a proper fuck, and maybe some punishment, too." I hoped the other predators would give him the same courtesy.

"Sir, I'm not going to have time to perform any tricks. I'll need to save my energy, so I can properly service you at the weekends. I'm going to miss you both, Sir. You've made my transition to California so much easier."

"It was the least I can do, Rufusboy, since I want you. Maybe I've even begun to fall in love with you. Just don't forget me." I'd said more than I intended.

"Shit, Sir, it's only a five-day week, I hope, then I'll be back in Hancock Park with you. I could suck you off before you leave, if you like, Sir."

Rufusboy took advantage of the moment. Without really waiting for permission, he slid down, unbuttoning my 501s and extracting the always-eager prick lurking within. I let him use his hands to arouse it more fully before he brought his lips into place. He began licking and laving both cock and balls in his inimitable style. Leaning against the headboard, I grasped his red hair and pushed fully into his mouth.

We were both hungry and eager. It didn't take long for me to spew a full load of my cum down his throat, which he swallowed expertly and eagerly. Then he dutifully licked and cleaned my fading penis and carefully tucked it back in place. We kissed a firm farewell before I strode out brusquely, surprising the others.

"I'm ready to leave, Tarquin. Let's get back to LA. Goodnight, James."

"Gg...goodnight, Paul, Tarquin. We'll need to get ss...something in writing about Rufusboy' sfinancial future."

It was a largely silent drive back to Hancock Park. My lover tried a little light conversation as he navigated the busy Interstate 5 Freeway. I was too far away and morose to respond. We parked his new Jag and let ourselves into the silent house.

"I need a strong drink," I grumbled. "I need to wash away the taste of James and his everlasting scheming. Why the hell won't he leave Rufusboy alone?"

"It's because Rufusboy has the potential of being a long-term meal ticket for him. That's why I decided to get involved and to keep a firm eye on the financial arrangements, and on James, as well. We both know how hot Rufusboy is. I suspect James and several other men can't wait to really get their hands on him."

"Fuck, if that was to make me feel better, I may need a second Scotch!"

"It needn't be too bad. Why don't you follow me upstairs and let my dick give you a drubbing instead?"

"I'll be coming up and getting UP in a few minutes. Let me lock up down here, first."

Tarquin lay naked on the bed, his large, obsidian eyes contrasting with his blond good looks. I shucked off my clothes, sighed and lay down beside him, welcoming his muscled arms that spread around me and his large cock that came calling at my back door. I rolled over to kiss him hungrily and deeply, trying to get myself and my emotions more fully under control. My kisses were returned slowly as our tongues probed each other, bringing me back to life.

"You want me to fuck you, don't you, Paul? Is it to make up for the boy you left behind and are afraid of losing? Or because you love me and want to offer yourself?"

"Shit, Tarquin, of course I love you and always will. A solid shafting would do me a lot of good, right now." We both were aware that I hadn't really answered Tarquin's question.

"Have you left your demons in Valencia? I expect…no, I demand your full attention!" My partner's disposition had turned serious.

"Yes, my Master, you'll have it. I want you and I want Rufusboy and I don't know where to draw the lines. I'm just so confused."

"It is time that you accept that he is going to be a public figure. Right now, I want you to show me how much I mean to you. Come on, excite me, stimulate me, and suck me."

I could see the smile on Tarquin's face as he said it. I needed to let go and lighten up. I responded with a light-hearted laugh and gave him my full attention. If he wanted me to suck him, then he was going to get the best blowjob he'd had in a long time.

I sank down to take a firm hold of his big, thick dick that was already rising for the occasion. His mushroom head reddened as I lipped it. Tarquin moaned in pleasure. So, I slid the whole pole into the warmth of my mouth, my tongue adding spit to the pulsating mix of erotic pleasure. It had been quite a while since I'd really given head. Reenergized, my mouth and hands set about their task. I continued working on his beefy balls as well as the weapon in my mouth for an enjoyable ten minutes or so.

"Okay, that is enough, boy, I don't intend to cum just yet. Roll over and get that ass where I can really rim it."

I was happy to oblige. My butt was soon on offer. I pulled apart my cheeks so my partner would have free access to my other lips with his tongue. It was my turn to moan as Tarquin worked his magic, stimulating and probing with his warm tip. My ass tingled as he burrowed deeper into my hole, his moist tongue opening the passage. It was exciting, different and I shuddered and gasped in answer to his efforts. His roving hands traced the brand he had burned into my right asscheek years ago. The circle with a "T" in the middle, the sign of his ownership, still served as an erotic stimulant. Then he came up for air, massaging his still slick prick to full erection.

"Now you're ready for me. Stick a couple of pillows under you, while I start to plough you, commando-style."

"Ready, and more than."

"You need to be tied down?"

"No. no, not tonight. Fuck, just batter the door down. I'm oozing for your dick." I had started to pant in my need. Tarquin was going to fuck me bareback that evening. How badly I wanted to feel the warm pulse of his shaft inside me.

"Then get your needy ass up, further in the air, to give me room to spear you."

We maneuvered into our familiar positions. Tarquin had been making use of my hole for over seven years now. When we had begun as Master and slave, his training had been vigorous, demanding and long. I fell in love with him before the end of my first year of servitude. When eventually his true feelings for me were aroused, they played havoc with our relationship.

It took us years to work through the labels and customs of the leather world and to arrive at our own safe harbor as lovers and fellow-Masters. Now we made love to each other because we wanted to. We enjoyed each other's bodies, and we were fucking good at fucking.

It felt good to be back under his control that night. That was what I needed to bring me back into my proper headspace.

I wantonly stuck my ass up with its lips quivering to meet his demands. Slowly and sensually, he slid his dong up and down my asscheeks as drops of precum spilled over and smoothed his path. His long fingers spread my bubble butt further. I twitched my winking hole eagerly, awaiting his battering ram. It came slowly. I could feel him lubing his poker before its probe began. He burrowed his way into my channel unhurriedly. My seething muscles accepted and welcomed the invader; clenching his cock, drawing him farther into my passage as he sank home.

I moaned in pleasure and then gasped as Tarquin's roaming hands found my own prick, which had begun to wag up and down in anticipation. My Master's hands then continued upwards, sliding through my chest hairs in search of my nipples and their piercings. I grimaced as he tweaked my tender tits and then dug in to twist hard on their heavy rings. His attempt to withdraw was quickly challenged by my ass muscles, and I heard his growl as I pulled him back into me. We were not done.

We picked up the pace, varying the speed as his dick demanded. Long, slow strokes gave way to harder demanding thrusts. Our glistening limbs began to slither over our sweating bodies as he powered into me. I was panting in the heat of the moment. My own cock punched the air as he pummeled ever more powerfully in and out of me. I clenched his rod harder. He growled loudly in appreciation and pistoned faster, as I released him. Yes, my Tarquin was always fierce in his fucking. The bed bounced beneath us as the pounding of his battering ram slowly drove my body into the headboard.

I humped in time with his strokes. His hands darted from my tits to my hips as he rode me home. We worked up a heavier sweat from our overheated bodies. He was getting close. I could hear him snarling and snorting in his usual way; in turn, I groaned and panted heavily. Then suddenly, his arms tightened hard around my torso as he made one final surge forward. My lover shot his cream into me once again. A minute later, my own penis exploded onto the bed with a rope of my cum. Then, to our surprise, we both came again together.

We were drenched and exhausted, but we were happy. He pulled out. We showered, washing one another slowly and lovingly. Then we lay back in bed and fell sound asleep in each other's arms. My world seemed a much better place, at least temporarily, with Tarquin's help.

The following weeks were long, but Rufusboy stayed in touch by phone and email. He texted during the few pauses in his workday. I would reply, trying to keep the tone light. We kept the weekends enjoyable—sexually adventurous, but not otherwise demanding.

Then came the first warning bell. Rufusboy was needed for some advance publicity work at the studio. There was to be a party for him, his fellow actors, and the media over the weekend. I was disappointed, but not too upset, until Tarquin ran into James a day or so later.

"Tarquin, we missed you on Ss…Saturday at the party."

"And what party was that, James?"

"The *Spycatcher* evening for the actors. I thought you'd be there as Rufusboy's new business manager."

"We weren't invited, James. I thought it was supposed to be just a publicity party for the actors and the crew."

"Well, it was, but a few of us thought we'd liven it up with some str…strippers—boys as well as girls. Rufusboy seemed to have ss… such an enjoyable time. I introduced him to some studio types who'd come along. One or two were interested in him, for the future. We need to go over some more details of his contracts; is next week okay?"

Tarquin called me immediately. I didn't know whom to believe. It was just like James to stir up trouble and maybe Rufusboy hadn't appreciated the size of the party. Still, I didn't like it. The tentacles of the entertainment world were reaching out. I didn't know how to stop them seizing my boy, or if he even wanted to be saved.

CHAPTER TWO - TARQUIN

I tried to keep one eye on my lover Paul and his troubled relationship with Rufusboy, while keeping my other eye on my own professional interests. The Century City entertainment law firm in which I was a partner had expanded its client base to include sports stars as well as overseas entertainment figures. This caused turbulent times, as we experienced the sudden growth with new styles of temperament.

My own portfolio now included several European personalities who had an interest in enhancing their Hollywood careers. I knew that my foreign language capabilities, impressive personality, and imposing body skills had helped me to secure this position. It didn't hurt to be six foot-two inches tall, with Aryan good looks, maintaining a hard and buff body, in addition to a Blackberry full of gay and leather contacts worldwide. The expanded position required more of my time and promised a considerable amount of European travel in the near future. I would have looked forward to the additional demands, if it were not for the problems at home.

Not only were there Paul's difficulties with his boy, now turned television star, but I decided I needed to end my own relationship with Slavegrant. There was nothing particularly wrong with the boy. He had a smooth butt, powerful haunches, and thick, strong legs that had been firmed from hours of horse riding.

Our relationship had stagnated. He no longer excited me. Yes, he performed his duties around the house more than adequately. His cooking and cleaning showed proper care and diligence. Now there was no spark crackling between us, such as there had always been between Paul and myself those years before, in our Master/ slave time together. Perhaps my decision was harsh; several of my relationships had run their course after a couple of years. Maybe it was partly my fault. After several years without Slavepaul, I seemed to need a more imaginative slave to arouse me fully and regularly. That wasn't happening with Grant, as I had hoped it might.

Part of the problem was Grant's "outside" life. In addition to his smaller professional acting jobs, there were his impressive riding abilities. Originally, I had approved of his continuing training, but this consumed a considerable amount of his days. He worked under horse master Tim Bronson, my friend and fellow Master. In the beginning, I tried to ride out with Slavegrant once a week. However, now he was usually exercising one of Tim's new acquisitions. A trail ride with me became much less of a challenge.

"Grant's gone as far as he probably can," Tim explained to me. "Certainly, as far as I can teach him. He'll be an excellent rider, but without that 'killer instinct,' he won't become Olympic or achieve international standard."

"It is that killer instinct, or something like it, that is missing from our sex life, as well."

"Why, Tarquin, you mean your slave doesn't perform to your standards? Fuck me, perhaps you need a change of pace. How about playing with a different Master—like me?"

I laughed. Tim had always shown his interest in me, but I had not wanted to pursue it, despite our one intense encounter.

"Yes, Tim, I will certainly tell you if that ever becomes more than a possibility. In the meantime, I have to decide what to do with Grant. I believe that a clean break would be the easiest and kindest."

Perhaps the fates were listening. A few evenings later, Slavegrant came to talk to me, in my study.

"Sir, that phone call this morning, at breakfast, that was my mother calling to tell me my father's in the hospital. The cancer has spread. He's only expected to live another month or so, Sir."

"My God, Grant, you should have told me right away. Have you thought about what you want to do?"

"Well, Sir, that's what I need to talk to you talk about. My father has always intended for me to inherit the family business, although I've had little to do with it for the last two or three years. I've always known it, even though we weren't that close. I want to honor his wishes, Sir. It's not as though my acting career has taken off. Master James kinda lost interest when I wouldn't remain one of his boys, Sir."

"I thought he still had you under contract?"

"Yes, Sir. He does, but all I've had recently have been one scene and a couple of bit parts, Sir."

"We could find you a new agent…."

"No, Sir, I've finally realized that I don't have the talent it takes to really make it. I may look good, but a real actor like Rufusboy can run rings around me. And, although I'm a very good rider, I wouldn't earn a good living doing that either, Sir."

"Well, you could stay here as my slave."

"Thank you, Sir, I really appreciate the gesture, more than you know. I've loved being your slave, Sir. But, it's time for me to move on, before you get tired of me and throw me out. I know a slave isn't supposed to do this, but I need you to release me, Sir."

I was astonished. In his own quiet way, he had seen through the façade of our relationship. The news from home had given him the spur to break away from his slave role. This was certainly a first for me.

"Well, you've certainly taken my breath away by changing the script." I chuckled to admit my surprise. "I think I understand. However, I want to have one final weekend with you, before you leave. Don't worry. It will be just you and me. Perhaps we will spend a couple of days in the woods again, or in Tim's cabin, near Idyllwild."

"Thank you, Sir. Your slave will be very grateful for the attention. Oh, one thing more, please, Sir."

"What is it?"

"Sir, the brand on Master Paul's buttcheek, the one you gave him to show he was your slave, your property? Please Sir, I want one, too. It will remind me in years to come that once another man owned me, Sir."

This was becoming too heavy. My mark on Paul's ass had been the final dramatic step into his slavery, the sign of permanent possession. It had been a traumatic and painful bonding for both of us. I would not allow a novice, like Grant, that privilege. It had not been earned.

"No, slave, you have to earn that privilege. Besides, the process would be too intense for you. You might well regret it in five or ten years. But I tell you what I will do. I will have my brand tattooed on your right cheek, rather than burned into it. That should satisfy you."

"Oh yes, Sir. Thank you, Sir. Indeed, it will, Sir."

"Fine. I will make the arrangements to have it done once we return from our weekend in the mountains."

Grant's quiet determination and guts impressed me. He had earned a solid weekend of servitude. So, I cleared my calendar to take him up to the rugged country about ninety minutes west of Palm Springs. I also made arrangements for an ink artist to come later to my dungeon. He would create the circle with a "T" tattoo when we got back.

Slavegrant had become too excited by the morning of our trip. I decided it would be best to put him into chastity. Before we left, he was sporting a CB-3000 which had pushed his package out nicely, but which prevented him from erecting fully. Paul was left to brood over Rufusboy. I hoped there would be no immediate further problems there.

It was a fine fall Friday morning, when we drove east on Interstate 10. We turned off and headed to Idyllwild in the San Jacinto Mountains. I had hired horses saddled and waiting in the town that would take us the rest of the miles through the wooded mountains, leading up to the cabin that I had borrowed from Tim. It was an easy hour's ride through the tall trees, a few with an autumnal touch to their leaves and the undergrowth around us.

Once we were away from civilization, the chastity device was jerked out of his jeans. I looped a thin cord around it and bound it to the saddle horn. My slave groaned happily as his cock was pulled and tugged in its plastic prison. I cuffed his hands behind him and pulled a spandex hood over his head. He could still breathe and see dimly. However, he could only guide his horse with his legs. I took the animal on a lead rope, so that, every time we went up or down a slope, Slavegrant's family jewels were punished. By the time we reached the cabin, he was leaking copious amounts of precum.

Leaving the slave mounted, I checked our weekend accommodations. They were more than satisfactory. I tumbled the slave off his horse onto the dirt. He rolled on his cuffed arms and then sat up, shaking his hooded head.

"There's work to do, slave. So, let's undo your wrists for the moment, while you can carry the supplies inside. Keep that spandex hood on. You can see well enough to get by. Take off the rest of your clothes. No—come to think of it, you had better keep the boots on. I don't know what might be underfoot. Now, put the horses away."

The tasks took my slave a full hour of solid labor. A light sheen of sweat covered his body by the time he'd finished. The slave showed at his slender, muscular best. I had changed, as well, into a leather thong and low boots. I thought a run through the woods would work up a good appetite for our late lunch. I removed the hood and tightened a wide collar with leash around his neck. A light weight was added to dangle below the CB-3000 between his legs. Slavegrant's wrists were again secured behind him. Off we went for a brisk mile.

On the way back, I kept him in front, encouraging him with swats from the riding crop that I was carrying. He hopped and jumped each time he was hit. That resulted in a fine thin line of welts by the time we got back to the cabin. His torso was glowing from the exercise. The effect made me feel horny, myself. I'd take him there and then.

"Come over here, Slavegrant. Spread yourself over this tree trunk. This will make a very convenient fucking bench, don't you think?"

"Sir, yes Sir. Whatever pleases you."

"That is correct. And right now it pleases me to fuck you. Do you need more restraints, or can you hold in place while I penetrate you?"

"Sir, I think I would prefer to steady myself for you, Sir."

"Fine, then move that cock cage and weight out of the way and spread yourself. I said spread yourself now, slave." I had my crop ready in the event that he needed further urging.

Both of us began to pant in anticipation of the fuck. His well-muscled ass, already striped by my crop, looked even better once I added another half-dozen welts. Slavegrant humped and groaned on the tree trunk. Precum drizzled from both our sex tools. I honored him by mixing both our juices and anointing his hole and my rubbered prick with the warm liquid. His butt was a bright rose red as I slid my fingers into him to stretch his eager hole. It didn't take long, as he had been well trained over the past year under my tutelage.

I aimed my ramrod at his winking rosebud to slide it easily and comfortably past his sphincter muscle. I stopped for a moment, allowing him time to adjust to his Master's dick. Then my large, muscled log shoved its head all the way in. He dug his body into the tree, his manacled hands twisting up his back. I forced them further up as I began to ride him. My penis lunged forward up his tunnel and then down back to his entrance. Then my weapon reversed its motion back up his velvety passageway. We were both sweating in the noon sun, grunting and gurgling. He fought to accommodate my engorged prick as I sought to prove my mastery over his now ravaged ass and hole.

"Good job, slave; now show some more effort. Squeeze those ass muscles. Grip my cock firmly. I am pounding back into you. Show me your skills. Come on. You know the fuck tricks you've learned from me. That's it. Clench those horseman's muscles. Buck with me. I'm tight in the saddle. You will not shake me off. Come on slave, let me see more of that slave spirit." Effortlessly, I let my crop remind him of the proper response.

Slavegrant was determined to give me his best. His naked body was grinding into the rough bark of the tree. The CB-3000 he wore kept hitting the trunk, too. He managed to hold himself in place as I drove further up into him, pulling on his manacled hands as a control. My torso drained its sweat onto his back. I grabbed at his hair with my free hand. Growling and spitting, I jerked up his head. Tears poured down his face. He was frustrated by his inability to erect his imprisoned cock. He was receiving pain/pleasure from his Master's pile driver in exchange.

The air grew warm around us as the primitive fuck reached its climax. This time, Slavegrant had really turned me on. My demanding penis thrust fully forward one last time. I roared my conquest to the skies and bellowed triumphantly as cum surged out of me. I filled my slave's innards. He lay there moaning and humping as I pulled out of him. I took pity on his battered torso, lifted him off the raw bark of the tree trunk, turning him over against the its rough bark. I then unlocked his cock cage. I had scarcely removed it when he shot two thick ropes of white cream that splashed across his chest as he lay with his back across the tree trunk. I reached over, carefully pulled off my rubber. I added its contents to the stream of cream already on his chest, then we rubbed our juices together, torso to torso.

For a few moments, I remained there leaning into him, breathing hard. My body was slippery with sweat and cum, and my voice hoarse from shouting. Finally, I pulled him upright to kiss him deeply. Despite the cuffs on his wrists, he ground himself into my body. Then my slave slid down to lick my penis clean of my seed, working hard on my balls as well. We stayed together, slowly coming down from a great high until we both felt we were safely back on the ground.

After his release, Slavegrant went indoors and I slowly followed. Soon he produced excellent, rare roast beef sandwiches from the supplies we had brought with us. The rest of the day was pleasantly peaceful. We splashed and washed in the nearby mountain stream. The water was cold and fresh. That night, I let him sleep with me in the king-sized bed. There he lay, leather hooded, leather restrained, with his cock and balls fully leathered in a tight glove-like sheath. He looked so appetizing lying there. For a moment, I almost regretted my decision to let him go. Then I remembered that it was really his choice and his future. It was time to move on.

The next morning, we went for one last horseback ride. I wore an old pair of brown leather chaps, that Tim kept in the cabin. I thought a cup and leather jock a good idea. That day, I also used a saddle and my boots. With my permission, Slavegrant seemed freer. He still sported the leather hood, without blindfold or gag. His wrists and booted ankles still wore the leather restraints. His cock and balls remained semi-erect in their leather sheath. Still, he rode bareback, showing off his skill, pushing his mount into jumping over obstacles and racing in wide circles. I felt like a mature and wise master watching and admiring an unruly student. The crisp, fresh air, when mixed with a light wind, was intoxicating. That morning, we enjoyed ourselves. I wanted Grant to have good memories of our last time together.

When we got back to the cabin, Slavegrant put away the horses. A few minutes later, still more naked than not, he came to me and presented, kneeling submissively in the grass to kiss my boots.

"Yes, boy, get up. There is still more training to be done this weekend. Get over by those trees; attach these ropes to your wrist and ankle restraints. The blindfold goes back on top of the hood for the moment. Next, you will spread your arms and legs wide. Start sucking on this penis gag while I tighten it around your head."

Slavegrant followed my instructions, checking the four ropes after they were attached. Once finished, I pulled his arms out and up to shoulder height, anchoring them tautly to tree trunks. I then followed with his legs, spread-eagling him. When I had his bonds tight, I added a rope through the D ring on the slave's collar. Now, he was fully secured between the two trees. My young stallion pranced in place. His rising cock had stiffened inside its leather sheath, fully stretching its skin.

My own weapon had been similarly excited. I pulled my cup and jock off, allowing it to erect proudly as I reached for my flogger. I moved in closer, pulling Slavegrant's stretched and naked torso into me. The gagged mouth was kissed hard. He quivered and hissed as I twisted his nipples, squeezing the nubs tightly between my fingernails. I stepped away, admiring the bound figure, loosening the strands of my flogger. The strands flicked around his leathered cock and balls. I changed my aim so that the cords slid past his perineum and across his asscheeks. A long hiss was the only sound he could make.

I followed this by walking silently behind him and checking the rawhide strands of my flogger. Now my focus was on that gleaming back of his, positioned right there, in front of me. I started on his shoulders, gently at first, then building up to a rat-a-tat of blows. This brought out a red blossom on the skin of the slave. He struggled, but to no avail. The five ropes held him firmly. I could hear only the strongest wails through the penis gag, firmly clenched between his teeth. My arm moved down to the well-exercised horseman's asscheeks. Again, I beat a steady tattoo of strokes, lighter and then heavier, as I worked out my escalating aggression. His body withstood as much as it could, struggling and shuddering. Only the sound of my own heavy growling and the whoosh of the flogger broke the silence of the woods. At last, I was satisfied. This was one beating that Slavegrant was going to remember.

The torment had only begun. There was going to be more punishment for his body to endure as the sun passed its zenith.

He hung there between the trees for about an hour. The sky began to cloud over, and the air became humid. I was setting my metal pegs in a stony area nearby. When I released the restraining ropes, his body waivered as if ready to collapse. I did not give him the opportunity. I pulled him along by his leather collar. An open-mouthed rubber O-ring now replaced the penis gag, which had silenced him. The blindfold was removed. He blinked as his eyes adjusted to daylight.

"Right, slave, your next torment awaits you. Lie down where you are. Yes, I'm sure the stones and pebbles will chafe your beaten shoulders and ass. Position yourself as best you can as I stretch you out again. Wet rawhide will bind your wrists and ankles to these pegs. You will be well stretched before I am finished. I want you fully spread-eagled. You need to feel the stretch. Your left ankle needs to be a little tighter, I think. Good, now you look like a true slave, soiled, beaten, helpless, and speechless.

"Now, let me add a few refinements. Your nipples need more work. They have not had any real training all weekend. A good twist will ready them for these bare crocodile clamps. Go ahead. Try to move away. It will do you no good. First the left tit, like this. Gurgling through your gag won't help. Here comes the right clamp. Now, I will test the connecting chain. Yes, that holds well across your chest. I am adding this additional chain. It will connect your nipples to your waving rod in its leather sheath. I am going to remove the top section of the sheath, so your cockhead is free in the breeze. The chain gets attached to the remainder of the stem of your cock."

I watched his attempts at struggle. Gradually he gave that up, settling down in his hard bondage. My foot slid over to his genitals. "How does your prick like my boot pressing down the other way into your balls? Puts quite a strain on the chain to your tits, too? You can try to howl all you want. Nobody can hear you out here. See how your dick bounces back when I lift my boot, kick it back up and pull on the two chains? The head is turning nicely purple in color. With a little more stimulation, I believe you will cream on command."

I detached another tool from my belt and looked down on my object of flesh. "This little cock whip of mine, working on the inside of your thighs, should help you obey."

I watched my slave struggle and sweat in the humid air. Perspiration was sliding off his naked torso as I tormented his dick. Spread-eagled on the rocky ground, his back was being further lacerated by his wild efforts against nature's tools of torture to evade my flogger and fingers. He gurgled and gasped noisily through the mouth's O-ring. However, he was helpless as the rawhide restraints tightened. A couple of minutes later, I growled the command to come again. Immediately, Slavegrant erupted. His jism splashed plentifully across his stomach. Spent, he groaned again before collapsing.

"You look very sexy, slave; stretched, tormented, emptied and spread-eagled. You are enough to get me excited, too. Let me add my cum to that puddle on your torso. Fuck, I'm feeling really horny. My balls feel full and churning."

Soon my own seed sprayed over the squirming bound body at my feet, firmly anchored to the ground. I panted in heat, looking into his pleading eyes. Fuck, the slave was hoping I had still one final gift to give him.

About ten minutes later, my cock began to throb and rise again. I knelt over Slavegrant's dirty, sweaty, and cum-smeared torso where I'd blended both our creams over his stomach. My knees pushed into his clamped nipples as he screamed in pain. That was enough; I guided my penis through the large O-ring and into his open mouth.

He had been trained to suck my dick. I was sure he was doing his best. His tongue wrapped around my excited cockhead. I shivered in anticipation. He had been trained to swallow whatever I provided. And I provided another rope of cum shooting into his gaping orifice. The whole experience was totally intense for both of us. My cream dribbled out of the corners of his mouth I sighed with pleasure, kissed his covered forehead before I got to my feet.

There he lay, fastened to the unyielding ground; tightly spread and clamped. Slavegrant still looked impressive with that slim musculature. His breathing was rapid and sobbing. His body was now soaked in sweat and cum. Flies and insects began to hover round the torso, gliding down to bite or feast. All my slave could do was to shake and writhe his battered body.

The O-ring forced his mouth open and my gift still trickled out of the corners. A column of ants began to climb over the leathered head toward the slobbering orifice. He shook it to clear them away, still they were determined to sample his liquids. A group of large flies droned over the drying cum on his stomach, landing, partaking, and biting as they wished. Further down, more insects were working their way to his exposed and still purple cockhead. He shouted through his gag as he sensed their imminent arrival. He sobbed and attempted a garbled scream through the pool of saliva, fluids, and intruders, in a haze of pain and pleasure as I looked on. Occasionally, I would wipe away the worst of the ants and other creatures, making sure that he was not in any real danger. My slave had requested a weekend of hard and intense servitude. That was exactly what I had provided. I took great pleasure in the result.

A crack of thunder and a sudden spatter of raindrops warned me of the weather change. I retreated back to the cabin, leaving the slave to face the now unfavorable elements, as well. I got the fire going again and watched occasionally from the window. The rain squall beat down fiercely for about thirty minutes, keeping the staked body protected from further intrusion. Eventually, the storm swept over the mountains as the sun broke through the clouds.

The bound body lay there, motionless. I could hear him still breathing noisily, occasionally twitching and groaning. I let him dry off for a while. Then, it was time to retrieve my property before the insects returned to their work. He smelled, looked filthy and exhausted. The slave remained still, not even turning his head at the sound of my boots crunching over the rocks. I untied his bindings, massaged the circulation back into his grubby arms and legs. After removing the O-ring gag, I pulled him into a sitting position by his collar.

"I think that's enough punishment for the moment, boy."

"Sir, your slave thanks you, Sir," came the whispered reply.

"I will take the clamps off. Do not wince or whine; it does not become your station. I know you hurt. That is the point. You and I both wanted to take you beyond your limit today. The leather hood and cock sheath are next. Shit, they're really sodden from the rain. We will leave them out here to dry in the breeze."

"As you wish, Sir," came a choked whisper.

"When you can move your muscles again, gather up the ropes and come on back to the cabin."

Sometime later, slowly, oh so slowly, the slave scrambled upright as I watched from the window. He collected the ropes and, with his bare hands, dug out the pegs. The well-used slave then slithered and slid on the still damp, rocky slope. Eventually reaching the cabin, he collapsed and crawled up the cabin steps. He hugged my booted feet as I opened the door. I stood for a moment, enjoying his service, before gathering him in my arms as Slavegrant sobbed and spluttered his thanks. His torso was chilled and dirty, but the very feeling from my body's warmth began to bring him around. I forced a bowl of hot soup and some herbal tea into him.

"Thank you, Sir. Your slave wanted to test his limitations for you, Sir."

"Well, I think we proved that you were capable of absorbing rather more training and punishment than either of us expected."

"Yes, Sir, it's all due to you, Sir."

I smiled and swept his wet hair off his forehead. My training and his regular workouts with horses had produced a strong and sinewy young man. He could be proud of his cock and his body. Maybe this last ordeal was what he needed to allow him to move confidently into the rest of his life.

He went out and took a swift bath in the nearby stream, shivering as he washed his body clean again. Right after, he began to run, then trot around the cabin, drying off in the afternoon's now warm sunny breeze. It was impressive to watch how quickly a young man was able to recover. I have to confess I was somewhat envious of the moment.

I slathered some ointment on his back. Slavegrant cooked our supper on the primus. Then, with wrists tied in front, he slid onto the large bed with me. He slipped off into a deep sleep immediately. Clearly, he had been exhausted by the day's intense display of his physical condition.

As I watched the glowing embers in the wood burning stove, I smoked a Montecristo and remembered my promise to have him tattooed with my 'brand' when we returned to Los Angeles. I also wondered about finding a replacement, when Slavegrant left in a week's time. I sighed as I joined him under the bedclothes. It was only a couple of weeks ago that I thought I'd decided that Slavegrant would not remain; after this weekend, I half-wished that he could stay a slave under my roof. Still, a suitable man usually seemed to turn up so I turned over and slept, as well.

That next morning, I tied the boy to the hitching post outside, his arms outspread on the rough wood. This time he faced me so that I could give him a good milking. I had told him in advance and allowed him to play with his cock and balls in preparation. When the actual moment came, he quivered in anticipation, groaned in expectation, and rewarded me with a full hand of fine, white seed. I gave him permission to lick me clean.

Slavegrant became quite frisky as I forced the plastic CB-3000 back on his now flaccid penis. He tucked it all away in his jeans before happily going off to saddle the horses and loading our remaining supplies.

It was a glorious fall day with a brisk breeze as we headed down the mountain. It almost seemed a shame to go back to the city. All too soon, we exchanged our horses for my Jag. The car headed back to Los Angeles and home in Hancock Park. I was relieved to find Paul and his boy spending a relaxed afternoon in the dungeon. That evening, Rufusboy had to head back to Valencia for another week on the TV series.

I kept my promise to Slavegrant and invited Baz, my favorite artist from Prix in West Hollywod, to tattoo him, scheduling the event for a couple of days later. In my slave's last few days with me he slowly gathered his gear together, giving the house a half-hearted final cleaning, He packed his saddle and riding gear to ship back to his family home in Virginia. Sensing the slave's needs that final day with me, I told him to get himself cleaned out and down into the basement. That brought him back to life. He hurried to obey.

For that final occasion, I chose to honor him by wearing my fine black leather uniform. I slid into the heavy black harness, breeches, boots, gloves, and cap. Once arrived in the dungeon, I found my slave had dutifully spread himself out naked over the fucking bench. I warmed him up with a light flogging—nothing too serious, as I didn't want to bruise the flesh that was shortly to be inked. I shoved a couple of gloved fingers into the hole that he had already lubed. He grunted with pleasure. My own cock responded, springing out of its nest, as I undid the buttons on my breeches. I smeared lube onto my eager prong, broke open and rolled on a black rubber, before throwing a quick final fuck into the slave beneath me.

Actually, I took my time, working my muscled tool inside the passage before me easily, but firmly. My slave wanted my dick deep within him. Slavegrant sucked me up his passage and gripped my cock to make certain I had a good time, as well. One gloved hand moved round to massage his penis, the other tweaked his right nipple.

He was happily panting, gurgling and sweating. I worked him, leaning over his torso. My pole scarcely needed encouraging to piston in and out ever more forcefully. The pace picked up. We shared the pleasure of our final moments. The heat intensified between us. I thrust demandingly and pulled his prick urgently. Our bursts of sexual release coincided. We were both cumming. I felt my seed surge from my covered weapon in his welcoming hole. His cream splattered over my glove and onto his chest. I lay there, almost on top of him, my body crushing his. He was snorting happily. I joined in a release of laughter, as I slid out of his hole.

The pair of us cleaned up again and relaxed for an hour, talking about our time together, before Baz, the tattoo artist, arrived. I had no desire for tattoos, personally. However, I had seen some examples of his ink-artistry on several of James Villier's slaves and knew he would do a good job with my simple brand symbol. We discussed the placement and size of the emblem, a circle with a Roman "T" in the center. I had already explained to the slave this was to be his farewell present. Baz positioned Slavegrant's hard-muscled right asscheek on the bench and carefully began the outline of the circle with his needle. I sat alongside and held my slave's right hand and arm, murmuring encouragement, like a doting parent., as time passed.

It took Baz about three hours of concentrated work, with a couple of breaks, to achieve the effect we both wanted. I was impressed by his degree of commitment to a relatively simple design. The result pleased us all. Most of all, Slavegrant, feeling both stiff and sore by this time, was delighted with the image he saw when I handed him a mirror. There was a thin black circle about four inches wide with a thick bold "T" at its center. The result looked just like the actual brand that he had admired on Paul.

Baz gave him advice on the care and the ointment to protect the new scab for the next few days, then departed, with both our thanks. Slavegrant flung himself onto the floor, weeping and fiercely licking my Dehners with his tears. I was touched by this gesture.

Actually, the whole experience was quite touching. Raising him up, I kissed his tear-smeared face forcefully and packed him off to bed.

A few days later, Grant was gone. Both Paul and I took him to LAX. I sat in the back seat with him and played with his tits and cock, one last time. After a few minutes of play, he exploded quite spontaneously and then licked his jism from his hand. We lip-locked and I savored the last of his cream. He tried to nestle in my arms as best he could with the seat belts, weeping silently.

It was a strange experience for me. For the first time in my almost twenty years as a Master, my slave was leaving me, rather than the reverse. I knew it was for the best. He had an open invitation to visit, should he come back to Los Angeles. Sadly, we both knew it would not be any time soon.

CHAPTER THREE - PAUL

The house in Hancock Park seemed very empty to both Tarquin and myself when we got back from the airport. Oddly enough, in the next few days, even I missed Tarquin's Slavegrant. He'd been a largely silent presence in our midst. From my point of view, he was a good slave, keeping our big house clean and tidy. He prepared our meals adequately enough. I imagined he serviced Tarquin reasonably well. I admired his spirit, breaking his contract, leaving his Master of his own free will. Slavegrant also found the courage to have his Master's brand tattooed on his asscheek.

I had asked to see his "Circle T" to compare it with mine. My brand had been burned into the flesh of my right buttcheek six years before. It was now a clean and dramatic symbol of my then slavery, an experience that I wouldn't want to undergo again. I rubbed my hand almost absentmindedly over the smooth indentation as I looked at Grant's more recent emblem. How far my relationship with Tarquin had evolved, through some turbulent times!

In truth, the brand would always remind me of the bond we shared. I hoped it would never again be broken. Grant's scabs would fall off and the circle would remain as a reminder of the time he had spent with us. Still, his brand was superficial. Mine was burned into my brain as well as my ass.

My mind went to my own boy, Rufusboy, the British actor I'd "acquired" last summer in Britain. I know that choice was made without really thinking beyond my cock. The sex had been exciting. His service then had seemed real enough. His stories of his harsh training were graphic. Now that his television career had taken off in the USA, I could only stand back and watch his work, as the star of the new series *Spycatcher*. There seemed to be the same whirlwind of publicity as in the rest of the entertainment world, snatching a piece of my boy. The whirlwind rocked and shook both of us, Rufusboy and I. Perhaps I was being too naive, but he seemed torn between the adulation and excitement on a large scale, and his humbler possibilities as my boy.

Tarquin was right. I was becoming obsessive in my fruitless efforts to keep him to myself. After all, I hadn't known him long in London. It had only been only a couple of months. I'd taken him on with very little actual training on my part. As I looked back on that time, I realized that Rufusboy had been at loose ends. His British television series had been reaching an end. He had some time to enjoy himself as my plaything. But that acting career would always be more important to him, and why not? My graphic design work was important to me. He was only in his twenties. He might become a good actor, as well as a handsome hunk.

My problem was that I thought of him as my own handsome hunk. I believed that Rufusboy had been content to go along with that. I preferred to hope that he really wanted to remain my boy. I also hoped that the excitement of his new starring role in an American television series would wear off with time. I thought that the circle of smooth flatterers and sexual predators would drift away as he became a regular TV commodity.

Who was I kidding, with James Villier, Rufusboy's agent and Tarquin's friendly rival, weaving an ever-stronger spider's web round my boy? At first, Rufusboy had come home to Hancock Park each weekend after taping finished, performing his service to me. I would fuck him fiercely, often spilling my seed into him, to remind him who was his Master. Gradually, the weekends were being taken up with publicity for the series, events to show off the new star and parties to which James conveniently 'forgot' to invite Tarquin and myself. In his professional capacity as Rufusboy's lawyer and business manager, Tarquin could keep one eye on him, reminding James of our interest. For that, I was grateful.

Finally, I told Rufusboy I would come up to Valencia for a

weekend about a month before Thanksgiving. He was to keep time clear for a day of service. I wanted to make it memorable. This was to be my way of 'branding' him, since I couldn't leave any physical marks on the actor's buffed body. So, on Saturday morning, I loaded my Escalade with half the toys from the dungeon, including the portable sling, and set off for Rufusboy's condo.

He was waiting for me, appropriately wearing his leather jock and low boots. Some time was spent on his large bed, after I'd shucked off my shirt, 501s, and boots. Rufusboy and I needed to get reacquainted and to explore each other's bodies. We were hungry for one another, exchanging tongues and saliva as I ran my hands over his warm torso. He shuddered as I flicked his large brown nipples and tugged on each in turn. Then, daring me, he reached over to twist my large heavy tit rings. In return, I took his freshly shaved cock and balls, squeezing them gently, but firmly. He hissed as the fingers of my other hand reached under his perineum and sought the entrance to his anus. He squirmed as I slid first one finger and then another into the hole he'd been ordered to clean out and lube in preparation. We lay panting and lightly sweating as my hands continued to play with his genitals and ass. I was warming both of us for the action to follow.

Then, Rufusboy carefully freed himself. He began to lick me all over, slurping my sweat as he slid down my chest. His tongue took my balls into his mouth one by one, washing them copiously. Then he switched to my twitching cock to swallow my prick as it grew with his stimulation. I pulled his head back up. I didn't want to cum that way. I needed more than a good blowjob at that moment. So, he squirmed back to my nipples, using his lips to carefully arouse the nubs and the heavy metal surrounding them. His teeth came into play to tease them more fully.

After a few minutes, I pulled him off again as I moved off the bed.

"Up, boy. Get the sling out and ready. Make sure the uprights are locked firmly into place. I don't want the fucking sling falling down at the wrong moment. I'm going to change into chaps and Wescoes. You, get naked."

"Yes, Sir, it will get the poles spread, attach the sling and the chains as you like them, Sir." His language change into the third person suggested he was finding his sub headspace.

"Get the leather seat at the right height for your butt."

"Will do, Sir. Can it strap on your black harness, when you're ready, Sir?"

"Maybe, boy. Make sure you're properly lubed for action."

"Of course, Sir."

We were smiling and sweating, ready for a good fuck session. The naked Rufusboy made short work of setting up the sling. Then he scrambled up into position. His head lay on the small pillow, his muscled body wide and open. He seemed to be in his proper headspace.

I looked at my boy, glowing with health and excited at the prospect of being speared by his Master. His cock was quivering with need. His hole was twitching as I pulled his legs up into the stirrups. Then I bound his wrists in the chains. Rufusboy needed to feel his Master today.

I would have him bareback. So, I smeared some hot lube on my own thrusting prick. I lined up my weapon. My cockhead was shoved through the waiting pink portal. He groaned as he felt my naked penis. Patiently I paused, letting him adjust to the size of the log easing into him. He gurgled as I inched farther up the familiar passage. Finally, my pubes were hitting his shaved cunt. He sighed as I moved forward. The sling swung away from me. My dick slid back to his entrance. Then I pulled on the chains. Rufusboy was spiked again.

Pleasure/pain took over. We swayed together, cock fully home and then sliding back. Still, his ass muscles suddenly squeezed my member to keep me inside him. Sweat dripped off us. Breath came in rapid pants. The tempo of the game picked up. I yanked on the chains. This forced him up the leather seat. Leaning down, I took his head in one hand. My kiss was hard, forcing my tongue toward his throat. He gagged and groaned as I let him loose. The swing forced him backward and forward on my prick. My hard shaft rampaged up his passage with energy and excitement.

I wanted to draw out this fuck. I wanted him to take all of me repeatedly, hammering his innards. He knew it, gasping and grunting on my pile driver. My hands held his penis, stroking it firmly as my cock rocked him back and forth. Our breathing was getting heavier and faster. My sweat dripped down my harness and splashed onto his chest. We were both slippery and sizzling with sexual excitement. I held back for as long as I could. The power exchange was powerful. Two men's bodies were tangled together in the most intimate way possible.

I prolonged the climax for a good thirty minutes. Then, the churning in my balls would wait no longer. I grunted and thrust all the way, pouring my cream into the waiting innards of my panting, perspiring boy. I gripped his penis while jabbing his innards with my own cock. He groaned as he sprayed all over his stomach. I slowed the sling to a stop and collapsed over Rufusboy in triumph.

A moment later, there came a pounding on the door of the condo. In walked James with a couple of his boys.

"Rufusboy, Rufusboy, I thought I'd dr…drop by and take you out to…. Oh, so so…sorry. I didn't realize you were already taken care of. Hello Paul, ss…sorry to have interrupted. You ss…seem to have been very busy to ju…judge from that cock of yours."

"Hello James. Were you expected today?" I looked back at Rufusboy with some suspicion as well as disappointment.

"Oh, I often come to ch…check on my protégé on weekends. I want to be sure he doesn't get into any mischief."

Since when was my Rufusboy his protégé? I thought. "I didn't realize Rufusboy was your 'protégé.' I thought he was his own man, able to look after his own interests. I know that he is capable of finding his own friends."

"Well, sh sh… surely you know what I mean, Paul. I like to think I've helped to uncover his talents, so to sp…speak. Does he need some help to get out of your sling? Maybe not. Anyway, don't overdo it, Rufusboy. Remember you have a sc…script to memorize this weekend."

"Don't you worry, I'll make sure he studies while I'm here, James." My anger at the interruption was coming to a boil.

"Fine. ...You are ss...such a careful caretaker, Paul. Or should I call you Master? My, but you have handsome tit rings. I don't know that I've really noticed them before. Well, we must be off. Tell Tarquin we need to have a meeting of the Circle of Ss...Six soon. I'm off to London in a couple of weeks, but I expect he already knows that. Enjoy yourselves."

Rufusboy had been completely quiet during this exchange. He was a captive in the sling, slipping his feet out of the stirrups and onto the floor. But his arms were still restrained in the chains. My dick had retired into its own bushy nest as I watched the visitors leave. Then I went over and released his wrists as he collapsed into my arms. The mood had been completely shattered.

"it's sorry, Sir. Please believe it when it says it didn't invite Master James. He seems to be developing this habit of checking up on it, Sir."

"Checking on you? What do you mean? Why do you address him as Master? I am your Master, not him."

"Yes, Sir, but, if it's alone, he wants it to play and service him. He gets the support of some of his boys who always come with him."

"Wants to fuck you, too?" My anger was coming to a boil.

"I've managed to prevent that happening, but it bugs me to have to fend him off every time, Sir. I don't think I can stand much more of this, Sir."

In his agitation, Rufusboy was breaking out of slave mode. To be forced out of his slave space—that was extremely unlike him.

"I'll kill the motherfucker!"

"Please don't, Sir. He's been a longtime friend to Master Tarquin and yourself. Also, he's my agent—and a good one, too. All this pressure is making it almost impossible for me to focus on work."

"He is no friend of mine. He's got to be talked to. He needs to understand that you're my property and nobody else's. Tarquin will need to deal with him, both as your lawyer and possibly the one that

James will listen to."

Rufusboy's voice dropped to a whimper. "I wish to hell it would all go away. Sometimes I just don't know who to turn to. It's hard enough keeping up with the television series, without these distractions. I'm sorry, Sir, I didn't mean you. Perhaps I could take you out for a meal, for a change?"

We both tried to relax and enjoy the rest of the day. Inside, I was still seething and wondering how to keep James at a proper distance. When I mentioned it to Tarquin on my return that evening, he volunteered to talk to James "on a professional level. I hope that would be more effective."

For the moment, it seemed to work. Rufusboy spent the next couple of weekends with us in Hancock Park. We made plans to get out of LA for a few days over the actual Thanksgiving holiday. Taping on the TV series was also moving along well, according to its young star.

§§§§

But, just before the holidays and our eagerly awaited vacation, I was shaken out of my obsession with Rufusboy one morning by a phone call from Cedars-Sinai Hospital. It was to tell me that my sister, Ellen, had been badly injured in a car crash. I put aside the design project I was heading at work. I raced through LA's heavy traffic, to the emergency room. My brother-in-law, John, was huddled on a sofa in a corner.

"Thank God you're here, Paul. Ellen's in surgery. It feels like she has been there forever."

"What happened, John?"

"They think it was a hit-and-run. According to the police, some guy in an SUV broadsided her. She's now six months pregnant. I am so afraid that I might lose both of them."

I collapsed on the sofa beside him and held him in my arms. John welcomed my attempt to comfort him. He needed the warmth and comfort of another human being at this stage. My involvement with Rufusboy had kept me from seeing much of my sister in the previous few months. Since the death of our parents, we only had one another. It made matters worse at that moment knowing that they had perished in a car crash almost five years before. I was distraught that my self-absorption had taken me away from my close relationship with my only sibling. She had always been there for me, since I'd moved to Los Angeles. She had seen me through some of my worst moments, never condemning me, always encouraging in her counsel.

"Let me see what I can find out. Maybe there's some update."

The nurses were empathetic, but I was told that we would have to wait until the surgery was over. They suggested we move into the family waiting room for more privacy. I went outside to call Rufusboy. When I couldn't reach him on his cell phone, I called Tarquin in his office and explained the situation.

"Try not to worry too much, Paul. I'll reach Rufusboy and bring him into the picture. Keep me posted as soon as you know anything. Give John my sympathy. Please let me know if he needs anything… And remember, I love you and I'm here for you."

"Thanks, Tarquin, I needed to hear that."

"I will get there later this afternoon, if they'll let me into that area."

I went back to comfort John. Together, we sat and endured the long wait. Eventually, the surgeon came into the waiting room.

"Mr. Braden, you'll be glad to hear your wife has come through the operation successfully. The pregnancy seems stable. Unless we need to, we would prefer that the baby not be delivered until further along in the pregnancy. We will need to keep them both here for a few days, in case of any complications. Her gynecologist will be in tomorrow morning to assess the case further. I know he will want to speak with you both then." Turning to me, he smiled and said, "You must be her brother. I can see a family resemblance. You can both see her for a few minutes, but she's very heavily sedated."

It was a nasty shock to see my big sister, who'd always been so vibrant and alive, lying pale and motionless in the hospital bed.

Both of us were badly shaken. I asked John what I could do to help. He wanted me to make a couple of phone calls to friends who were looking after their son. I made him drink some coffee and halfheartedly eat a sandwich.

Tarquin arrived that afternoon, comforted John, and then turned to me. "Are you okay?"

I nodded.

"I have not been able to reach Rufusboy, yet. They are probably working late to finish before the holidays. I'll keep trying. I did place a message on his phone, asking him to call me."

Tarquin took John home to comfort his son and put him to bed. He could also take a shower and put on fresh clothes, while I stood watch. The doctor said not to expect any change overnight. That didn't matter. I felt I needed be there just the same. Word was trickling out about Ellen's accident and by answering questions on his cell phone, I could take some of the pressure off John's shoulders.

I was kept busy, caught up with my own office manager. My thoughts only occasionally strayed back to Rufusboy. There was still no reply from his Blackberry, or the landline in the condo. Much later in the evening, Tarquin called back.

"I'm at LAX and don't have much time. No one seems to know where Rufusboy is. Taping finished early this afternoon. So I got one of the gofers to go round to his condo. He wasn't there, and it looked as though he'd gone on a trip."

"Well, yes, we're supposed to be going away to Baja."

"I'm sorry, Paul, but I don't think that's what happened. He got the production office to book him a ticket to London for this evening."

"London? Why would he go back there?"

"I don't know, but I intend to find out. Peg, my assistant, will keep checking at this end. I'm booked on a red-eye to New York and I'll take a London flight tomorrow."

"No, Tarquin, I'm the one who should be doing that."

"My dear Paul, you need to be near your sister. She and John need you more at this moment. Let me try to find out what's happened. Oddly enough, James has been in London for the past few days."

"Fuck, James said he would be going to England when he appeared that day at the condo. I'm coming, too. If James has engineered something…."

"Don't get hysterical. What could you do over there? You've no legal standing with Rufusboy. Yes, he's your boy, but you're not a blood relative. You're not even his Partner. Why should anyone tell you anything, particularly in a foreign country?"

"But I love him!"

"Perhaps you do; or perhaps you're just infatuated. At least I can use the fact that I'm Rufusboy's business manager in my search. We don't know that James is involved. You're much more use here, helping your sister and brother-in-law."

"I just feel so helpless."

"You can work with Peg on this end, if it will help. We'll keep you fully posted. Now I've got to go and catch my plane. Just remember, Paul, I do love you, Paul, and that's for real."

"I know, Tarquin and I'm truly sorry I've been such a wimpy bastard. I love you, too. Thank you and thank you for doing this for me. Have a safe flight. Good luck."

The phone went dead. I sat back, drank John's cold coffee and wondered how the fuck I had become so screwed up with my real priorities in life.

CHAPTER FOUR - TARQUIN

Usually, I fall asleep quite easily on long distance night flights. It's certainly comfortable enough in first class on British Airways to London. This time, my mind was buzzing with questions about the activities of the past few days.

Was I right to go charging across the Atlantic looking for my partner's boy/love/obsession? How could I be certain Rufusboy was running away? Maybe he was just in Britain to see his family? I didn't think so, since he and Paul had been planning a trip to Baja, California over this Thanksgiving holiday. Had James Villier driven him to alter course? Was it the stress of his imminent television stardom or the industry gay hangers-on?

Should I have allowed Paul to come with me? After all, Rufusboy was his concern. But he also had a sister, with an unborn child, in "stable but critical condition" at an LA hospital. He was part of a very limited family support there.

As I'd brutally told him on the phone, he had no legal rights or connection to Rufusboy, especially in the boy's native country. He would be a gay guy looking for a man, who seemingly wanted to disappear. As his lawyer and business manager, I had limited, but legitimate reason to have concern and search for him. I hoped that James was not the reason for this inexplicable disappearance. We had not had any communications from Rufusboy or the studio.

Fortunately, I had Rufusboy sign the necessary papers a month ago. A copy was emailed to me, in my company's New York office, where I dealt with some legal work before I boarded the plane for London. No, it was better that Paul stayed to help his sister's family and keep his mind occupied.

How did my friend and competitor James Villier fit in? True, he was Rufusboy' agent and a damned good one. But he had wanted more than that, as I'd seen for myself. James, himself, was hot; I knew that fact well. He held the key to professional opportunities. Rufusboy had been torn, though he had resisted, much of the time, I hoped. Had James arranged this last-minute dash to London? He was already there, meeting with Rufusboy's UK agent and others of his own contacts? It did not seem likely. James had sounded genuinely startled when I phoned him from LAX. We agreed to meet for lunch as soon as I arrived Friday morning, before most offices closed for the weekend. Fortunately, Thanksgiving was not a holiday the British observed, or I would have been completely thwarted. Rufusboy was due back at work the following week. There was no time to lose.

I sighed and tried to relax. The 'beds' in first class were comfortable, though a little cramped for a guy of my size. I'd spent the dinner hour mulling over the problems. There was not anything I could achieve, until I landed. So, I drifted off into a light sleep for several hours. Of course, James had sent a car and driver to Heathrow who took me straight to The Ivy Restaurant to meet him.

"Tarquin, you made good time from the airport. And what did you think of the new t… terminal?"

Stammer still in place, I noticed.

"Hello, James, it's good to see you. You are looking very English, or is that Scottish, in your tweeds. Thank you for sending the car. I needed that, after two long nights on planes, however comfortable. Seriously, we need to get down to business. Is there any fresh news?"

"Nothing very much. Do you mind ordering right away? I've decided to have some ff…fish. I have already talked to Norman Jones, the boy's London agent. I hadn't met him before this week. He didn't ss…seem to know anything about this. He wants to see us right after lunch. He's trying to reach Rufusboy's parents in Edinburgh but doesn't think he'd go there. I'm very concerned about what's brought this about."

"So am I, James. Frankly, I wondered whether you'd engineered it."

"My dear Tarquin, why would I do that? Ah, here's the soup."

"James, I've known you for how many years? Well over fifteen. When you decide you want something, you stop at nothing to get it. We both know you'd like Rufusboy for more than just a client. Paul found him first. He has already trained him for himself."

"Well, you're certainly being bb... blunt today. So, I'll match your style. I'll admit to being personally interested in Rufusboy, but I had nothing to do with this. He's due back to work on *Spycatcher* next week, even though most episodes have been shot. He's still got a cc...contract to live up to.

"And you seem ss...sufficiently intrigued to dash across the ocean, so I've a proposal for you. Whoever finds him first gets to ss...spend a night with the other as a reward. You know how mm... much I want to get back in your ass, Tarquin, don't you?"

"I don't know about that. For the moment, we need to forget your personal interests in Rufusboy or me. I was going to suggest pooling our resources and working together. But I'll take your wager. It could be the spur we need. We're in a foreign country, even if they speak more or less the same language, and without the resources of our offices. It's also a holiday weekend back home."

Previously, I had casually asked Paul how much he knew about Rufusboy's past, and the answer was "not much." Hopefully his agent could clue us in. We ate hastily, paying little attention to the excellent food. I wasn't really hungry, but heaven only knew when we might get another decent meal.

James's driver got us over to Norman James' office efficiently, and the agent was waiting for us. By Beverly Hills' standards the suite wasn't luxurious, but it seemed to be humming effectively with staff bustling and phones ringing on a damp November Friday afternoon.

"It's a pleasure to meet you, Tarquin. Of course, I've heard so much about you from our boy and what a help you've been to him. I'm so sorry to hear about Paul's family problems. Pity he couldn't be with you." Rufusboy's British agent was shorter than I'd expected, agreeable and clearly in charge of his operation.

"Thank you, Norman. Paul and Rufusboy have said the same about you. I'm hoping you can shed some light on Rufusboy's sudden flight. It seems out of character. Paul and Rufusboy had planned to spend the long weekend in Mexico."

"Yes, James gave me the main outline of events. I have seen neither hide or hair of Rufus for almost three months, since he left to start work on the American version of *Spycatcher*. I thought I'd wait until you arrived before phoning his parents in Scotland. I think that's an unlikely bolt hole. He rarely saw them in all the years I've known him. But it's a place to start. My assistant is setting up the call now.

"Could it have been this new series? Perhaps the new surroundings? Or different ways of working, with a different crew? I do know a deal of work was involved, but Rufus was always very professional in that way. It's one of the reasons he's done so well. He's such a dear boy. Ah, here's the call now."

James and I sat silently listening to one end of the phone conversation. It soon became apparent the Rufusboy's mother had no idea where he was. She thought he was at work in Los Angeles. She could not think of any other UK friends he might have gone to see. Norman thanked her, promising to keep her informed and turned back to us.

"So, there's nothing there. All I managed to do was to upset the good lady. I think her surprise was quite genuine. No, we need to look elsewhere. James, do you think he was overworking or had major problems on the set? I know the pace of production is faster in the US than over here."

James seemed on the defensive. "I don't think so. He ss...seemed to be managing the job well enough, despite the demands on his time. That part he was enjoying, I'm sure, although it was keeping him more than busy."

Norman decided to pursue the problem with me. "So, it sounds like something in his personal life. I need to ask you, Tarquin, is all still going well with Paul? They certainly seemed happy enough when I saw them last year. But these things can change."

Norman then darted a look at James.

"And other people, other men, I should say, may become interested. I should know. I really enjoyed playing with him when he was starting out, fresh from university. Then he met Paul and I was back to being merely his agent. He really is a hot hunk and a very marketable commodity."

The two agents smirked at one another. I interrupted. "How about other men, or women, in his life back here? You know, people with whom he might have remained in contact?

My friend/competitor still seemed oddly defensive. "I pulled some ss…strings. He took the ss…second flight from LAX, two nights ago. BA had no note of any booking beyond London."

"Norman, there must have been friends, or some men before you?" I asked again.

"Rufus never seemed to need friends or have much time for them either. I certainly kept him very busy when he was with me. He'd been a 'rent-boy' at university; a 'trick' available for hire, while he was studying drama.

"We worked out a suitable financial arrangement between us for our play sessions when he was starting out professionally here in London. After that he kept active with the gym, voice lessons, and later rehearsals and his increasingly large television parts. No, I'd have known if there was another man, or woman for that matter." Norman seemed certain on the point.

"Ss…so what about a Master before you?" queried James, "He must have got that training ss…somewhere."

"I'm trying to think back. One name I do remember is Simon Dacre. He's a banker, now here in London. I run into him sometimes. You know how small these circles are. He often boasts of severely putting Rufus through his paces early on.

"Then there was Bart, who got him started. He's a very successful, but uncouth, building contractor, near Brighton, where our boy went to university. He sent him to me, but I don't think they kept up the connection. I can give you their phone numbers. You might just catch Simon before he leaves for the weekend."

"Excellent, Norman, give me the nu…number and I'll try Si… Simon right away."

"Thank you, Norman, this has all been helpful. I suppose I could give this man, Bart, a call. What is his number and last name?" I wanted to do something, take some action.

"I'm trying to remember. Let me check my address file. Here he is, Thompson. I believe he has a house not far from Brighton." Norman wrote the information down and handed it to me. "Let me know if you find the boy. I'm really concerned for him personally, as well as professionally."

James was pleased with himself; he'd managed to get hold of Simon Dacre on the phone. Dacre had been intrigued and agreed to see us in his office, "Just for ten minutes. I need to get home and change." We said a rapid goodbye to Norman, promising to stay in touch.

James's driver maneuvered his way through the wet and busy streets of the city. Simon Dacre's place of work was an imposing piece of 90s glass and metal architecture. He had a dark paneled corner office, rather like James's suite in Beverly Hills. In fact, they had already established a rapport on the phone, two tall dark-haired men with a darker taste in other men.

"Mr. Villier, Mr. Charlton. Gentlemen, what can I do for you this dreary Friday afternoon? It's not often I get to entertain American guests, particularly from the film and television world."

"It's ss…so good of you to see us at ss…such short notice, Mr. Dacre." James' stutter was working overtime.

I cut through the pleasantries. "We need help in locating one of our clients who appears to have gone missing in the UK. We understand you may know him, Rufusboy McLachlan. He is now a television star."

"Was he a client of the bank? I don't recall the name immediately." Mr. Dacre was professionally smooth.

"No, not that I'm aware of. I believe you knew him in a more personal way."

Simon Dacre's polite smile did not fade, but the light left his eyes.

"I don't quite see what this has to do with me. What is your professional interest in Mr. McLean, that was the name?"

James interrupted. "We're his American mm…managers. He's shooting a new US TV series, adapted from the British version of *Spycatcher*. He ss…suddenly flew back to London a couple of days ago unexpectedly. We need to ff…find him and get him back to work. We hoped you could help us."

"Ah, now I remember him. He was a handsome young devil who lacked discipline, which I enjoyed providing. He had considerable potential. I'm glad he's doing well. But I haven't seen him in, oh, two years, I should think."

"Have you heard from him?" I queried.

"No, Mr. Charlton, not really since I moved to London with the bank. So, I'm afraid I can't be of more help. He really needed a regular dose of specialized training. Of course, I'll let you know if he contacts me. Where are you staying?" He rose from the table. Clearly the meeting was over. "Well, if you'll excuse me, gentlemen, I've a dinner to go to this evening…."

There seemed no pointing in wasting each other's time further. We were left with Bart Thompson, the builder, who seemed to be a slender chance. Still I had followed it up earlier. The deep gruff voice had been noncommittal but concerned on the phone. I was eventually given his address and directions to a house in the country, about eighty miles south of London.

"Tarquin, I'm not ss…sure it's worth tt…trailing all the way down to some deep-in-the-country place on a cc…cold wintry evening. Let's ss…stay in town and think it through over a proper meal."

"Why, James, where is your detective spirit? I know the clue is not all that promising. We still need to check it out. Are you sure you are not backing out because this is my clue and I might just win the bet as well as your hot ass?"

"Fuck you, Tarquin! All right, but it better be worthwhile."

Even with a car and driver, it was slow going down to Brighton on a dank Friday evening. Darkness fell. Ahead of us was an endless motorway, followed by country roads. I was getting very tired and wondered what kind of fool's errand we were on. Would Mr. Thompson just give us another name, another clue, another dead-end and then send us on our way?

We finally drew up in front of a large, well-kept, Georgian-style house, seemingly located in the middle of nowhere. The door was opened by a tough-looking guy, about fifty, in jeans and boots.

"Yea, what do yer fucking want?"

"Hello, I am Tarquin Charlton, and this is James Villier. We are looking for our friend and client Rufus McLachlan. You are Mr. Thompson, is that correct?"

"Fuckin' right, I'm Bart Thompson. You rang from London about some guy. I don't know that I can fuckin' help."

There was something solid and knowing about Bart Thompson that gave me hope. I shoved my way inside.

"We think Rufus may need some help. He left work in Los Angeles, flew to London and has disappeared. That is so unlike him."

"Since you're already here, you might as fuckin' well finish comin' in, though I don't see where I fuckin' fit in. You want a drink?"

"That would be great. We have been on the move since I arrived in London, this morning. We really want to find Rufus."

He led us into a surprisingly comfortable room with a fire blazing in the hearth and offered us beer or wine.

"This is very gg…good of you, Mr. Thompson, ch…chardonnay please. We're his American agent and business manager. We've got to track him down and get him back to LA."

Clearly, James was also tired and being clumsy. I was not going to let him foul up even this slender thread.

"The fact is, Bart, we are at the end of our rope. You are the only lead that we have got left. We do not know why Rufus did a bolt for London. He was supposed to be going to Mexico for the weekend with Paul."

"What the fuck makes you think I'd know where 'e is. It's been years. And who's this fucker Paul?"

I took a deep breath. Bart Thompson had not thrown us out yet and I grounded myself.

"Okay. Fuck it...all right. I know you trained Rufus and made him a successful 'rent-boy.' How do I know? Because he and Paul told me so. Paul is his new Master and is going crazy back in Los Angeles."

"So why the fuck isn't 'e here?"

"Because his very pregnant sister was in a very serious car accident a couple of days ago and is in hospital. Because Paul has no fucking legal rights to Rufus either here or in California. He just loves him and wants him to be happy."

There was a slight noise outside the closed door, but we all heard it.

"That's a pretty wild story you're spinning. What did you say was yer fucking name?"

"Charlton, Tarquin Charlton. I have known Rufus all the time he has been in the United States. He has been staying in our home. James here is his film and television agent. We both know Rufus is a hard worker and would not duck out on his job without good reason."

"Well, what proof have you got that I know this fucker Rufus? You don't seem to know anything about me. Where's the fucking connection?"

I took a serious gamble.

"I am willing to bet that you are Bart, the Buttmaster that Rufus told Paul about. If this is true, you are the man who first taught Rufusboy his 'trade' while he attended college here."

A slow smile spread across Bart's face. I knew I had scored a touchdown.

"Okay, motherfucker, you better come in and explain yourself."

Bart called out, as he stared straight at the door from where the noise had come earlier.

The door slowly opened. An embarrassed Rufusboy shambled slowly into the room.

"Hello, Master Tarquin. Hello, Master James. It's good to see you both. I'm sorry. I've been such an idiot. I needed to get away from LA for a few days, to sort myself out. Bart here is the only one I could really trust. So, I called him from Heathrow, got on a train for Brighton and here I am."

"The kid knew I'd fuckin' well look after 'im. It's been a while. Still, we've always stayed in touch. I throw a good hard fuck into him every so often to keep him on the right fucking path. You fellas wasted no time in tracking 'im down."

"Well, it certainly was not easy. It is a great relief to find him in such safe hands. Now, if you do not mind, I am going to call Paul and you, you miserable fucker, are going to apologize to your Master." I was too tired to be more than mildly angry.

"That's the way to treat 'im, Tarquin. While you're doing that, I'll rustle up some food. I'll bet it's some time since you fuckin' ate. I s'pose we better find a couple of beds for you. There's plenty of spare rooms here for tonight. Fuck, might 'ave been good to keep 'im here for a couple more days. Then we could 'ave had a fucking orgy. Just like the good old days. Any chance I can get you gents to stay over?"

We all laughed and relaxed. I managed to reach Paul on his cell phone and made Rufusboy apologize and confess his sins. Bart supervised a decent dinner, with Rufusboy in proper slave mode. I discovered a fellow cigar aficionado in Bart. We each enjoyed one of my Montecristo's. But I was dead on my feet, and Rufusboy seemed in no mood for significant questions.

The beds were very comfortable. I slept soundly. The next morning, the sounds of the countryside woke me up. The sun was shining when I finally opened my eyes. Rufusboy was sitting on the end of the bed, avoiding eye contact.

"Master Tarquin, I'm sorry I've screwed you and Master Paul

around."

"And good morning to you, young idiot. Why the fuck did you not let us know what you were up to?"

"I'd just had enough of LA and all the demands, the schmoozing and stuff. I thought if I came back here, I'd have time to sort myself out."

"Well, you left Paul half crazed with worry about you, in addition to his concern for his sister and her baby."

"I'm totally sorry. I didn't know about that. I just felt I was being pulled in so many different directions. Of course, Paul is my Master. I owe him—and you—so much, for my career in America. Then there's Master James. Look, I know he's a friend of yours, Sir, and I mean no disrespect. He's been a great agent. He's made sure I have a good contract for the series; but he isn't content with that. He wants more of me. What I mean, Sir, is that he wants my body, as well. He's made it clear that he is prepared to offer all kinds of bribes and incentives, Sir. Why, only last week…."

"So, James is the real reason you left town, rather than go to Baja with Paul?" I did not think Paul needed to know all this right then. Besides, he almost certainly already had his own suspicions about James's intentions toward Rufusboy.

"He wanted me to stay in LA and 'meet a film producer with a script and a leading role for me.' I knew, he was just pimping me out, again. Just like a 'rent-boy' all over again. It was my tits and ass the guy wanted, not my talent."

Rufusboy began to choke up. Rather foolishly, I put my arm around his shoulder, allowing him to snuggle up against me and relax.

"It was a spur of the moment thing, Sir. I couldn't face Paul after I'd almost whored myself the night before. I just needed to get as far away as possible. England and my past contacts seemed so much safer. I was coming apart at the seams. You can understand this… can't you, Master Tarquin?"

"I believe so. Although, that does not change the fact that you should have, at least, left Paul a message. Come on, boy, there is no reason for tears. Yes, you have certainly fucked up, but you are safe now. Relax here for a day or so, before you return to work. And you are going back to work?"

"Why yes, of course, Sir."

He cuddled closer into me; behaving much like an overgrown puppy. But I needed to remind myself that this was a buffed, handsome man. I could not help but feel a stirring in my loins, to use the old phrase. I was not certain he knew the effect he was having on my body. His was a powerful aphrodisiac, which I had to resist. I almost believed his story. Rufusboy did seem guilty and upset. I changed the focus of the conversation.

"But, why did you come here, to be with Bart?"

"Oh, that's simple enough, Sir. I knew nothing of Ellen's accident, I swear. I'd plenty of time to think on the flight to London. I couldn't stay around work, with Master James constantly shadowing me, with his gang of boys and gropers. Because of my new celebrity, I wasn't sure Mexico would be any better.

"Here in Britain, there was Sir Norman, my British agent; but I was afraid he would immediately tell Master James. I knew he was already over here and that was the last problem that I needed. Then there was Master Simon Dacre. Master James mentioned last night that you met him, briefly in London. I've sworn never to go near that sadist again.

"So, Sir, Bart was my best bet. He may not have a college education and he 'fucks' every other word, but he is strong and tough. His heart is big, and I knew that I could trust him. He seemed the natural choice. I'm glad I did. He settled me down and gave me a good, no-nonsense talk about my responsibilities to all the others in the *Spycatcher* team. It wasn't really necessary. Of course, I knew I was going back, to get on with the work. I just needed time for myself, Sir."

I moved off the bed, before my naked and interested cock became too obvious and climbed into a pair of fresh briefs and jeans from my travel bag.

I observed something that didn't quite ring true. Rather than disgusted or repulsed, when he spoke about the various men, who had been attracted to him, Rufusboy seemed proud and excited. My observation was reinforced, as he poured out the details of his abusive apprenticeship with the sadistic Simon Dacre.

"I'm sorry, Master Tarquin, I didn't mean to unload on you like that. I've never told anyone about my time with Sir Simon before, not even Master Paul. Oh, I gave him a brief outline once last fall, but not all the details."

My instincts were smarter that to give real heed to his claimed innocence of intent. I knew his words were more premeditated than that. I decided the issue would be dealt with by his Master, Paul, once he returned to LA.

"That's all right, Rufusboy. Confession is indeed good for the soul. You needed to get it out."

"Yes, Sir. But why should I choose you, at this moment, Sir?"

"Because, you consider me a friendly and sympathetic ear, I imagine. You feel safe with me, as your Master's partner and you are in Bart's house."

"I guess you're right, Sir. It's probably time to let go of my earlier Masters and the darkness of my past training."

"Your training may have been brutal and painful. Every boy needs to go through that kind of treatment. To get back to the point, I do not see how all this bears on your reason for running from LA?"

"I'm not really sure myself, Sir. Part of it is that Master James reminds me of Sir Simon. I don't think I'm capable of going through his kind of kinky torment again. Master Paul flogs me and fucks me hard, but it's not the same, Sir."

"Master Paul trains you, because he loves you and wants you to be the best boy you can be. That is the way I trained him. Only the best will do."

"I guess so, Sir; now that you've put it that way. I get a real sense of belonging with Master Paul, as well as with you, Sir. I only wish you had come along first. I would have worked harder to become a perfect slave for you, and then your lover, if you'd taken me, Sir."

Rufusboy' insolence had gone too far.

"Watch yourself, boy. Paul came first, and he is my partner!"

"But, Sir, you still need a new slave, don't you? I mean now that Grant has gone; it would be an honor and a pleasure to be of service to you, Sir." Once more, he snuggled up to me.

Rufusboy had just confirmed his insincerity. "You are already spoken for, boy. You are Paul's boy and he needs you."

"I don't know who really needs me, Sir. It seems so many people have made claim to me, that they're pulling me apart. There's the television company and their hangers-on; then there's Master James and his boys, and, of course, Master Paul and you, Sir. I feel safe with you, Sir. I know that I need a dominant man, an experienced Master, Sir."

Rufusboy was not impressing me with his attempts at persuasion; still his words went on.

"You're the one who came to find me. It was you that searched all over southern England, Sir, not Master Paul. I know the strength and determination that it required. If you're really not interested in me, why did you fly to London and not Master Paul? Yes, I know about his problems; but it doesn't change the fact that it was you. You deserve to be honored whenever you want me, Sir."

Fortunately, for Rufusboy, we were interrupted by Bart.

"Are you fuckers ever coming out of there? Hell, it's after eleven and James is pacing the fuckin' floor wantin' to get back to London."

"We will be right there, Bart. Okay, Rufusboy, that is quite enough of your trying to seduce me. It will not work. In my eyes, you are and will always be Paul's boy. We should all fly back to LA, late Sunday morning. Will you be coming back with us?"

"If I can sit with you, Sir."

"I am not sure we can arrange that, or that I want it. I will however do my best to protect you from James, during the rest of this journey. You will stay here with Bart and relax. James and I have some unfinished business to attend to in London. We will meet you at Heathrow. Now get dressed."

"Sir, yes, Sir. Thank you, Sir."

He leaned over to kiss me. It was a full lover's kiss and I felt my mouth opening automatically in response. Rufusboy could be a very sexy bastard when he wanted to be. I cursed myself for not being less caring or concerned about him. Rufusboy was a full-time taker. I cut him short and opened the bedroom door to a very curious Bart.

"Come on, motherfuckers. Stop playing around. I've arranged to take you out for a fuckin' good lunch and then get you back on the London road."

It was easily arranged. Bart was happy to have Rufusboy's full attention for another day. He promised to sort out the ticket arrangements and to get the boy out to the Heathrow in time for the Sunday flight. After our return from lunch, James's driver started on our journey back to town. I reminded James that I'd won the bet about Rufusboy.

CHAPTER FIVE - PAUL

I was so relieved to hear that Tarquin had found Rufusboy in England. It was the middle of the night, at our Brentwood house, when I got his phone call. My sister and her baby were out of danger, but still in the hospital. I'd been sent home Saturday evening, to get some rest. After his call, I was restless and couldn't get back to sleep. It seemed strange that Rufusboy's past connections were reappearing a few years later.

As I wandered around, the house seemed very empty with Tarquin away, Grant gone back home and Rufusboy causing problems in England. I found myself in the kitchen, looking for comfort food. Milk and oatmeal cookies sounded good. My mind couldn't stop pulling at the threads of Rufusboy's history, as he'd told it to me during our time together in London. Yes, it had been useful both Tarquin and I knowing something of Bart Thompson. That had helped solve the mystery of Rufusboy's disappearance.

But there was another name that Tarquin had mentioned on the phone. He described how he and James had eliminated a short list of other men from Rufusboy' past. It took me several minutes that night to remember how Simon Dacre's name fit in Rufusboy's colorful and painful sexual history.

Gradually the details of Rufusboy's involvement with his second master came back to me. We had been sitting in Rufusboy's London apartment one rainy Sunday afternoon last fall when I first heard Dacre's name. My boy had been in a confessional mode after we had enjoyed a lengthy fuck session with Rufusboy in severe bondage. For some reason Simon Dacre was on his mind.

"And what about this man, Dacre?" I had asked. "You and he did share some history together?"

"I'd be surprised if he remembered me, Sir Paul. But, yes, I spent almost a year in his service, the most painful of my apprenticeship. Yes, from how he talked and looked, I began to think he could be a sadist."

That day Rufusboy was happy to delve into what had to be painful memories. "it met him at one of Master Bart's occasional orgies, early in its training." Rufusboy was slipping into full third-person slave mode. "You'll remember I told you how Bart had taken it on when it was a student at the University of Sussex. He trained it how to please other men and trained it well. I think we both enjoyed ourselves, as well. He also paid it more than enough to cover its tuition and board, as a drama student.

"Yes, Master Bart gave it a thorough apprenticeship, in offering itself and its open holes to any suitable man. Sir. it became a good 'rent boy' and Simon Dacre became its first 'outside' Master."

"You mean while you were still a student?" He was obviously trying to turn me on with his story. I was fascinated and wondered where he was leading; so didn't stop him.

Rufusboy continued, "Yes, Sir. It was during my second year at Sussex. I was already becoming an accomplished actor, both on and off the stage. Sorry, Sir. I mean 'it' was becoming an accomplished actor. In the beginning, Sir, it was Bart's 'pig-boy', trying to satisfy him and his friends at parties and learning new tricks. Sir Simon came late to one of those orgies. it was chained to a St Andrew's cross, naked, hooded and high on endorphins and poppers. its anus had already been well worked that evening, with cum and juices dripping out of it. its own cock was still thrusting, desperate for release, when it heard a deep voice telling it to settle down.

"He ran a police nightstick across its back and walloped its asscheeks a few times. Then he began shoving the metal rod up its hole. This was an exciting new experience for it, to be sure. Fortunately, its passage was still slick with cream and juice. So, the thick cold stick didn't have too much trouble making its way home.

it rose in its chains onto its tiptoes to take as much as possible. That seemed to please Sir Simon. He rapidly substituted his own thick, warm penis for the metal stick. Then, he proceeded to give it a hard and violent fuck, that kept it on its toes. At the climax, he ordered it to cum and milked it not once, but twice. So, naturally, it was very interested in him."

Rufusboy appeared to smirk. I sat down on the bed again. We continued the discussion.

"So, later Bart rented you out for a weekend? Is that how it worked?"

"Well, Sir, it never actually saw any money change hands, when it was rented out. It must have happened, but all it ever got was a few presents. You know, Sir, like clothes, a watch or some expensive chocolates. A month or two passed, before Master Bart thought it was prepared for Sir Simon's 'more extreme interests.' One Saturday afternoon, he sent it over to this big house in Brighton.

"it was nervous, Sir. This was to be its graduation from 'pig-boy' to 'rent-boy.' it was determined to do its best, by cleaning itself inside and out, as Master Bart had taught. its 'costume' was a pair of torn tight jeans, polished boots, and a clean tee shirt, with a strategic tear near one of its nipples, covered by a black leather jacket for the bus ride.

"Sir Simon was ready when it arrived at his door. Sir wore black leather from cap to high boots. His dick already peered out from his tight chaps. Sir was a good-looking man, a bit on the dark side. He walked around it, poking with his fucking metal nightstick. First, its cock and then its tits were slapped with the hard police weapon. Then, Sir Simon ordered it to undress completely and to follow him down to his cellar.

"The room was set up as a dungeon. This was the first dungeon it had ever seen. The room was lit with dim, recessed lighting, that reflected on piles of rope and chains. There were cupboards with whips and strange implements. In the center of the room were two long leather-covered tables. it was ordered over to one of them, Sir."

Rufusboy seemed to have a remarkable recollection of these

previous events and was more that enthused to share the whole experience with me.

"Come on, bend over. Let me inspect that hole of yours. I want to make sure that it's open enough to take my prick or my nightstick. I must say it doesn't look wide enough, right now. I will start getting you ready with a two-fingered lube job. You need not grunt so hard. Now this metal butt plug will be screwed in, to get you started. Keep it in there or you will be punished even more severely.

"Now, lie down on your back while I restrain you. Come on, pig-face, put your arms above your head. Now get ankles flat at the other end, so I can strap you down properly."

"Thick leather was wrapped around its wrists, its forehead, its neck, its waist, its knees and its ankles. He cinched each hard. It felt him come back, to pull them even tighter.

"First, I am going to shave you. This red hair is too distracting. Since you have to go back to the university on Monday, I'll leave your head for the moment. However, I am going to lather up enough cream to smear across your chest and armpits, your cock and balls and that nest of red pubic hair. I'm surprised that Bart hasn't trimmed you already. Hmm, I can see he has put some effort into enlarging your tits and stretching that ball sac. He must have remembered that both are prime interests of mine; yours could still do with more work.

"Right. Now, be still, while I use this straight-edge 'round your cock and balls. I said don't move; or my hand might slip, and you'll find yourself a eunuch way before your time."

"it was scared and did as it was told; remaining quiet and still as he began at its groin. Slowly, he worked up across its chest, circling round the nipples that Master Bart had already started to grow. When Sir Simon was finally content with his work, he ran his hands over its denuded skin. There was a cool draft over the family jewels, as he picked up its balls and ruthlessly pulled down its eggs to the bottom of the sac. He then picked up a heavy metal stretcher and locked into place with his Allen wrench."

"That should keep them comfortable for this first session. If you please me, we will stretch them further. You will wear this all weekend. Now to work on your tits. They are not big enough for my use. I'll be adding some clamps, each of increasing severity, heavier tools, every few hours. Ten to fifteen minutes of pulling and twisting will keep them sore and alert.

"Yes, go ahead, shout and groan this first time. Then I can tell if I am hurting you enough. The mere thought of sexual training should already have your nipples rising and reddening. So let's get started, applying the clamps one at a time and, oh, so slowly. Scream away, my young pig.

"That cock of yours is going to have to learn to be patient. It gets no release until I say so, and that will only occur once you please me or should I say once this weekend.

"Now let's move to your feet."

"Its eyes widened as he produced a small thin cane from one of his cupboards. He aimed it at the soles of its feet. At first, he tickled its toes, selecting each for individual treatment. But, then, he slid the Malacca cane across the soles. Gently at first, it tapped from top to bottom, from left to right. Then slowly, he began to escalate. Gradually and painfully, the strikes grew to become a rain of blows.

"The tender bottoms of its feet had never felt anything like it. it was later told 'Bastinado' was the name for this torture. Sir Simon would come to apply this pain frequently. its feet felt as though they had been held in a fire, by the time he finished. After he was through, he applied a thick, soothing paste 'to start to harden them,' he said.

"Once the straps were loosened, he hauled it upright by its wrists. He fastened them to a chain on a pulley. it couldn't bear to have weight on its bare feet. Sobbing and screaming, it was dropped to the floor and was left there, for what must have been a couple of hours. Then Sir Simon came back with a large pair of heavy work boots with liners and forced its feet into them. Once it could bear to stand, its new Master pulled the chain back up, over the pulley. He twisted the metal plug out of its ass. In its place, he forced his fucking hard, black nightstick, slowly and carefully into its hole. Sir Simon fucked it, with his police stick for the next hour, sodomizing it successfully.

"The torments were all repeated the next day. it was exhausted, by the time he deigned to take it with his own prick. Even that was to be a fierce and hard fuck. Soon he'd filled it with his warm seed and then gave it a reward. Ruthlessly, he edged its still hard cock. it was finally allowed to cum. Yes, Sir Simon was truly a sadist and it earned whatever fee he paid for it that weekend."

"Yet, you went back to him again, afterwards?" I queried, as Rufusboy leaned closer into me again.

"Yes, Master Paul. At first, it begged Bart not to send it there. But he was its Master then and insisted that it learn to take whatever clients wanted to dish out. its job was to accept whatever punishment came with the pleasure.

"The masochist in it responded to Sir Simon's abuse. A pattern was established; using the canes or nightstick, always on the soles of its bare feet; which became hardened, as he predicted. That meant the length and severity of the bastinado were increased to achieve the heightened threshold of pain he desired.

"Sir Simon would awaken its cock and balls ahead of time. its ball sac was gradually stretched, until it could take a third cold heavy steel band locked in place. its penis continued to be lightly whipped with the bastinado, until its mind associated the two. In the end, its dick sprang to attention, as soon as he ran his fingernails across its feet. Beads of precum formed as the cane began its work. it wasn't allowed to cum. That climax, it had to earn, by enduring Sir Simon's torments over a weekend.

"Sir Paul, he said he enjoyed hearing my screams and groans, for the first month or so. Then he got bored. One Saturday afternoon, he forced a bit gag into its mouth and locked the gag tightly round its head. it could only gurgle back at him.

"Over the next two weeks, he built a framework of thin straps to fasten around its face and jaw. Strips of fine black leather ran around its chin, to keep its mouth closed and slobbering over a gag. The strips of leather continued up its face so that Sir Simon could force its eyes closed while he worked. The leather ended by binding its forehead as tightly as possible. Sir Simon would rub his gloved hand over the leather, plastered across its face; as though caressing an animal he was grooming."

Rufusboy boy continued on with his blow by blow tale.

"Of course, his other area of interest was the training of its tits, Sir."

"Yes, my red-headed bugger, be proud of your big brown nipples. They are being educated, especially for my pleasure. Your hot spots need to be connected. When my cane paddles your feet, your cock must obey my unspoken command. When I bring your tits to attention, your dick will rise in salute.

"Eventually, when I think your training has progressed enough, I will consider displaying you to my friends. I may even pimp you out. But there is much work to be done first."

"Sir Simon began to rent it regularly from Master Bart, so he could develop its erogenous zones. There was a routine. it stripped naked; first, its new Master would close it in the latticework of black leather straps and gag. Then its balls were tied down and stretched. The tit play began to take longer. As its nubs grew stronger and bigger, they were subjected to a good fifteen minutes of brutal pulling and twisting.

"But that wasn't the end of its special training, Master Paul. A light whipping with his special small flogger would follow this. Afterwards, clamps and weights were applied to its nipples. They were left in place for longer periods of time, despite its pleas. Finally, came the regular bastinado. its feet learned to harden and suffer. As Sir Simon predicted, its prick began to make the connection. Soon it became hard and leaking. My penis was left thrusting vainly, into the empty air.

"Sir Simon liked to provide variations in his torments. One weekend, as we began, it was made to stand upright, at parade rest. it had learned the correct posture with hands behind its head. He produced a new set of clamps with sharp metal teeth. Soon they hung with weights on its tormented tits.

"The sharpened teeth bit into its flesh. Drops of blood began to seep out and run down its chest. It chomped down on the leather bit that was forced into its mouth. it gasped at the heightened pain. But that was not enough, Sir. its new Master brought out the nightstick in order to enthusiastically attack its butt, shoulders and already wounded chest."

"Stand still, rent-fuck. You are a nothing but a piece of shit that needs to be disciplined. You are at parade-rest. That includes thrusting out your chest, so I can reach those clamps, properly. Suck your gut in. They must be feeding you too well, at that university of yours. That's better, but not good enough. I'll just lube up my metal rod and shove it up your rectum.'

"That was one of its worst experiences. He seemed to relish every minute of it, Sir. In fact, its torments made Sir Simon even more excited. He commanded it over to his fuck bench. It was forced down with its bloody and clamped tits squeezed beneath it. No restraints were allowed. it had to hold its position, while he drew out the metal stick and roughly inserted his lubed and rubbered prick. It was as hard as a log of wood.

"By now, it realized that it was indeed becoming his masochist pig. It had come to take pleasure in the violence and degradation of the fucking that followed; it was bewildered, yet it kept coming and suffering. It was ashamed but enjoyed the pain. It had been truly mastered and Sir Simon knew it. Before the next visit, Sir informed it that he'd invited a couple of friends to join him."

"You'd better do me proud, as I put you through your paces, slave-scum. Your job is to show off that body of yours. You will shave yourself from the neck down. Clean yourself out thoroughly, just as I have taught you. Be sure to get here promptly.'

"It was frightened and yet fascinated. Eight months had passed since it had come under this new Master's spell. Now, it did indeed accept Sir Simon as its Master. This was to be a graduation exercise, Master Paul. It arrived right on time and undressed quietly, just as directed."

"Good, you may yet make a worthwhile slave. First, rub this oil lightly all over your body, from head to feet. It looks as though you did a good job shaving. Now, bend over. Let me see your ass hole.

Looks satisfactory. Be sure to rub plenty of oil in that spot, as well. I hope you gave yourself at least three enemas.'

"You will serve as my centerpiece this evening. You will be blindfolded and fully restrained, with a new gag. Tonight, your body will be completely accessible to my guests. You will obey them, just as you do myself."

"He began to work its sac down, so that all three of the metal ball stretchers, each freshly polished, could be locked in place. Its cock paid attention and lazily uncurled in its turn. Then, its feet were forced into the very heavy black boots, with Vibram soles and a metal stud pattern across the leather. Heavy, two-inch thick irons were locked around its boots. A spreader bar pushed its feet apart. That weight alone, was enough to keep its feet in position.

"Its nipples were given their usual, painful 'warm-up,' as it stood at 'parade rest.' After fifteen minutes or so, Sir Simon produced cruel, biting clamps with chain. They were forced onto its sore, but toughened nubs. The weights he attached were different. They were a brighter metal, with sharp spikes, that tormented its freshly denuded pecs, as they swung with every movement."

"An interesting addition, don't you think, my rent-boy? They will prick you every time you move and boy, you will be moving. Here is your new gag. This has a thicker metal bar. It is a real horse bit, instead of the soft leather. Now, open your mouth wide and take it in so I can lock it in position. Now comes the usual network of straps 'round your head. I have changed some of the soft leather strips for shiny metal strips, to give you an overall metallic look. Even the new blindfold is metal. Don't worry, I have cushioned it with soft leather round your eyes.

"Yes, yes, indeed. The whole effect is enticing and erotic. It will be even more enticing when I wind these chains round your waist and down your legs to those ankle irons. Then they will circle up your arms to these leather and iron restraints, which I am attaching to the chain that will be run though the pulley then, ratcheting you up, tightly stretched, but left with your toes on the ground."

"It felt enmeshed and excited, Sir. The chains and metal bound it tightly in place. it was fully exposed. its dick was loving it. That wasn't to be allowed. it felt its prick being pushed into a heavy metal chastity egg. No erection was to be permitted. Finally, almost as an afterthought, Sir Simon lubed its hole with his gloved fingers to slide a thick metal dildo into place. it felt the device open inside it, clearly meant to stay in play until the intended time of entry. The plaything was made ready.

"Within a few minutes, the doorbell rang. Two other voices joined that of my Master."

"Klaus, Bill, how good of you to come. We're in the spare room with some drinks and some nibbles.'

"The first voice was dark and European-accented."

"And so, this is the new possession that you have told us about. *Ja*, he looks like a handsome specimen, hanging there."

"You've trussed him up good.' The other voice was definitely American. 'He's available to play with, of course?"

"Of course, Bill. I thought he would be something to entertain you both, after we've had a drink. He's quite well trained, but still needs some discipline. I have brought out some toys for you to try on him. Please, help yourselves."

"Master Paul, it shivered silently, determined to do its best. The voices faded slightly as the visitors took their drinks. Soon enough, a pair of hands flicked the spiked weights on its chest. It couldn't help but gasp as the fun began. Its Master provided lighter floggers for his guests and his nightstick for himself.

"The European wasted no time, applying the flogger to its butt. It hissed through the bit gag, trying in vain to dodge the increasingly heavy blows, until the visitor pronounced its cheeks red enough. Movement was almost impossible with iron restraints on wrists and ankles. Still, it tried to move away, as it felt him pull out the metal dildo that had kept it well opened. Its passage soon felt a thick dick exploring, sliding down its asscheeks."

"You will keep still, *schwein*, while I honor you with the gift of my penis. I will use a condom, *ja*, I will add some hot lube, so you can accommodate my thickness. Slowly, I now enter, so that the pigboy may feel me."

"He was right. His weapon felt thicker than any other prick it'd taken up its anus before. it was grateful for the visitor's slow progress, as its passage tried to adjust. He wore leather. It enjoyed the scent that it could smell. Thin leather gloves reached around to flick the spiked weights and tit clamps. It gasped through the bit gag. The visitor moved further inside it. It tried humping back, as Master Bart had taught it, in early training. The log began to slide further up the chute, Sir Paul."

I had to wonder whether Rufusboy was exaggerating his torments for my benefit. Still curious, I let him continue.

"A few centimeters more, then I will be satisfied. Then, we will work together. Relax, *schwein*. Bear down."

"By now, the pain made it dizzy. But it was chained upright and forced to endure. The German grunted and pushed again and again. Finally, it was filled tightly, now fully penetrated by a fireplug prick. It sweat and panted hard. However, the visitor waited a minute or two, before slowly sliding out. It almost cried out through its metal gag, as it was emptied. That was only for a moment. Almost immediately, he was shoving back in again, Sir.

"His leathers creaked behind it as the mating dance started. His hot breath warmed its back. Evidently, he was shorter than it. Still, he was powerful. From his cock to his arms, he was all muscle. The European pushed and pummeled it with his log, as well as with his hands. It felt as though its innards were being pulled apart. The man's lust became contagious. Soon, it found itself pushing its ass out, reaching for the German's dick. It clenched its butt muscles in time to the guest's unhurried movements.

"He was skillful, too, using his hands to keep it constantly excited and on edge. He played with the cock-in-chastity and batted the metal egg, forcing it to open its hole wider, in surprise. He alternated with tormenting its wounded tits or sliding his gloved fingers round the metal bit in its mouth for it to suck on.

"All the while, his fireplug pistoned up and down its innards relentlessly and with increasing speed. Soon, he began cursing and shouting in German, until it felt the final thrust, deep in its passage. It knew the visitor had cum. He rested inside it for several minutes, while he quieted down. Still, it remained frustrated and unsatisfied. its cock was unable to be erect or to even move."

"*Gut, mein schwein*, you did well with me. Not all men can take my big cock, but you worked hard for it."

"Great show, Klaus. You really put on an excellent display of fucking. Now, I know why you're considered such an accomplished Master."

"Thank you, Simon. *Ja*, I enjoyed myself. Your pig has potential. I'd enjoy another deep poke sometime."

"Of course, my friend. Whenever you wish. Now, Bill, you've been very patient. What's your pleasure?"

"Yeah, Simon. His ass has been well used. So, I'd like access to his other hole. But not until after I've used my handy little whip on the front of him."

"Fine, When you're ready, he's all yours. I'll loosen his gag a bit for you. He is going to find my nightstick up his bum again, to stop his dripping on the floor."

"Sir Paul, it gritted its teeth, as Sir Simon ruthlessly shoved his metal pole into its sore asshole. Fortunately, there was enough lube and juices to protect the passage; but it still hurt. Yet the hurt was not as much as the 'handy little whip' did, in the hands of the visiting American. He began with its inner thighs. There the blows also bounced onto its balls. They swung in their metal stretchers. It hissed and gulped as he flicked expertly, over its tender flesh. Then he focused on the metal egg itself; rocking its imprisoned and leaking dick.

"Finally, he delicately tickled its clamped and bleeding tits and their spiked weights. The blows were light, but focused. They produced the most pain and punishment. His sadistic treatment was exhausting. it gasped as it hung from its chained wrists. Its whole body quivered and sweat. This was almost too much to bear, Master Paul."

Rufusboy again sounded like he was outright bragging. I began to wonder how much Rufusboy liked to dramatize his sufferings and tortures.

The boy continued, "The American had a fresh idea for torment. 'Okay, Simon, that seems to have warmed us both up. Now let's see if your pig knows his oral service. Would you lower him to his knees? And remove his gag, please?"

"It fell to the floor. The heavy boots and spreader-bar kept it in an uncomfortable position. Its arms remained in irons, drawn well above its head. It felt the metal gag being unbuckled and slid out of its mouth. It gulped the air in eagerly. Still it could see nothing around the blindfold. There was the sense and smell of another man in leather in front of it. Helplessly, it stuck out its tongue, still salivating from the gag."

"Here, pig. I'm feeling generous this evening. Take my cockhead on that tongue of yours and warm it for me. I guess, in your bondage, I'd better help you find my rod. Not bad. Keep licking as I ease my cock into your mouth. There's plenty of prick for you, so stretch open your mouth muscles. My thick PA should add some additional spice for you."

"It did as it was told, as it had been taught. Its upper body was still hung from its wrists, still chained overhead. It tried to reposition its knees, to make room for the metal chastity device on its cock with its stretched and iron-bound balls. The repositioning was uncomfortable, but bearable.

"It leaned forward to accept a long, thinner cock, that reached towards its throat. Master Bart's lessons in cocksucking had trained it in the basics of swallowing and salivating carefully. It knew to keep its teeth out of the way. But this monster seemed to grow in its mouth. The hard metal of his PA thumped and tickled its uvula.

"The American guest shoved his jewelry further back, seeking its throat. As he found the track, his long penis with thick PA, it attempted to swallow. The PA blocked the unused throat and airway path. It tried breathing through the nose, as Master Bart had taught. Still it was choking, as the American grabbed its leathered head to push even further. He took pity as he heard the gasps and choking. The visitor released it momentarily, so it could suck in as much air as possible. But only for a few short moments.

"Then he shoved penis and PA in again. He held its head, as it swung from the chains. He pushed his seemingly endless snake into its throat. It was lucky. Its automatic reflexes kicked in; it relaxed enough to allow his passage. Feeling the heavy metal PA dangling down its throat was certainly erotic. its mouth was filled with saliva, as its tongue caressed and washed the rod nestling there. Its lips closed around him as he started vigorously to move, slipping in and out.

"No more than a puppet, dangling from an iron leash, it gasped for air whenever possible. its imprisoned cock thumped the ground, in a vain attempt to find its own pleasure."

"Take it, pig. Take it. Take it all in. Give me a good ride. Let me reach down. If I tickle those weights on your fucking tits, that should give you extra incentive.'

"He was right. The fresh pain spurred its efforts to please. Its closed lips sucked, tasted the veined pole pulsing in and out, like an express train. As the American puffed and grunted, he even sounded like a train, puffing and gasping in his excitement. His hands went back to its head. He held tight to the leather and metal straps around its face. His PA bobbed in and out of its throat. He groaned, as it moaned. Saliva slid out of the corner of its mouth."

"Now, pig. Now, I'm going to face-fuck you. I'm going to rape your throat. Come on. Take my seed. Swallow it, cunt. Now.'

"Sir, it felt his surge and then the warm salty flow, bypassing its mouth and filling its empty stomach. There were two full loads of cum in less than an hour. It felt both honored and abused. The American Master drew back, carefully into its mouth. Then he slapped its head, as its tongue made fast duty to clean his prick head and PA. He even sprinkled a final few drops of cream for it to sample.

"When he came out, he wiped his cleaned cock on its chest. That harsh motion set the spiked weights jangling. He released it. At that point, it just hung there, like raw meat on a hook. It was glad that the visitors seemed satisfied. However, it was not. it was left exhausted by the torments and the whole ordeal."

"'I'll give you a few minutes to recover, pigboy.' It was Sir Simon's voice. 'You have done well for my guests. I'm going to release your cock and balls. But you may not cum. I am going to stick-fuck you, as your reward. If you groan like that again, fucker, I'll shove a rougher gag in that cheeky mouth of yours.'

"It couldn't help the groans, as it was hauled upright again, forcing it onto its toes, still wearing the heavy boots and spreader bar. Clearly, Sir Simon expected better discipline. Once it was standing, still tied and taut, a thicker rubber cock gag was forced into position. The nightstick was still firmly up its still dripping hole. Its own cock rose in appreciation of its momentary freedom. It could only stare ahead blindly, still blindfolded and covered by the web of leather and metal straps, as the rubber was inflated to fill its mouth.

"Once more, its breathing became difficult. It had to force itself to inhale and exhale, largely through its nose. It was a helplessly bound animal again, a living object for other men's play and punishment.

"Sir Simon wasted no time in working his metal nightstick up and down in its ass chute. Sweat slid down its face, as his visitors joined in. One was using the cock whip again, stimulating its already purpling bruised dick and quivering balls in their tormenting stretchers, while the other alternated with Sir Simon between flogging its shoulders and forcing it with the stick.

"It only took a few minutes before its anguished and imprisoned penis spewed a load of thick cream onto the floor. The tormentors laughed together and continued until a second spray of cum burst forward.

"It was just left there, hanging. The steel nightstick was still in its rectum. Thankfully, the gag was deflated to let it breathe. The guests, still chuckling, returned to more drinks and food before leaving. When they slowly departed, they paid no further attention to the exhausted pigboy they had molested.

"Finally, Sir Simon came back over and gradually released it from bondage. His hands helped get its circulation going again. He gave it a beer to drink and some of the now stale sandwiches to eat. Sir even provided a damp cloth to clean itself. Once back into its clothes, the Master called for a taxi and sent it back to the university dorm, still grubby and over-used.

"After that event, it pleaded harder for Master Bart's mercy. Thankfully, it only spent a few more evenings with Sir Simon and his whippy canes and bastinado torture. Then he was transferred to London, by his bank.

"When it moved there a year or so later, Master Bart came to see it acting in plays in town. By that point, there were not even social exchanges with Sir Simon. Besides it had a new Master, Sir Norman, by then. It stayed well away from that nightstick sadist.

"With that, Sir Paul, I think you know all my sex life."

Neither of us ever brought up Dacre's name again.

§ § § § §

Now months later, sitting in the house I shared with my lover Tarquin, Rufusboy's history seemed to be more ammunition for my increasing feeling, that Rufusboy's psyche had been severely twisted as he emerged into a young gay man. He had to fight to survive, enduring almost endless abuse from older men. Now he expected it. He almost needed it to perform. That is why he'd accepted my aggressive BDSM-tinged approaches so easily the previous summer and fall in England.

I saw that none of his previous relationships had been long-lasting. Perhaps he would need such violence from other men in the future. Would the feelings he claimed to have for me last much longer? I needed reassurances from Rufusboy, himself.

There would be one more surprise that night, or rather on Sunday morning. This one was far more pleasant and made my day, as I awaited the return of Tarquin, Rufusboy, and James.

It was a phone call from John Bishop, the realtor from Palm Springs, calling to tell me the house I was buying there was now in the agreed thirty-day escrow. He'd called the day before, while I was still at the hospital. I'd been too tired that night to check for phone messages.

I suddenly realized I would be a house-owner before Christmas. My signature was going to be needed on papers he would be emailing me.

With all that had occurred, I had forgotten that weekend in Palm Springs, that Tarquin had arranged some six weeks before. I sat on the bed to let those memories wash away the dark ones about Rufusboy.

It had been only a couple of months before that I'd decided something had to be done to take our minds off of our current domestic difficulties.

Charles, one of the original members of the Circle of Six, had died a couple of months before. He had become a good friend to Tarquin, as well as his personal banker. Charles had even appointed Tarquin executor of his estate. Part of his holdings had been a pleasant vacation home in Palm Springs. We had envied Charles's secluded and spacious 'hideaway' when we had visited.

Apparently, the house was now on the market, perhaps not the best of times to be selling. We had been toying with the idea of acquiring a 'retreat' for Tarquin and myself. We needed somewhere away from our hectic professional and private lives in Los Angeles. We had enjoyed most of our recent visits to the warmth and relaxed atmosphere of the gay-friendly resort area.

On the spur of the moment, I had suggested to Tarquin that we drive there the following weekend, to take a serious look at the Charles's property. We were in a position to afford it at a fair market price. Somewhat to my surprise, I actually got excited by the idea. I thought I might even buy the house in my own name, if we liked it well enough. That way, we avoided any conflict of interest. I think Tarquin was also glad to find me not brooding over Rufusboy for a time.

The weather was still warm as we set off the following Saturday morning. Southern California looked golden brown in the autumn sunshine of late October as we finally left the cities behind and climbed through the Banning Pass. Our friends, Ian and Stuart, had promised that our favorite room could be made available at *Chaps Inn*, for the night. Tarquin had even wrangled a reservation out of Ginger for dinner, at *Shame on the Moon*, for that evening. We looked forward to relaxation and a time to enjoy ourselves, as we took the Highway 111 turn-off toward Palm Springs.

Charles's house was in the foothills, just northwest of the city center. The property was on a less-traveled road, leading to half-acre lots and clumps of large, but scattered rocks. I had called ahead and John, our realtor, was waiting for us with the keys. John Bishop was a big, happily flamboyant character, but a total professional in business, as we knew from past experience.

The house seemed larger than I remembered, very impressive with a sliding glass wall that opened onto a sunken terrace and swimming pool. There was the typical great room, spreading across the width of the house. The main house was comprised of a comfortable living area with oversized furniture, an adequate dining area, together with a very modern and well-equipped kitchen. Three bedrooms were more than we needed, but I thought one could easily be converted into a necessary play space.

We wandered all around the property separately and together. Both of us poked into closets, checked the sprinkler system and grew more interested, while trying to mask our enthusiasm. After an hour or so, the realtor decided to push us along.

"Will this meet your requirements, Mr. Charlton, Mr. Everest? It's a very attractive property. I'm surprised it's still on the market, even in these times."

Tarquin decided to open the bidding. "For goodness sake, call us Tarquin and Paul, then we may call you John. Yes, it is as we remembered it—very comfortable and livable. Still, it is rather large for a second home. I don't know how much time we would spend out here."

"Oh, gentlemen, you'll find the desert grows on you. However, as an alternative, you could always rent it out during the season. A home with three bedrooms and three baths is very desirable. It's largely furnished, as you can see."

"I'm not sure we'd want to do that, John, but we are seriously interested, right, Paul?"

I smiled in agreement, amused by his typical 'take-charge' attitude, even when I'd decided that I was going to be the owner.

I thought I'd show a more positive interest. "We'll talk it over while we're here and get back to you tomorrow. You don't mind us calling you on a Sunday?"

"Hey, in this market, realtors have to available 24/7. Well, at least in theory. I'll be happy to handle the sales and escrow details at this end, when, or should I say if you decide to go ahead."

"Thanks, John, we do appreciate all the help; we will give you a decision before we leave in the morning."

We talked about the property back and forth that afternoon, as we shopped at *GEAR,* for a new 665 leather hood for me. Our conversation continued that evening, rather than focusing on the delicious dinner at *Shame on the Moon.* My growing excitement about the house was the crucial point. Yes, it was large, but, as I pointed out, we needed room for slaves and boys.

When we eventually checked into Chap's Inn, we laughed the sight of my original posture collar and Tarquin's flogger. I'd left them behind there, when I'd stormed out of his life almost four years earlier. Ian and Stuart had faithfully kept and displayed these trophies ever since. Yes, now we could laugh, but that had been a traumatic turning point in our lives.

Now, we were confident in our partnership together, proving the point once again that night. By the time I was tumbled onto the large, comfortable bed, our property decision was a foregone conclusion. We rolled together, naked, and began to warm each other up with deep kisses. Next came tender bites and fierce embraces. Finally, Paul and I fell into an energetic session of sixty-nining, going at it until we were breathless, sweating and savoring each other's creamy juices.

I offered my asshole to my lover. His swiftly lubed and probing fingers stretched me slowly. He slid a thick butt plug into place, until he could get his second wind. At that stage, I enthusiastically went to work on his nipples, heating us up for the main event. Tarquin took me slowly and easily, enjoying the pleasures of my well-known but still narrow passage. I humped back on his prick, pushing and squeezing my muscles. I actively encouraged his efforts as he growled and roared in his inevitable style. Sooner than expected, he emptied a second load into my larger hole, while my penis erupted a moment later onto both our stomachs.

By the following morning, we both felt refreshed and restored. John was delighted when I told him I wanted to put an offer on the house. I told him that I wanted a thirty-day escrow. I knew that once we had made a deal, I would be anxious to take ownership.

We only quibbled a reasonable amount over the purchase price. That was part of Tarquin's job as executor of Charles's estate. We drove back to LA. I looked forward to soon being the owner of my own home, for the first time.

We chuckled on the way back. Here we were, two Masters without a single slave-in-residence between the two of us. Rufusboy's being away, working hard during the week, was making me increasingly edgy. Tarquin felt he had to find a new slave candidate for himself. It hadn't been a problem before, but he thought he needed "a different breed of man," whatever that might mean.

CHAPTER SIX - TARQUIN

I immediately observed that James was on the defensive, as our car left Bart's house for the return to central London. He had not expected to have to honor our bet, about finding Rufusboy He certainly did not want to lose, especially to me.

"I don't ss…see why you sh…should expect to collect, Tarquin. After all, it was really a jj…joint effort."

"Oh, come on, James. Remember, you were the one who did not want to drive down to Brighton at all."

"Well, you haven't gg…got any gear with you." James was clearly refusing to accept his loss. I wondered how much he had heard of my conversation with Rufusboy.

"Never fear, James. By know you should know me well enough to know that I always travel with a bag full of a basic set of leathers. Why, I will bet even money that you do, as well. Besides, I borrowed a few toys and other items from Bart before we left."

James had the good grace to start to chuckle. Soon, we were both laughing. I sat back, satisfied that I had won.

"You always were a determined bb…bastard, Tarquin. But I won't make it easy for you. I promise."

"I would not expect you to, James. However, I have waited a long time for this opportunity. I am armed with proper motivation. How about dinner at the hotel this evening, fully leathered and booted? We will play after."

"Your ss…suite or mine?"

"So that is what you were arranging on the phone this morning. Adjoining suites, I should hope. What else have you planned, James?"

"Jj...just you wait. I want to ss...surprise you, Tarquin. I've booked you on the same floor at the Rochester, as me. They have butler service on the executive floor, you know. Please, don't be concerned. I am ch...charging it all to Rufus's account!" Clearly James was using every angle. But with what we had just been through, it felt well justified.

With our conversation over, I gazed out of the window at the fall landscape. The green fields were always lush, and there were trees with the last yellow and red leaves drifting off in the pale sunlight. I remembered how England could look its best at this time of year.

Of course, with James in charge, check-in at the Rochester Hotel went smoothly. We were soon in our adjacent suites, just as James had required. A minute or so later, there was a knock at my door.

"*Bugger it, James, let me get settled in,*" I thought, but out loud I said, "Coming."

Rather than my next-suite neighbor lounging there, a very well-built younger man with a freshly trimmed crew cut, stood before me in a dark grey suit.

"Good afternoon, Sir. I'm Roger, your butler. How can I be of service? Do you have everything that you need? May I unpack for you?"

We both took a second look, possibly a third. I liked what I saw. I hoped my young butler did, as well. Roger was my height, cropped blond hair and military bearing. I thought fast. I definitely wanted to know more about him.

"Please come in, Roger. I am having some problems with the television. Perhaps you could explain the controls and channels to me."

I knew it sounded feeble, even to my ears. Despite my feeble invitation, Roger entered with confidence and ease.

"Certainly, Sir. The remote can be a little tricky."

Smoothly, he talked me through its simple operation. I watched and listened, though I was checking out more of the man, than the machine. He appeared well muscled under his suit jacket. My young butler looked to be about thirty, I would say. He carried a very slight London accent. He had a square jaw, slightly long nose, and chiseled cheekbones. My hand grasped the remote before his fingers left, just for a few seconds.

He looked up. His eyes sparkled.

"I want to have dinner in the suite this evening. It will be dinner for two, around seven o'clock. Can you arrange that for me, Roger?"

"Of course, Sir. There are menus in the folder on the desk, or I can ask the chef to make something special for you, if you would like. If you'd call me on extension forty, when you've decided?"

"You would serve our meal, of course?"

"If that's your pleasure, Sir."

"Excellent, I will give you a call shortly. I am Tarquin Charlton, by the way."

"Yes, Mr. Charlton, and you are from the Hancock Park area of Los Angeles, I believe."

I chuckled, "You have done your homework."

"It's our policy at the Rochester, sir. We want to get to know our guests…and their needs, sir."

"Thank you, Roger. I will be in touch."

James arrived promptly at seven. He looked smart in his leather uniform, which sported a thick red stripe down the breeches and his always polished Wescoes. I had slipped into my leather shirt and breeches and pulled on my Dehners. They were the basic black leather that always came with me, in my second travel bag.

"Good Evening, Tarquin. I hope you're ss…satisfied with the suite and the ss…service."

"It is excellent, as I am certain you knew it would be, James. Come in. I have your Scotch and water ready for you. Dinner should be along shortly."

"I told you that you'd enjoy the Rochester. It's new. A friend ss…

suggested it. Now, I think I'll always stay here, especially with such an impressive butler ss...service."

"Yes, Roger is certainly impressive. You picked the right type for me. So, here is to the success of our mission and getting back to LA."

We chatted amiably enough for a few minutes. I have known James since I first arrived in Los Angeles, over fifteen years ago, now. I was a recent graduate and fledgling entertainment attorney, as well as a freshly declared Leather Master. Our friendship has been sexually contentious ever since. Thanks to the Circle of Six, we have both prospered in our professions. James's specialty as a talent agent was young male hunks, with...shall we say...an explorative nature and plausible acting talent. He made sure they had good training in their craft and even better training sexually, under his harsh, personal discipline.

A discreet knock announced the arrival of Roger along with another attractive young male, as assistant, to serve our dinners. While he was too discreet to acknowledge our leathers, I could not fail to notice one eyebrow go up. There was a hungry, but appreciative gleam in his eyes, as he set out the simple meal.

"Would you like me to remove the covers and serve you, gentlemen?"

"No, thank you, Roger. It certainly smells very good. I will let you know when you may take them away. We will have moved next door, won't we, James?"

"If you say so, Tarquin. It's your evening."

James's eyes were fixed on the young assistant, while I exchanged a glance with Roger, who stood erect and at attention. I thought I noticed a large cock beginning to tent his pants. Yes, there could have been possibilities if we were staying longer in London.

The staff slowly withdrew. James sighed as I motioned toward the table. We ate lightly crusted lamb chops, with some excellent *al dente* vegetables, followed by small, fresh, fruit tarts.

Our conversation turned to the Circle of Six—our close-knit

group of Leather Masters in LA. We were linked by our common interest in slave ownership, as well as our common professional connections. I had survived their tough initiation rites, when invited to join, shortly after I arrived in town. Paul had been initiated, as my slave. Now, that there was a vacancy, I wanted my partner to be admitted as one of the six Masters. James was against it in principle. As chairman for the year in question, I was determined to push Paul through. He had all of the right qualifications.

"You just cannot accept that a slave can evolve into a Master or that a sub can become a Dom, can you, James?"

"No, Tarquin, I can't. Oh, I realize there can be exceptions. After all, you tried it in reverse for a week or so yourself, but your Dd... Dom nature prevailed. For me, a ss...slave will always be a ss...slave. If he becomes uppity or dd...demanding, out he goes."

"Well, you've always maintained a revolving stable of healthy young bucks, in need of training. Apart from your house slaves, tim and tom, you seem not to want any form of permanent relationship."

"No, I guess I don't. I like to pp...pick and choose and move on after a while. Unless, of course, I cc...could persuade you to change your ways, Tarquin. Cc...could you accept a 'pp...permanent relationship' with me?"

I chuckled contentedly. "Come on, James, you keep trying to get into my breeches, but I'm not interested and definitely not available."

"But there was that one night...."

"Yes, and that was part of my initiation. That is not something I care to repeat. Besides, it is your turn this evening. I am curious to find out whether you are worth the wait."

I called Roger on the house phone to let him know we were finished. I hustled James and the bag of toys into the adjoining suite.

It was not like being in my own dungeon. Improvisation would have to be the name of this game, as I tipped the contents of the bag onto James's bed. Restraints, rope, a double hood with gag, plus a few other interesting choices fell out. I ordered James to strip down to the big cock ring that he always wore. Then, he was to put his boots back on while I wrestled a heavy metal ring over my own, by now, plumping dick. James fussed for a moment, then, after a frown from me, he obeyed.

"Come on, look lively there or I will be forced to encourage you with the flogger."

"Sir, yes, Sir."

"Begin by putting on these wrist and ankle restraints. I will affix the ropes to the bed. Good, there seem to be adequate spaces to attach them to. I hope you cleaned yourself out ahead of time, James. Did you bring an enema kit?"

"Shit, Tarquin, Sir. I may not have practical experience as a bb… bottom, but I do know what is expected. Besides this hotel has first class medical supplies. Ss…surprising what they could find this afternoon, Sir."

"I am glad to hear it. Now get your super-clean ass over here and up on the bed. Let's get to it. The hood goes on next and then the gag. I am not sure how soundproof these walls are. Here. Let me smooth the leather over your face. Now, open and take the gag in, or do I have to shove it into your mouth? Next, I pull the outer layer round your face and zip it closed. You will still breathe easily enough. Yes, the hood makes you look like the devil you can be, James."

I slapped his butt hard with my leathered hand, before I began to fasten him to the headboard ass-down with some pillows and towels placed beneath him. James grunted as I pulled his booted legs further apart. I then lifted them, one by one, up above his shoulders. It had been years since I had seen him totally naked. He had always taken special care of his body. He still had good abs, outstanding pecs and very little body fat. His cock and balls had always been impressive. This evening, they were already excited, and his cock was erecting. His large PA glimmered in the lighting in the room.

It was a pleasure to restrain him. The muscles in his shoulders and legs were made to assist, as I pulled the ropes taut. Typical of James, he tried to find a comfortable position on the bed, bent double. I made certain to rectify that, with some well-placed slaps across his hooded head, which resulted in a less comfortable position for the sub in short order.

"James, there are a number of dildos here for us to try out on you. Unfortunately for you, there is only a limited amount of lube. I am sure it has been some time since you have felt an intruder up there. So, I will start out easy."

I was true to my word. The first plug was little bigger than a beginner's size. It slid in and out much too easily. I jumped to a broader, ten-inch penis shape with muscle markings and a thickening base. He started taking it easily enough as I proceeded slowly and cautiously. Still at five inches in, James began to moan audibly through the gag. I sensed his muscles clenching instead of relaxing.

I stopped for a few minutes and ran my hands along his body. I checked the small nipples and flicked his blood-engorged prick, sticking straight up against his stomach, with his PA gleaming. He squirmed some and shuddered, as I drove the dildo in another three inches.

It was becoming hard, sweaty work for both of us. I decided to change my tactics. The flogger I had borrowed from Bart was of fair size. It had a handle that fit nicely into the palm of my hand. I turned around and swung it into ass-action. James's body jumped with the force of each blow. I started playing a gentle game of warm-up. I tested the power of my arm as the flogger flared against his firm asscheeks. It felt good as the leather snapped across his butt, parting round the dildo, which quivered between the strands. Ten minutes of this intense action brought up the color of his ass, as well as the heated color of my body. I was thoroughly warmed and satisfied thus far.

James lay doubled up, shifting in his bondage. The dildo had sneaked up his passage another inch. It was in almost to the base. I snarled at him.

"Come on, motherfucker. Surely you can swallow the rest of this little rod up your anus. Push out. Relax those muscles. That's better. You are almost there. One last effort by both of us and you should be fully spiked."

And he was. James groaned as the black dildo was soon fully

seated, with my aid. A fine film of sweat covered both our bodies. His butt muscles clenched and unclenched as they fought to accept the balance of the large rubber invader. It was probably longer and thicker than any he had taken before. Being fucked by me should be a pleasure after this.

"I want you to watch as I sink my shaft into you. I want you higher and tighter, so I am going to pull your ankles up farther. Then I will unzip the top hood. No funny business. Remember you lost the bet. You are mine for the evening. Nod if you understand."

The head, still silenced in the double leather hood, slowly nodded agreement. I lowered his booted legs for a moment. James winced as his ass sank down on the bed with the dildo fully inside him, and his cheeks red and bruised.

"Well, now we know you are properly penetrated. I have got your wrists repositioned higher on this 'contemporary iron' bed frame. I need your legs back alongside them. Come on, up in the air. All the way, boy."

James's eyes glared at me through the now unzipped hood; the inner layer of leather still covered his face. Slowly, he raised his heavy Wesco boots. I took the trailing ankle-ropes and secured his boots up, next to his bound hands. He was now fully exposed. His tanned torso sweat. His breathing became laborious. I could hear him pant, the sounds from behind the gag guttural and garbled.

James was now my prime meat. His flushed, purple cock thrust into the air, with his 00-gauge PA mounted tautly on its head. His ass quivered from the impaling. He was probably anticipating my engorged prick that was more than ready to pierce him.

Slowly, I twisted the dildo. It soon began to slide out of its own volition. James was emptied with a loud plop. I rolled on a rubber, added some lube and positioned my cock at the winking, red entrance. Reaching forward, I sucked on his gagged mouth. My tongue ran along the leather as he gasped beneath me. My victim's body shuddered. His boots banged on the headboard. He was ready now, for my pole to enter him. My eyes stared intently into his. Then, his gaze wavered and dropped in submission.

I decided to force the pace and shoved straight in. His passage was well opened by the broad dildo. My cock slipped in easily. His body tried to resist. He clenched his raw muscles. Mine would be the victor. This time, I was in the saddle. He had no choice but to take me in, all the way.

My smile told him all he needed to know. He was mine. James slumped in defeat.

"Come on, James. Show a little more spirit. My penis is fully home in you. Enjoy the ride; or I can make more of a fight out of it. You know damned well which I prefer."

James accepted the challenge. His ass muscles clamped down on my cock as I slid backward. His body was shaking with the effort. I shoved back, breaking free of his muscled restraints. I was working him. I entered then retreated, repeatedly, from his hot, velvety passage. I was growling loudly in my usual way. My arms used his booted legs as a lever to transport myself even farther inside him. He would not soon forget this night of conquest, if I had any say.

We sweat and swore. At least, that is how I interpreted the guttural sounds coming from around his gag. Our strong torsos challenged one another, our muscles strained and flexed. I leaned over him and tweaked his small nipples. I massaged his desperate cock. His grunts grew louder. That earned him a slap on his leathered head. We were both in heat. My prick plundered, playfully. Now, he was reciprocating. His body pulsed and slithered, in rhythm with mine.

I took the two large fingers of my right hand and slowly slid them alongside my dick inside his hole. He wanted it all. So did I. I reached farther with my rubbered weapon. I shouted with pleasure and then tamped down the noise, remembering where we were. His body trembled, as was evidenced by his involuntarily thumping of the headboard. I slapped him again as I fought to keep his eyes focused on mine. My intent was that he would remember who mastered him. His eyes glazed over with lust. James needed to be fucked hard. I was his true Master, if but for the moment.

Now came my final deep thrust, powered by the energy in my balls. I rode him home. He stiffened, then relaxed. My cream shot into my rubber. My fingers slid out. He was mine. It was not until then that his cock exploded, without being touched. The splatter of his cum even reached the leather hood.

We hung there for minutes. I was satiated, but not completely fulfilled. There was something else that I wanted to do with James, something I rarely tried in my play sessions. I wanted to fist him. I coached him to relax in his restraints. I pulled the condom off my still-quivering penis, then smeared its contents over the cream, already on his stomach.

My preparations took time. I exchanged my black leather gloves for black rubber ones, that ran up my lower arm. They had to be liberally coated with the available lube. I lubed his anus as well; though it still leaked our joint juices. James became very quiet. He was probably tired, in his double-trussed state. He watched the proceedings, carefully. I wondered whether he had ever been fisted before. Slowly, I flexed my fingers in front of his face. My hands are not small.

"Yes, James, I am pleased to tell you that you're going to feel the power of my fist. I am going to loosen your gag, so you can spit it out if necessary. However, I am going to add a blindfold. You will not see what is going to happen. My guess is that you are a fist-virgin." He nodded vigorously. His eyes widened, looking both excited and alarmed.

"Well, I will take it slow. I think you will find that you enjoy it."

I pulled forward on his leathered head, to add the blindfold. I wanted to make sure his eyes were well covered. Then I loosened the leather gag, to make his breathing easier. The ropes around his heavy booted ankles were tightened. They were starting to tremble from either desire or dismay.

"Fuck you, Tarquin. You always want to gg…get that extra ounce of pp…pleasure and pain, don't you?" He managed to gasp out.

"And fuck you, James. I had to put up with your shit during your long night of using me. I have waited a long time for retribution. Now, shut the fuck up. Take it like the man that you claim you are, or you will have that gag tightened, back in place."

I was surprised by my vehemence and tension. It did shut him up. I could almost hear his teeth clench. I slowly slid three of my gloved fingers into the well-reddened hole that vibrated so invitingly. They went in easily, searching for his sphincter muscle. I widened their spread very slowly. Gradually, I soothed the wall of his passage in preparation for two remaining digits Then, I eased out my hand to taper all five digits together. This time I began by curling my thumb in with my fingers, before easing through his gate. As I entered fully, I could sense my hand beginning to blossom in his innards. Carefully, I unraveled it, well-covered with thick lube and our remaining juices, and formed an open fist inside him, as I crept up his widening passage.

We both breathed heavily. Our minds and bodies became fully engaged in this ultimate act of sexual possession. James lay perfectly still. He was tense as a bowstring. I could feel the sweat trickle down my face as I edged my way farther up the tunnel. My arm felt weightless as my lust for possession was satisfied. James was beginning to relax as he could begin to feel a new ecstasy caused by my careful and delicate invasion.

I gently played inside him with care and reverence. My lower arm stayed inside him for maybe four to six minutes. My friend and rival had been fully conquered. Then, carefully I eased back out of his passageway, compressing my fist in on itself. With a slight turn, like an exotic flower, my wrist and fingers slipped out of his hole.

James was so exhilarated by his induction into fisting that he orgasmed again. This added a further load of spunk onto his hooded face. Not to be outdone, I followed suit and his stretched torso was now well-covered in pungent smelling cum.

Our endorphins had been raging. I needed to release him, so that we both could rest. Later, we showered together, soaping each other lavishly, then toweling the other off. It seemed only natural to collapse together onto James's bed. We were more relaxed together than we had ever been. There we lay, quietly, in each other's arms. An hour or so later, I slipped away to my own suite and slept deeply until the following morning.

§§§§§

At seven a.m., Roger brought me the light breakfast I had ordered. He then stood, hesitatingly.

"Is there something I can do for you, Roger?"

"Sir, if I may presume, do you have a moment or two to speak?"

"Of course. I hope that you don't mind my eating breakfast while we talk?"

He nodded his head and began, "Sir, I recently got my visa for the United States. I wondered whether you might know of a vacancy for a skilled manservant or bodyguard? I'm ex-Army—ex-Cavalry as a matter of fact. I finished my tour about nine months ago, sir."

"Yes, I did notice your military air and haircut. You certainly sound like a man who has given good service. Tell me, what kind of position are you *really* looking for?"

"Ideally, sir, I'd like to join the household of a gentleman like yourself or Mr. Villier. I was batman to my colonel for a while, after I'd been wounded in Iraq. I looked after his gear and other things. He helped me to get the correct visa through some American friends of his, sir."

"Do you have any experience in cooking or running a house?"

"Yes, Sir. I passed the Cordon Bleu Basic Course, before I signed on here."

"Well, I might have interest myself, although I do have specialized tastes and requirements."

"Sir, forgive me, but I think I've got a fairly good idea of what your demands might be. Sir, if I may say so, you and Mr. Villier looked really hot in your leather and boots, last night."

"Why thank you, Roger. Are you aware of the significance of our uniforms?"

"Yes, sir. I believe I know the service that's required to go with them. I did, er, find a dildo on Mr. Villier's floor this morning. I think it was too big to manage by himself, if I may presume to say so, sir."

I laughed. "Okay, Roger, you may presume, this once. Normally we're both Masters, but last night was a special occasion.

"Yes, I am in the market for a new slave, who would be willing to submit to my style of discipline, for a year or so. That amount of time is needed so that we both may make up our minds as to whether or not we are suited. Of course, you do know that slavery does not legally exist today. Nevertheless, a man can bind himself over to another man to learn and provide full service, by contract. That is what I require. No outs. A man would essentially turn over all control to me and become my property."

"Yes, sir, I think I understand. The army's a bit like that, at times."

"Well, if you find yourself in California and you are still interested, please get in touch. Here is my cell phone number. I will give you the opportunity for an interview and inspection. You do understand that I can make no assurances or promises beyond that.

"Now, I do have a few quick questions; then I must finish packing to leave. And Roger, I expect honest answers. You have had previous queer experience or relationships?"

"Sir, Yes, sir. Experiences a plenty, but only one long-lasting relationship. I can give you details, sir."

"Are you healthy? Positive or negative?"

"Shit, Oh, excuse me, Sir. You really do get right to the point. No known diseases. I had a complete check-up about three months ago. I am negative, sir, and I plan to remain that way."

"You are a free man? No matrimonial or domestic partner entanglements?"

"None, sir. I will be traveling alone. I've always had a hankering to see Los Angeles, Sir."

"Good. Do you have a resume that you can leave with me?"

"Yes, Sir. I'll have it for you in five minutes."

"I will need a reference or two. When are you expecting to travel?"

"Sir, I've saved enough for a return airfare and for an apartment or something for a month or so, in order to get me settled, Sir."

"It sounds as though you have really thought this through. Don't wait too long. My partner and I can muddle through without someone to run the house for a week or so. Then we will need to find a suitable candidate or two."

"Sir, I would have to give my fortnight's notice here. The bosses have been very good to me, Sir."

"I can understand that. I think we could manage that long. If this is truly your purpose, you should proffer your notice today and plan to see me soon. I would expect to see you within the week that you arrive. Please let me know your flight details, as soon as you have them made. Then, I will know that you have actually set the date. If we do not hear from you, with your plans soon, we will fill the vacancy."

"Understood, Sir. You mentioned a partner, Sir? Would I be performing sexual services for him as well, Sir?"

I chuckled. "Not necessarily. He has his own boy, for now. No, you would be trained to service me, alone. Still, you would be responsible for running a large house, cooking and serving our meals, primarily dinners. Do you think that you can handle that?"

"Sir, yes, Sir. I'd give it my fucking best, Sir."

"Fine. What is your full name, Roger?"

"Roger Barstow, Sir. I thank you for your time and interest. I don't think I'd disappoint, if you took me for training, Sir. I'll go and get what I have for a resume and be back shortly, Sir."

He was gone in a flash. I pondered our conversation, as well as his intentions, as I spread the orange marmalade on my toast. Roger had all the outward attributes that I was looking for. The man was tall, well-muscled, certainly handsome enough. He had a subservient manner and seemed to have a reasonable idea of what would be demanded of him. If he did make it over the Atlantic, he would certainly be worth a full inspection, even if we had already taken someone on.

He soon returned, carrying a manila envelope containing his resume and his passport photo. I slid it into my briefcase. I would read it on the plane, if I could have some privacy, away from James's or Rufusboy's view.

To my surprise, he swiftly knelt and kissed my right hand, then placed it on his head. I was impressed. Indeed, there had been some basic training.

"Thank you, slave. Now, get yourself up. That is enough for the moment. You are certainly a promising prospect. Make sure you get your ass over to Los Angeles, as soon as possible. Remember, notify me of your arrangements soon and call me a day or so before you leave, so we can set something up."

"Sir, thank you for your time and this opportunity, Sir."

I joined James in the lobby. He looked tired and out of sorts. We made it to Heathrow in time for the flight. As Bart had promised, he and Rufusboy were waiting for us at the check-in counter. I returned the bag with Bart's toys, with my appreciation. He informed me that he had paid for Rufusboy's upgrade. Then the all-too-familiar PR team prepared to spirit us away. It was a nice perk, but I was still not certain that I wanted Rufusboy traveling in the same cabin.

"You fuckers look after my boy. I think I've fuckin' well straightened him out. Maybe I'll come out sometime and take a look at your fuckin' Beverly Hills for myself, again."

"You would be more than welcome to stay with us, anytime, Bart. Thanks again for all your help," was my genuine reply.

The flight back was uneventful. I had to smile, as James kept shifting in his seat, obviously still feeling the result of our activities the night before. It appeared that he finally found some comfort by lying down. "My ass hurts too much," he claimed innocently. I decided to follow his lead and stretched out to enjoy a needed rest after the hectic 'holiday weekend.' It appeared that Rufusboy did the same in the seat he was given, a couple of rows behind us in the full cabin.

We were all worn out by the time we touched down at LAX. Paul was there to meet us. He greeted Rufusboy warmly, but warily. I persuaded James to go home by himself, which was probably just as well. I was too tired to focus on what could happen next.

CHAPTER SEVEN - PAUL

I was so relieved to see Rufusboy back in LA and in Tarquin's care. I was even glad to see James. It had been a hellacious Thanksgiving weekend. At least my sister, Ellen, was now out of intensive care. Her unborn baby seemed to be safe, too. She remained in Cedars-Sinai, but color was coming back into her cheeks. Thankfully, John, my brother in-law, was in better condition to handle the situation.

My Rufusboy hugged and kissed me, in an embarrassed sort of way. He'd apologized a couple times on the phone and again in a text message, before he left England. While I knew that he was certainly a responsible actor in the middle of production on his television series; I did wonder whether he really would have returned, if Tarquin hadn't gone searching for him. When he turned to my partner and asked if it would be okay to spend the night at home, in Hancock Park, we immediately agreed and staggered to my car in the parking garage.

We were all tired, so the ride home in my Escalade was unusually quiet. I decided that any play session had better be postponed. We had Chinese delivered and tried to unwind. Between Rufusboy and Tarquin, I pretty much got the full-length version of their adventures overseas. It was noticeable to me that Rufusboy deferred to my lover's every comment. It seemed excessive; I put it down to Rufusboy's tired and dependent state.

"Paul, why don't you and Rufusboy share our master bed tonight? He'll have to get up very early in the morning."

"But where will you sleep, Tarquin?"

"I'll be fine in the guest room. I assume the bed's made up?"

It seemed that Rufusboy had other ideas for the first night. "I could do that, Sirs. But I was hoping we could all share the big bed for one night, Sirs."

"Fine with me." I didn't really give much thought to any motives, "Tarquin, does that work for you?"

Tarquin seemed reluctant to agree, but he finally did so. That night we all slept together, for the first time. Rufusboy, between Tarquin and me, went straight to sleep. Tarquin and I were so restless that Tarquin finally left to sleep in the other room.

The studio car collected Rufusboy at dawn. We agreed that he should spend the week concentrating on work and staying in his condo. He would come back home to Hancock Park for the weekend, if he could.

Even though all we back in town, I was still wound up from all the stress. There were no slaves or boys to release my pent-up energy that day.

Finally, Tarquin looked up from the papers he was reading. "Come on, Paul, settle down and try to relax. You need to get your mind off the problems of Ellen and Rufusboy. Perhaps, getting in shape for your initiation into the Circle of Six would be a good way of doing it."

"With everything going on, I'd completely forgotten about that."

"Well, it has not been in the front of my mind lately either, but I was looking in my diary and your evaluation meeting is next month."

"That's when I have to be voted in by the other Masters, right? I know that each of them has to have had his own private inspection time? Does that include you? You are the president, or whatever you want to call that position."

"That is correct, I get my turn as well. I'm looking forward to some 'quality time' together. Perhaps, we should get some practice beforehand." He chuckled.

I thought back to my previous initiation about five years earlier, when I'd been merely Tarquin's slave. But this presented a much greater challenge.

"Are you sure I'm really eligible? This would be the first Master application who'd previously been accepted as a slave. I doubt that everyone can be welcoming that."

"I have had to argue long and hard. There are still one or two who don't really agree. But I am the president and I had the deciding vote. You will still have to prove yourself in the preliminary rounds with each of the other four, as well as myself."

"So, how do we start?"

"Well, I thought you might begin with the one you know, Master Lancelot. He is our doctor and the one friend who knows most of our history. I will let him know you are 'in play,' so to speak."

That conversation temporarily took my mind off Rufusboy. I still felt compelled to phone him every evening. I was afraid he was going to disappear again. The boy accepted my calls cheerfully enough. The series was nearing completion of its first limited season of thirteen shows. So, the actor was having to work hard in order to make up for that one lost day at the studio.

Dr. Lancelot called the very next day to set up an appointment for that following evening.

"I don't want to delay the voting, Paul, so get yourself over here around six. Peter or Paul will let you in. You don't need to bring anything special. Just make sure you're freshly showered and cleaned out. Oh, I should tell you that the boys are looking forward to seeing you again."

"Thank you, Sir. I look forward to submitting."

I was also getting excited. The twins, Paul and Peter, were among my oldest friends in LA. It was thanks to Peter's initiative that I had initially met Tarquin. We each, in turn, had become a slave to a demanding Master. Paul befriended me at a traumatic time, in my earlier submissive apprenticeship. I was glad that the two now belonged to Master Lancelot. With everything going on with my career and life with Tarquin, we hadn't had a chance to spend much time together. Once I had become a Master in my own right, it was inevitable that a gap would open up between myself and Master Lancelot's two slaves. We remained good friends and were always happy when there was an opportunity to see one another when I visited Dr. Lance, professionally.

The following evening, I left work a little early so that I could take a quick shower and clean out, as expected. I presented myself at the doctor's office a few minutes before six. Peter let me in. We hugged and kissed and laughed before he led me to a separate examination room I'd never seen before.

"It's always good to see you, Paul. Your namesake will be along in a minute or two; he's making a few preparations for the doctor. We need you naked, before our Master walks in."

It didn't take me long to strip down. Peter reached over for my cock and balls, "fluffing" them up in a surprisingly professional manner. I tensed at first, then gave in to his ministrations.

"Good evening, Paul, are you ready for your first initiation exam?"

"Good evening, doctor. Yes, Sir, whatever you wish."

"Good. You certainly look fit enough, but then you usually do. Hop up onto the examination table. It's been quite a while since I've conducted one of these tests."

I remembered what Tarquin had told me, as I climbed onto the long, padded table.

"*Lance is into mummification and electro play. I have fond memories of that session and the sack he gave me is still around here somewhere.*"

I had little experience with either fetish, but thought I'd enjoy the challenge. I felt cool rubber on my back as I lay down. The twins drew my legs together and fastened a thick Velcro restraint round my ankles. Then my feet were thrust into the bottom of a red rubber sleep sack. My ass was raised. I felt a well-lubed metal dildo thrust up into my hole with wires attached.

Music played softly in the background. The twins worked, silently and efficiently. They threaded the cords through the fastenings in the suit and the eyelets at the edge of the table. The doctor issued instructions from time to time.

"Make sure you keep his arms close to the torso, boys. Peter, fluff up his prick and balls again. Make sure that they are fit correctly inside the detachable rubber jock."

My rubber enclosure had been well powdered. The suit clung tightly to my body. In no time, I started to sweat. Inch by inch, I was bound tightly in red rope, over my red rubber enclosure. Soon, I could only move my upper torso. My genitals were packed away inside their own compartment, with the detachable flap. The twins eventually restrained my shoulders. My body began to throb in its rubber cocoon.

"Okay, boys, get the hood on him. Make sure you are using the one with the penis gag and the breathing holes. Make it good and tight."

I had no experience with rubber hoods. I could tell that the twins knew what they were doing. They expertly got my chin in place and proceeded to pull it snuggly over my ears and scalp. Then I heard a zipper. That really cinched the hood tightly in place. My eyes couldn't see anything. They adjusted the breathing holes and left the gag out for the moment. By now, every pore on my body sweat. I was breathing in great gulps of air, as I tried to calm down. The heat and tautness of the thick red rubber, along with the tight bondage was spooking me. Dr. Lance came over. He ran his hands soothingly and sensually over my torso. As I relaxed, hands ripped off the jock cover over my testicles. My cock fell out immediately, eagerly sensing the fresh air. Other hands pulled the covers from over my nipples; exposing my tits and their heavy metal rings to the audience.

Fingers began to flick both of these erogenous zones, as I moaned and tried to struggle. I slithered slightly in the rubber sack, as the rivulets of sweat increased. The cords kept me restrained tightly. Fingers increased their playful activity, pulling on my nipple rings and massaging my dick into a hard erection. I ground my plugged and rubbered butt into the table as the penis gag was thrust into my mouth. I did my best to keep my breathing under control with the now limited supply of oxygen. Silence reigned. There was only the faint sound of the electro music and my faint groans. Then, I roared as I felt my tits pulled up and clamped. They were pulled even harder. I could only guess that they were being attached to some kind of pulley that was overhead. The stretch on my nubs was beyond painful, but at this point there was little that I could do.

Dr. Lance continued to run his hands slowly over the rubber in which I was encapsulated, massaging my limbs and soothing my nerves. Perspiration ran down my entire body. If not for the codpiece, I might have thought that it was urination that was pooling beneath the small of my back. I squirmed in the red sack, feeling the gathering of my perspiration around me. I felt the pinch of small clips being added to my scrotum, cock, and balls. Then I felt more clips being attached to my already stretched tits. A loud groan attempted escape from around the gag that silenced me. I could only guess what was to come.

"Boys, play with our visitor. See if you can relax him while I connect the wires that we have attached to my power pack. Then we may begin my test by electro play. Make sure the ass probe is still well in place."

"Yes, Sir, we'll keep him excited and ready for your examination."

I'd never experienced electric toys before. I had certainly heard enough about the experience from friends who had been through their ordeals. I tried to brace my body as well as I could, for what I was certain was to come. I could not even begin to imagine what electric current would feel like, while I was held tight in my slippery, sweat-filled encasement.

At first, all I felt was a mild tingling in my balls. Soon, it spread to my dick. Then, a jolt jerked through my body. My stretched nipples suddenly vibrated from the shock that echoed through the clamps. I felt them project higher. I strained in the sack, vainly trying to move away, as the tingling became a series of oscillating shocks.

Then, the dildo in my ass joined in. A shudder ran through my entire body. I was not sure that I was going to be able to withstand the attack that seemed to make my whole body rigid. I bit down hard on the gag filling my mouth. The shocks continued to ease. Then, suddenly, they spread, touching the different parts of my torso that the hands had clipped the wires to.

The pattern was irregular, leaving me to be surprised and obliged to react each time. I could tell that my cock had hardened, being fully exposed in the air-conditioned exam room. I could feel it pulsating and full of energy. The pulsating vibrations from my asshole only served to encourage my cock's muscle to harden and thrust further into the cool air.

I heaved and strained as several hands reached over my rubber-clad outline. But I was tied too tightly. I became blind to everything except the pleasure that now concentrated around my balls. My body tried to arch as best it could as another round of more powerful shocks caught me unawares. Finally, my cum thrust up and out of my piss slit. Penis and balls were covered by not one, but two torrents of thick, pungent cum.

As I lay there, panting and dazed, I sensed fingers removing each connection. I had not realized how many clamps wired me to the electrical master that had control of me. Once the clamps were removed, I felt the restraint ropes gradually loosening their grip on the bondage sack that enclosed me.

"Remember, Peter, roll the hood off carefully. Cover his eyes and sweaty face with the dampened towel. That will help shade his vision while he adjusts again to the light. Paul, unthread the cord from around his shoulders. You can both work on freeing the cord from around this Master candidate. I know he has my vote."

The process of freeing me took quite a while. Lance, who was both doctor and Master, was on duty, checking my pulse and body temperature as I emerged from the red rubber cocoon. I was both exhausted and exhilarated. I was slowly propped up and then slid off the table, but only after a gentle sponge bath. Lance smiled as he enveloped me in a warm, congratulatory bear hug. More significantly for me, Peter and Paul knelt to kiss and lick my bare feet in homage.

"Well done, Paul. I didn't really have serious doubts about you. I appreciate your total acceptance and submission. Here, take the rubber suit with you. It's yours. I gave Tarquin his leather sleep sack over ten years ago. I hope he still has it. I'll be delighted to propose you for the Circle of Six next month."

"Thanks, Doc. That means a lot. I really appreciate it and your efforts tonight." Turning toward the twins, I added, "Thanks, guys, for all the hard work. It was a mind-blowing experience, one that I won't soon forget."

So, with Lance, I had my first vote. Now I needed to move on to the other members of the Circle. Two of them, I didn't know very well. I wasn't sure how to approach them. I had no need to be concerned. They called me in rapid succession. Clearly, word had gone around from Lance and these men wanted to inspect the new candidate in plenty of time before the crucial meeting.

§ § § § §

Next would be Kenneth. All I knew about him was that he was a banker, a senior vice president, in his fifties. I had only met him casually, as Tarquin's partner. Like Charles, his late predecessor in the Circle, he was from back East and into corporal punishment and young boys. Other than that, according to Tarquin, he was different—a tough and intense executive.

His phone call was brief and to the point. The voice was polite, but not overly warm. I was to present myself that very evening. His place was nearby, in Hancock Park. There was no explanation for the short notice. I had no choice other than to go with the flow. So, I drove the few blocks. I was not sure what to wear. Tarquin recommended 'boy gear.' So, I dug up an old white T-shirt, threadbare jeans with no underwear, and pulled on my black Wellington boots. We laughed. It had been years since I'd dressed that way.

The house looked much the same as ours. It was the typical LA vintage, executive mansion. From all appearances, the residence was highly respectable and well maintained, at least on the outside. As I arrived on the front porch, the door was opened immediately by a younger boy wearing only a thong, and a thick gag that covered the lower part of his face. He signaled that I was to follow him into a side room. The room was spartanly furnished like a gym. My host was comfortably seated in a high-backed wooden chair. He was also naked, except for his studded leather jock and low boots. Another boy, wearing a similar leather gag, but with a flaming red butt, was rubbing his thin and leaking cock over the boots, coating the its leather surface with precum.

"Evening, Paul. Good of you to come over so promptly, with so little notice."

"It is my pleasure, Sir. Thank you for your invitation, Sir."

"Now, let's get straight to business. Strip down. Good, no underwear. Put those Wellingtons back on."

My mind had a momentary flashback to ten years past and my early days as a submissive. Even here and now, I nervously presented myself for inspection by a new Master. Thank God, my body was still in good physical shape. I'd maintained my washboard abs, bubble butt, and I proudly projected my chest to show off the metal rings that gleamed from my still well-developed nipples. To me, any master would be pleased to have a view of what I had to offer.

Master Kenneth checked me out thoroughly. He quirked an eyebrow at my nipple jewelry. In turn, I looked at him before discreetly lowering my eyes. He was in great shape, for a man his age. There was a mat of curly grey hair on his broad chest. His arms were well-muscled, as were the legs on his 'corporate body.' His face was without expression, but his eyes did sparkle. His lips looked full and voluptuous.

"Tarquin has told me that you haven't much experience with my particular fetish. I like to spank and paddle ass, especially the asses of young boys. I like to hear them cry out and beg for mercy. For some, I will show them mercy, for a certain price."

He kicked the boy away from cock-polishing his boots. The lad crawled between his Master's legs. His gag was loosened and slipped down his neck. Then the slave started to lick its Master's studded leather jock, energetically.

Master Kenneth grunted his approval. "Not bad, Pablo, but put more effort into your work. Still, good enough for a small reward."

He stood up and unlaced the side of the codpiece. It fell down to reveal a handsome thick weapon that was already swelling towards an impressive eight inches. There was one marked sign of individuality. The cock and balls were shaved and smooth to show off a tattooed bull's eye, radiating out like a sunburst. The inking was Native-American in style, vivid but discreet.

The kid knelt up on his red-marked ass to take the great tool in one gulp. Obviously, this was not his first effort at cock sucking. But he was not allowed to chomp for long. His Master pulled out his glistering dick and proceeded to pack it back into its studded leather cave.

"That's enough for the moment. I don't want to get overly excited yet. That's for later. Bring over the usual toys, put them on the table beside me. Then get the fuck back in the corner with Carlo. Paul, come on over and check out the tools of my trade."

There was an array of gloves, thin and padded, paddles and straps, all ready to be used on my cute bubble butt. I hesitated.

"Get over here, motherfucker, and stop behaving like a virgin fairy." Kenneth's voice coarsened and deepened. "Now lie across my lap, face down. Make sure your prick is between my thighs. My boys will hold your hands and feet in position while I slide on my leather gloves. Right, I'm ready to begin,"

I'm not sure what I expected. I know I felt stupid, at first. I wasn't a child being punished by his parents, but a fully-grown guy sprawled across the legs of an older man for his pleasure. The slaps from the thin leather-gloved hands at first were pleasant, a gentle rhythm that lulled the senses. But gradually they increased in intensity as the rhythm became more discordant. My right cheek was getting the majority of the attention. I could feel the blood pounding to the surface there.

Then came a pause as I felt him move above me. His studded jock was digging painfully into my torso. A gloved hand reached round to caress my right nipple and to tweak the heavy ring. I jerked in surprise. A sudden pain exploded on my left asscheek as a heavy paddle hit the surface, not once, but several times.

"You will hold your position, cunt, while I play with your body.

If you can't manage that, then the punishment will get much more severe."

To demonstrate, he twisted my tit ring. I gasped. The paddle descended, and I groaned again. His boys held my wrists and ankles more tightly as the paddling continued with increasing authority. My own cock began to enjoy the pain. I could feel it uncurling between his legs and the first drop of precum forming. We were both panting from the exertion, as I was beginning to sweat.

"Not a bad beginning, pigboy, your bubble butt is blooming the way I like it. Now I need to get the surrounding area to color up, too. So, I'll take the small strap to your inner thighs and then to your asshole itself. Then you'll hurt equally all over."

This was becoming ridiculous. Here I was, a mature Master in his early thirties, naked on another man's lap. Desperately, I tried to hold still as light, sharp slaps flicked around my upper thighs. Then, as a gloved hand parted my cheeks and reached into my delicate asshole, my uncomfortable position had to be maintained. The pain was becoming almost unbearable. Biting my lips seemed my only recourse. as I felt tears flood my eyes and roll silently down my cheeks. No man would be allowed to break me this way. I was my own Master. Besides, I had endured worse in my early years of submission training.

But my prick betrayed me. Now excited and fully extended, it bumped against Master Kenneth's leg, allowing a few pearls of precum to dribble down it. This made him even more excited and angry.

"So, the slime bucket can't control his animal urges. I'll soon put a stop to that antic. A couple of slaps from my strap on your cock head will calm you down. But punishment is required for such gross behavior. I'm going to use my heavier gloves and you will call out each blow, adding 'more please, Sir."

Two hands hit my rump heavily.

"ONE, more please, Sir."

The boys stretched me out as taut as though on the rack.

"TWO, more please, Sir."

These were not ordinary leather gloves; they were heavier, and the palms lined with ridges.

"THREE, more please, Sir."

They were like knuckle-dusters in reverse, with lead lines in the palms.

"Four, more please, Sir."

Each blow laid a fresh bruise across the already enflamed surfaces.

"Five, more please, Sir."

I wasn't a baby. I could withstand a severe beating.

"Six, more...please, Sir."

My ass felt it was dissolving in a cauldron of heat and pain.

"Seven, more...please, Sir."

My voice was choking up as the tears flowed.

"Eight...more...please... Sir."

And my fucking cock was starting to stir again.

"Nine... please...."

"What did you just say, shithead?"

I tried to focus through the haze of pain.

"NINE, more please, Sir?"

That's better, but you get an extra couple added."

"TEN, more please, Sir."

Each fresh blow felt like a live coal, each in a slightly different place.

"Eleven...more...please, Sir."

I was losing it; body on fire and taut as a bowstring.

"Twelve...more...please...Sir." My voice was a mere whisper. My lips tasted blood where I'd bitten through them.

"Thirteen...more...please....Sir."

And then the blows stopped, although I was hardly aware of it. The waves of pain washed up and down my body. My voice was a husky croak. Once again sweat was pouring out of me, as I lay panting across his also sweaty lap. But Master Kenneth's voice came, still cutting, if not so cool.

"All right, boys, get this lug off my lap. I want him ready for his final round of service."

I was tumbled off his lap. A boy turned my body to face the Master on my knees. As I started to sink back on my haunches, the fire in my butt forced me back upright. As my vision cleared, I found myself faced with the sunburst tattoo. His thick dick thrust eagerly towards my mouth. I strained up on my knees and glared up into his excited eyes.

"You know what you have to do now, don't you, cock-sucker? I'll let you use your hands, so get working. If you don't try hard enough to pleasure me, I'll apply this crop to your butt—just like this."

One touch of the crop on the fire that was my rectum was more than enough to get my tongue reaching for his prick. It was big and bulky. My mouth was dry at first. Then, mercifully, my saliva started to flow again. I was able to coat the weapon in front of me and slide it into my mouth. I somehow managed to eat most of it and closed my lips tightly so my tongue could massage the log within.

Fortunately, Master Kenneth had been excited by the beating he'd administered and was soon happily face-fucking me at full speed. We grunted and sweated together. He grabbed my ears, pulling me fully into his crotch. I tried to keep my balance as my own fucking penis slithered over his polished wood floor. I used the few extra ounces of strength I found to lick and saliva his muscled pole. Cursing and swearing in a very non-executive way, he came in two bursts in my mouth. I was swallowing his thick cream and using it to lube my tired throat. Then my own cock exploded and sent a pool of cum onto the elegant floor.

He sank down into his chair, after he'd slid out of me. I fell sideways onto the floor. For a few moments the only sound came from his two naked boys who having crept out of their corner, were busily slurping up my jism.

Suddenly Kenneth started laughing, great bellows of laughter, slapped his knee and moved over to me. Carefully he drew me back upright, pulled me against his furry, matted chest and gave me a hearty kiss.

"Congratulations, Master Paul. That was a great show we just put on. You gave a pitch-perfect performance. I think that's one of the toughest beatings I've ever given, and you took it, face-fuck and all. You're one tough Leatherman. I'll certainly give you my vote for Master membership in the Circle."

Then Master Kenneth turned solicitous "Now let's get some relief for your ass; I've got some very good anti-bacterial soothing cream. Also, I tried not to break the skin too much. But it's going to take a few days before those bruises go away. By the way, that's a really cute bubble butt you've got there. Let me know if you want a change of pace and play bottoms up with me."

I did manage to chuckle. Kenneth wasn't so bad, when he relaxed out of his corporate mold.

"Sorry, Kenneth, I really appreciate the offer. However, I basically gave up bottoming some years ago. The only man who still gets up there occasionally is my lover and partner, Tarquin. That was one shit-hard beating. But at least it's more than broken the ice, so to speak. So, I thank you and your boys."

"Hold on, Paul, let me drive you home while you sit on this contoured cushion. Pablo can follow in your car."

By the time I got back to the house, I felt thoroughly worked over. Tarquin put me to bed, ass-up with icepacks and liniment. The next day was Saturday. For once, Rufusboy arrived as promised, but I was too sore to sit, let alone play strenuously. I was beginning to wonder if the price of joining the Circle of Six as a Master wasn't too high.

By Sunday morning I felt recovered enough to hustle Rufusboy down into the dungeon for a slow fucking. I decided he shouldn't be allowed to cum. That required a clear plastic CB-3000 being closed over his cock, before it had a chance to get excited. He groaned as the tiny spikes touched his tender dick. That earned him a couple of hard rump slaps in return. I lubed him and my rubbered weapon quickly. My eager cock slid home as he sprawled over the fuck-bench, gripping the handles and holding his position without restraints.

It wasn't one of my better efforts. As a result, Rufusboy was half-hearted in response. But I needed to blow my load after my bottoming treatment earlier in the week. After about fifteen minutes of 'tug-of-war,' I felt that familiar churning. My juices swept up and into the sweating boy beneath me. It gave me release, but not him, by design. However, I did unlock the chastity device before we got into the big shower. He dutifully soaped and washed me all over, working very carefully round my asscheeks and that still bruised area of my torso. I winced as he patted it all dry and then toweled himself.

We joined Tarquin, with Rufusboy kneeling between us, listening to the conversation. We talked about a number of things—principally the house in Palm Springs—my house, if I remembered correctly. It was now in escrow and Tarquin had helped me secure the bank loan for the mortgage. My lover, typically, now insisted on paying a share of the closing costs. By the time we settled that, we were all restless. It was a sunny day outside, typical of Los Angeles in the late fall and we all agreed we wanted to get out of the house.

"We've got an invitation to an AIDS Project fundraiser over in Holmby Hills for later. It says, 'smart casual or leather attire'," Tarquin chuckled. "Could remind us of that afternoon in Silverlake when we first met, Paul. Fuck, that must be almost eight years ago. Do you remember?"

As if I was likely to ever forget that day! We looked at one another, my handsome partner's smile lighting up those dark obsidian eyes. I found myself eagerly responding to these shared memories.

"We could go in the same outfits we wore that day—if we can still get into them. I'm sure you can. I bet you haven't added more than an ounce or two to your weight since then."

"Then it's agreed; we can be ready by five, I'm sure."

We took Tarquin's Jaguar the short distance to a large, slightly overblown residence in the Holmby Hills. I looked at us as we walked into the party. My lover's black leather shirt and custom breeches still fit him superbly. His Dehners had been freshly shined by Rufusboy that afternoon. He looked every inch the part of the successful, mature Master with his Circle of Six cap and smoke curling up from his Montecristo. My boy was obediently behind him, talking earnestly. We'd agreed that his new professional position was more important that afternoon than his role as my boy. So he'd put on a pair of tight black leather jeans, low boots, a leather armband on his right upper arm and a beige silk shirt that set off his russet head of hair. As for me, I'd decided that I should also show off my relatively new status.

Eight years before, I'd been a young cub looking for a Master on that previous afternoon. Even now I could still climb into the same pair of black leather chaps, after loosening the tie at the back a little. The new under chaps were now matched leather with a discreet codpiece, But I'd left the original harness at home, in favor of a dark spandex shirt. I hoped the total effect suggested the Master I'd become. From the attention I was getting, it looked as though I'd succeeded.

Tarquin circulated and, as I watched his easy manner, I thought again how lucky I had been to attract his attention years ago, and how well his maturity suited him. Rufusboy dogged his heels, but then got swallowed up in the crowd. Of course, James was there. First, he insisted on telling me his version of the search for Rufusboy in England. Then he reminded me that I needed to make time for his evening inspection for the Circle of Six in the near future; that was easily arranged. Finally, he dragged me over to meet Vittorio, the last of the four Masters who had to approve me. I'd only met him at the time of my slave initiation and I sensed that he was still undecided.

"You think you have the balls for the Master's test, kid?"

"Yes, I'm quite sure my package will meet your standards, Sir. I can be available whenever you want me to prove it."

He grinned. "Okay, kid, you're on, for next week. I'll call yer."

I nodded, walked across the large reception room to Tarquin and looked around for Rufusboy.

"I haven't seen him recently; he's around somewhere, I expect."

The crowd was beginning to thin out, as I strolled through the downstairs of the over-stuffed home. An evil impulse led me to venture upstairs. Most of the rooms were open, One door was firmly closed and I could hear men's noises. I hesitated a moment. Behind the door could be the owner of the house and a guest; it could be two of his other guests. Or it could be Rufusboy and not alone. That decided it and I turned the knob.

Perhaps I shouldn't have been so surprised. There were two men on the bed, naked as jaybirds. One of them was Rufusboy with his dick firmly up the other guy's ass. The older was squeaking and moaning softly, as my boy pounded him. Both were so completely caught up in the fuck, they didn't notice me for a minute. I marched over to the bed.

"Fuck, Master Paul, what the shit are you doing up here?"

The two of pulled apart. Rufusboy's cock slid out, but remained rock hard, covered with a rubber, slimed with lube and juices. The florid other man, panting, was gathering up his clothes, ready to leave. "Hi Paul," he mumbled as he slid by; I'd seen him before somewhere.

"Why, Rufusboy? What the fuck are you playing at?"

"It's simple, Master Paul. I needed to get my rocks off; Alan was just the receptacle."

"But this morning in the dungeon…."

"You got what you wanted, Sir. I got nothing, nada. I'd been waiting all week, not wanking off, waiting to come for you. You didn't want me. You even put me into that spiked CB-3000."

"That's hardly fair, and why pick up some old man you don't know?"

"*Au contraire*, I've fucked Alan a couple of times before. I ran into him downstairs. he's always ready and willing. I like to Top once in a while."

He'd turned away, as he climbed back into his clothes, leaving the condom on his slowly fading dick. I was silent, stunned, and uncertain of what to say.

"There's a lot you don't know about me, Paul. You've never really asked, and I've been content to let it slide. Oh, don't get me wrong. I really care for you, and Master Tarquin. You've both been good Masters. I really lusted for your body last summer in Britain. Still, I do have physical needs. I have to take care of them once in a while, if you won't, Sir."

"You mean unsafe sex is a regular thing for you, without my knowing it?"

"It wasn't unsafe. I was wearing a rubber, and I know Alan gets regular check-ups. And it's only occasional, when I get too tense and need a hole to release in. I saved my cum all week, and most of that crazy week before. I didn't even get off this time, thanks to your interruption, Sir. It's no biggie as they say. I'm going to clean off, Sir."

Rufusboy wandered off into the bathroom. I stood there like a fool, smoothing the bedclothes, on automatic pilot.

He was back in a few minutes, looking as hot and as desirable as always. Was I really such a fool as to believe I could keep him for myself, alone? The evidence against that was mounting by the day.

"I'm ready, if you are, Sir. I'd be grateful if you wouldn't mention this to Tarquin. I don't want to lose his good opinion as well, Sir."

We went downstairs together to find Tarquin looking for us.

"Just what have you two been up to? No, don't tell me, but I think it's time we ought to be going."

It was a quiet, short ride home. Tarquin chatted pleasantly to Rufusboy, who had slid into the front passenger seat. I sat silent in the back, trying to process what had happened.

Rufusboy left early that evening, pleading the continuing heavy load as his series was grinding to the end of its first season of taping. He kissed my partner exuberantly, embraced me rather more dutifully and drove off into the night.

I sat back down, still silent. Had I misjudged Rufusboy all along?

Had he always been promiscuous, or was this a recent development? There had been no visible signs to me before the flight to England. Had he always been this variable, slipping from one man to another, without caring about commitment or duty? Suddenly I flashed on a memory of the leather bar in London, last summer, with a crowd of men around Rufusboy, before he saw me. How much did I really know of his previous life? Only his edited version. Was this carelessness and total focus on himself the result only of the tensions of the TV series and the endless demands being made on him? Or was his erratic behavior somehow the result of his earlier training?

My mind just went in circles. How much more did I need to do for my sister in hospital? Was I crazy to be buying a house in Palm Springs right now? Did I seriously want to undergo the rest of the Circle of Six initiations? I sighed, said goodnight to Tarquin. I went up to bed, somber and a little scared. Part of me felt I still needed both Rufusboy and the affirmation of the Circle. But how could I manage it all?

CHAPTER EIGHT - TARQUIN

Winter in Los Angeles is mild compared with most of the world. But that year, the emotional turmoil in our small household in Hancock Park seemed to be growing more frigid and turbulent as we reached the last month of the year. Both my partner Paul and his boy Rufusboy were unhappy and querulous. Their relationship seemed to be tearing apart after Rufusboy's strange flight back to his homeland, Britain. To some extent, I had successfully distracted Paul with the initiation process to enable him to join the Circle of Six group as a Master. He was working on that when he was not gloomily obsessing on Rufusboy.

Actually, running the large house was proving a chore, too. Ridiculous as it seems, we were both used to having slaves/boys to do the cleaning and the cooking, as well as providing alternative sexual release. Paul and I each had a busy professional life that filled out our workweeks and sometimes spilt over into the weekends. To get away from that hectic pace was one reason we were buying the second house in Palm Springs. Now, we were without either a slave or a boy for the first time in many years. My old houseman/slave, Virgil, had been loaned for a couple of mornings a week to do the basic cleaning, but he actually belonged to another man.

So a call on my cell from Roger Barstow, the British butler I'd met during our recent stay in London, was a welcome relief. As we had agreed then, he was calling to let me know he would be leaving for Los Angeles in a couple of days and would be "at my service." I smiled at the turn of phrase.

"Thank you for letting me know, Roger, and, yes, the position is still open. However, we need to fill it just as soon as possible. I will want to inspect you the morning after you arrive here. That would be Saturday, the tenth, would it not?"

"Sir, yes, Sir. I can be available whatever time you want, Sir."

"Ten a.m. should be fine. Find yourself an inexpensive motel near LAX for the night when you arrive and take a taxi over to the house in the morning. I'll pay the cost."

"Thank you, Sir. But I do have money, Sir."

"Well, we'll see about that. And you better call me that morning, so I will know you have made it and to give you directions."

"Sir, Yes, Sir. I'll report in that morning and thank you again, Sir, for the opportunity."

I sat back in my comfortable chair in my Beverly Hills office and pondered. Yes, we definitely needed someone to run the house and prepare the meals, but I also wanted a new slave I could train up for my special pleasures. It wasn't an easy combination for any man to take on. The last real success had been Paul, himself, six or seven years before. Then there had been only me to cater for. Now Paul was my partner and lover who lived in the same house, but had needs of his own. I mentally crossed my fingers and hoped Roger would be the answer to our prayers.

There was to be another surprise that afternoon. Peg, my ever-efficient assistant, put her head around my door.

"Tarquin, you've got an unexpected visitor. Rufus McLachlan is here. He doesn't seem to have an appointment, and he's busy charming the ladies for the moment."

"Rufus? I thought he was working. Give me a minute and then show him in."

Rufusboy—what did he want? I couldn't think of any problems with his contract. True, the 'Spycatcher' series had almost finished shooting. It wasn't likely there would be any word of renewal until the programs started airing in January. Well, it must be something important and personal to bring him to my office rather than the house. I moved out from behind my desk and into the more relaxed sofa arrangement 'for important clients.'

Rufusboy came bounding in, looking particularly buff and cheerful. Peg brought in some bottles of Evian water and left us alone. He sank down beside me and gave me a full tongue kiss, which I failed again to fully resist.

"Hello Tarquin, sorry to barge in like this. But I had an afternoon off and I needed to do some Christmas shopping in town, so I thought I'd drop by."

"It's always good to see you, Rufusboy, as you well know. I thought you'd be working today?"

"I wasn't needed for the full day. Besides, everyone needs to get into Beverly Hills for gift-buying. There isn't much choice in Valencia."

"Well, what can I do for you today?"

Rufusboy slid across the sofa, almost into my lap. His hands moved into my crotch, seeking my prick through my pants.

"We don't get many chances to be alone together, certainly not at the house. So, I decided to track you down in your lair. I want you to take me, Sir. Take me and fuck me, here and now. That's why I've come in, to be with you privately."

"Come on, Rufusboy, this is a public office, and you're Paul's boy, not mine. Even if I was interested, I would not play behind his back."

"But I know you like me. So, you must want me, too. You showed that when it was you who came looking for me in England. And you've no one to serve your sex needs right now."

"Yes, you're quite a hunk, Rufusboy, but you're another man's hunk."

He was starting to get undressed; I got up quickly, went over and locked the door. Rather stupidly, I went back and stood in front of him. Yes, I suppose he did turn me on, and I wasn't used to being almost celibate for weeks on end.

"Stop it, Rufusboy, right now. We are in my office, not a dungeon."

He slid down and started unzipping my pants before I realized what he was up to.

"I can suck you off right now. That will show you just how good I am. You don't know what you've been missing. Come on, Sir, let that weapon loose."

"That is quite enough, Rufusboy. Get up off the floor, right now. I mean it."

I pushed his hand away and slapped his face hard.

"Oh, I love it when you show who's Master, Sir. If you won't do it here, come on back to the condo. Or I can take a room in a hotel in town. Please, Sir, it needs to be fucked now—and hard."

"Forget it. That is not going to happen, Rufusboy. Yes, I do find you very desirable in my present mood. But I am not going to cuckold my partner for a quickie."

"I'm not looking for a quickie. I want to become your new slave, Sir."

"That cannot happen, and it is not going to happen on my watch. Time for you to leave, before I do something to break the friendship we have. And that is all it can ever be—a friendship."

"I hear what you say, Tarquin, but the bulge in your crotch tells me something else. All right, I'll leave for today. But I'm not going to give up on you. Oh, by the way, say hello to Paul for me."

"I think it would be better to keep this meeting to ourselves."

"I don't care. I think I'll be moving on from Paul in the New Year, when *Spycatcher* goes on the air and the offers start coming in."

"Don't count on that, Rufusboy. You're going to need a solid anchor like Paul to hold on to. That's what Bart would want for you, and that's what I want for you."

"We'll see. I may be back for the weekend. Later, Tarquin."

He marched out, so sure of himself and his sexual allure. I heard him chatting up my colleagues, while I sat there, shaken and disturbed. Yes, I had to admit he was very sensuous and tempting. Still, I realized that there was an underlying trait of selfishness, and maybe also self-preservation. Rufusboy would always think of himself first, and not always of the man he called Master. I determined to stay out of his way as much as possible.

I did mention the meeting casually to Paul the following evening, when we were in the kitchen, enjoying a dinner he'd pulled together from leftovers in the refrigerator. At least his old culinary skills had not completely left him.

"Two news items—first, you remember I had mentioned the butler in our London hotel, Roger, who wanted to come over and apply for service with me? Well, he has followed through. He will be flying over on BA at the weekend."

"That's great, Tarquin, he's evidently serious about applying for both jobs, your slave and also butler or whatever in this house."

"Seems so. Although, as you will no doubt remember yourself, it is really one and the same job. Anyway, he is supposed to come over on Saturday morning for an inspection. Can you be here to meet him?"

"Of course, you couldn't keep me away. I think Rufusboy may be here. At least he's due home this weekend."

"That reminds me—second piece of news—Rufusboy dropped into the office the other day."

"Oh, I didn't know he'd been in town."

"He said he had to do his Christmas shopping. There did not seem to be any real business reason. I think he's getting concerned about his future out here."

Paul grunted. "He's always so restless, trying to second-guess where his life, or rather his career, is going. I get tired of trying to keep up with all that crap. I think he's beginning to fall apart from his mental turmoil. In addition, his interest in serving me is slipping, too."

So, my partner wasn't completely unaware, and I'd planted another seed. I didn't want to intrude on their relationship. Still, it did seem to be getting more one-sided every week that went by.

The doorbell rang promptly at two minutes before ten on Saturday morning. I knew it would be Roger, since he had called earlier, very excited, to say he'd arrived in LA and asking to confirm his appointment. This promised to be an important meeting for all of us. I decided to wear my best dress leathers and Dehners with spurs, adding my Muir cap with the Circle of Six insignia. I wanted to impress. So did Paul, who'd slipped into his new VK-79 breeches and uniform shirt. I opened the door and was pleasantly surprised. Roger looked even better than I had remembered, with hair trimmed to a shining buzz cut. His arms were well defined by a black muscle shirt and one striking tattoo. Tight leather jeans and highly polished Wellington boots completed the package.

"Sir, good morning, Sir. Presenting for inspection, Sir." The lightly London accented voice was loud and clear, but trembled slightly with excitement, or fear.

"Come in, boy, and welcome to our home."

As he crossed the threshold, before I could even close the door, I saw his eyes glaze over as he checked the leather in front of him. There was a soft sigh of satisfaction. Immediately, he sank down on his knees, kissed my right boot and then my gloved hand. I raised him up, hugged and kissed him. The kiss was open-mouthed and enthusiastically returned. Then Roger remembered himself, drawing himself up into military rigidity and correctness.

He marched forward, rather than walked, as we advanced into my study where Paul was waiting.

"Paul, this is Roger Barstow, and let me introduce my partner, Paul Everest."

"An honor, Sir."

And down he sank again and performed his obeisance. Paul smiled as we looked over the shining head and nodded slightly.

"All right, slave, you can relax and come and sit down. How was the flight?"

"Please, Sir, I prefer to stand in the presence of my Masters, or rather the two gentlemen I hope to be allowed to call 'Master,' Sir."

"As you wish, but at least relax into parade rest. You're making my neck ache already." I chuckled.

He was very nervous, fists clenched and bearing still rigid. A few beads of sweat dotted his forehead. I needed to loosen him up, even before we got to the dungeon.

"Let's show you some of the house."

We 'marched' through the dining room into the kitchen. Here, Roger clearly felt more at home, looking carefully at the appliances and asking politely, if rather timidly, about our food likes and dislikes. He began to feel more secure, as I intended, describing a couple of dishes he could prepare. This wasn't the way I normally conducted these interviews. But I needed to break through the military façade first, before I could discuss my own main interests. Paul and I sat down at the kitchen table, and I asked Roger to make us some coffee. He hesitated, looking around. Paul, bless his heart, jumped up.

"Here, let me show you where everything is. You couldn't know it yet, but once, back in the dark ages, I was Tarquin's slave. I still remember the terror of making my first pot of coffee for him."

Roger looked very grateful as Paul showed him where the coffee beans were kept and so on. He gradually took over, as Paul intended. Two steaming mugs appeared in good time.

"I've got some work to do, Tarquin, and you two need time together anyway." Paul tactfully took his coffee and left.

There was a moment of charged silence. Then, smoothly and gracefully, Roger sank down on his knees again beside my kitchen chair. I was surprised at how well he moved for such a big man. I ran my hand through his crew cut, feeling some of the tension dissolve.

"You have made it this far, Roger. I'm impressed with your determination."

"Sir, thank you, Sir."

"Now I am going to need to find out much more about you before I can decide whether to take you on in any capacity. It looks as though you could find your way around a kitchen, but what about the management of this house? More importantly, what about giving yourself completely into my service?"

"Sir, whatever you require. I think I can learn to manage the house as well as the cooking for you and Master Paul. I would be honored for the opportunity to serve you in every way, Sir."

"You realize that I am demanding one year of your time and complete submission? There are no limits for me, and no backing out for you. If I don't think you can cut it after six months, I can throw you out. If I don't think you have progressed into complete submission and slavery after a year, you will be shown the door. After that, I decide whether to keep you permanently."

"Yes, Sir. I believe that's what I need and want, Sir. Though I've never had the chance of proper training before, Sir."

"Then, I think we understand one another. You have left everyone and everything behind in Britain?"

"Sir, yes, Sir. Just have a change of clothes and shaving kit in my holdall here, Sir."

"Now, tell me about yourself. You grew up in England, I presume?"

"Yes, Sir, born in Pimlico. That's in London, Sir."

"Yes, I know. And how old are you?"

"Sorry, Sir, I should have known better. I'm almost twenty-five, Sir, spent my childhood in London. My dad left when I was about six; I don't remember much about him—just a tall good-looking bloke with blond hair and a great smile, Sir."

"Rather like you, then, Roger."

He beamed. "It's kind of you to say so, Sir. Well, then, my mother went back to work. She was a cook, and a damned fine one, too—excuse me, Sir. She worked her way up to being cook in the home of a film producer, Mr. Bill Farnes. Maybe you know him, Sir?"

"Yes, I have met him—produced some big international pictures a few years ago."

"He had a house in London and one in Surrey, out in the country, so we went backwards and forwards."

"Must have been hard for you with school and friends?"

"Not too bad, Sir. I stayed with my Gran in London, when Mum had to be in Surrey, during term time. But we were in the country mainly during the school holidays, in the summer, and I could join her. Mr. Farnes had a son, Billy, about my age. We got to be friends, explored the neighborhood, played a bit of tennis and rode his horses. There wasn't any Mrs. Farnes, as I ever saw, only the occasional lady friend. It was great for a while."

"Why, what went wrong?"

"I don't know as I should tell you this part, Sir. But I guess it's important you should know how I got started. It was the summer I left school after I was eighteen. One hot day in August, Billy and I were fooling around in the stables. You know, playing with each other's cock and balls and experimenting with sticking a finger up each other's arsehole. It wasn't anything too serious. We'd taken our clothes off to keep cool when Mr. Farnes came back from a ride and found us, Sir."

I chuckled. Roger was a big man. Probably he would have been well grown by the time he was eighteen. I could imagine his employer, or rather his mother's employer, finding him butt naked with an erect cock and balls waving in the breeze.

"So, what happened?"

"Well, Sir, Mr. Farnes ordered Billy back to the house; he'd deal with him later. Then he told me I'd have to be punished, too. I was older by a couple of months and should know better."

"I think I can guess what happened next."

"Yes, Sir, Mr. Farnes took me into one of the empty horse stalls, naked as I was, shoved my underwear into my mouth to keep me quiet. Then he gathered up some straps, tied my arms up to the hay feeder and beat my butt with his horse crop."

"Why am I not surprised? And was that all?"

"Oh no, Sir, when he'd got my arse good and bruised, he noticed that my big dick was fully out. We were both panting, short of breath. But he was turned on, too, I could tell. I was like sobbing from the pain. Still I could hear him unzipping his breeches and then spitting on his own cock. He was moaning as he did that."

"You've got a cute arse there, boy, and I'm going to fuck it. Ever been fucked before, Roger? Not while you were playing with Billy—ever?"

"He pulled out the underwear gag.

"No, Sir, Mr. Farnes, I ain't fucked anyone either—Billy nor any girls either yet, Sir. Please Sir, will it hurt?"

"Damned right it will at first, but then you'll get used to the feel of my man-rod back there and you'll enjoy it. I'll get some Vaseline or something from the medical kit for my condom and then I'm going to bust your cherry. I've had my eye on you since Christmas. You seem a likely lad for spearing."

"And that's what he did, Master Tarquin. Got his poker rubbered and greased and gently stuck it up my hole. Of course, it hurt, being the first time. So I squealed, and had my wet briefs stuffed back in my mouth. But he was fairly careful. He kind of moved in slow motion, so to speak. He took his time, so as I could take it all in, before he 'popped my cherry."

"I assume he succeeded." I was listening carefully.

"I guess. I remember it was like having a log of wood moving inside me, Sir, but it was warm and muscled. Gradually the pain got less, as he slid up and down my virgin chute. He began going faster, his arms coming around my body and working my own dick."

"Hold it, boy. You don't cum before me."

"I grunted something in reply and tried to hold it in. Fortunately, that seemed to excite him. Finally, I felt for the first time that hard thrust before any man masters me and fills me with his cum. And then I let loose my own fountain. When you're eighteen, you've lots of juice to spend. Some of it landed on his riding boots. A few minutes later Mr. Farnes had me on my knees in the straw, licking my cream off those tall brown boots. He looked so powerful, standing over me, smartly turned out in his cream shirt, breeches and those fine boots. I was instantly addicted. It had been painful, but I'd kind of enjoyed it. My butt was sore. Still I knew I'd want some more, sooner or later."

"So it wasn't your only time with Bill Farnes?"

"No, Sir, there were a few other 'lessons' in the stables, but not many, as he got busy with a film he was making.

"I really didn't know what I wanted to do after I left school. My mother insisted I learn a trade and got me a job in the kitchen of a good hotel restaurant. But I had no interest in 'hospitality industries' at that time. Finally, Mr. Farnes took me on as an assistant gardener and stable hand. I enjoyed that a lot more, being out in the open air working hard. It built up my muscles, what with pitching the bales of hay and such, Sir."

"So how did you end up in the army?"

"You see, Sir, Mr. Farnes used to go riding with one of his neighbors. This was a military gentleman who could ride anything on four legs, or two, as I was to discover later. Major Trevor was in the Horse Guards; he also came down to the country at weekends. He was a good-looking man, tall, dark, with a mustache, about thirty I'd guess. When you're seventeen, everyone over twenty looks so much older than you, Sir. He noticed me one day when I was saddling up Mr. Farnes's stallion.

"A couple of weeks later, the boss told me to take the stallion over to the Major's for the weekend and to stay as long as I was needed. This was a treat, I thought, that called for my best jeans, boots and a clean tee shirt. I was dismounting in the Major's yard, when he came out in what I came to know as 'cavalry undress uniform.' Sir, I'm sure you know about the breeches and tall brown boots for an officer, riding crop under his arm. My cock perked up at the sight immediately. He led the way into a cavernous barn, where another couple of horses looked over their doors at the newcomer and me."

"Crosstie him here in the middle, Roger, if you please."

"I was fumbling innocently with the second rope, when I heard the taps on the Major's boots behind me, saw his hand with the white cloth in front of my nose and then blackness.

"When I came to, dizzy and confused, I was naked. I was also crosstied, wrists and ankles roped in place between two beams. It must still be daylight, I thought, but a leather hood covered my head completely, except for my eyes. In addition, I could feel what seemed like a small log up my arsehole. That was a butt plug, as I was to learn to call it."

"Good, you're coming to, Roger, and may I say you look like a stud yourself this morning, as strong and as enthusiastic as the stallion stamping behind you. Yes, I did take a good look at you over at Bill Farnes's place. A week or so ago, I asked to borrow you for the weekend. I enjoy having likely lads to service me at home and at the barracks, and Bill assured me you'd be very trainable. I know you can hear me through the hood, so just nod if you're willing.'

"I hesitated, not fully understanding what he wanted. At eighteen, I was new to the queer world. Two sharp thwacks from his crop helped make my decision. I nodded.

"The taps on the Major's boots told me he was coming closer. The sound of his crop whistling through the air told me he was near. The pain in my butt told me he'd arrived. Encased in the leather hood, I could see only, but I surely felt the thrashing he gave me. Throughout it all, I remember my dick remained strong and hard. I can remember very clearly what he said and did next."

"Yes, my young stud; you definitely like the rough side, don't you? Well, so do I, so we'll get along very well. Bill tells me you're a virgin in most queer things. There's no time like the present. I'm going to start your training now, starting with your tiny nipples. I'll pull and twist your tits until the nubs start to harden. A couple of plain clothes pins is a good way to keep you aroused. Take a deep breath as I apply first one and then the other. Oh, don't whimper, you'll get used to the pain.

"Fuck, I can hardly believe it. The sight of you twisting in my ropes and the sound of your groans have already got me horny and hard enough to take you. Bill says you're beginning to like being fucked. I'm here to tell you, you'll be begging for it shortly. Let me see how much you've learned. I'll just slide on a condom and add plenty of my lube. I've got a big penis, Roger. Expect be pronged by it regularly if you prove a satisfactory fuckboy."

"While the Major was talking, he got himself ready for the fuck. He pulled the plug out of my bum and slowly slid his monster into its place. I braced myself against the ropes as the lubed and rubber-covered weapon pushed past my sphincter muscle and farther inside me. I moaned inside the hood, my face sweating into the leather. Inch by inch, his man-rod battered its way, stretching my passage farther than I would have believed possible. I strained in my bondage net trying to ease the pain within me and to take his entire pole inside me.

"Slowly, I was mounted on the Major's prick. He roared his delight and slapped my bruised cheeks. We worked hard for about twenty minutes, gradually coming together. My naked body also had to absorb the pinches and twists of his constantly shifting hands. My cock grew even longer, as I could feel him stiffening within me, enjoying every minute of the pain and pleasure. Finally, of course, he came. I thought I felt the rubber tip filling inside me. After a couple of encouraging slaps around my leathered and sweaty head, I came, too, splattering on the concrete floor.

"Afterwards, he first lowered me down to lick his cock clean, once he'd emptied the contents of the rubber into the pool I'd made on the floor. Then, I had to lick up this combination of his seed and mine. Following that, I was told to lower my leathered head onto his boot in submission. He raised his other boot, grinding my head between them. I was his, and he knew it.

"That is why I joined the army and why I became Major Trevor's boy. I soon discovered I needed to be near him. Because his was the kind of discipline I needed at my age. With his help, I enlisted in the Household Cavalry, Master Tarquin."

I stirred Roger with my foot under his cock and balls. He sighed with satisfaction on the kitchen floor.

"And was the army what you expected, Roger?"

"Yes, Sir, I think so—at that stage of my life. I was eighteen, big and strong, anxious to please and I knew something about horses. So, I was a very suitable recruit. In time I became a good competent soldier, a fierce fighter, and a crack shot. Won a medal for my pistol work. My mother, I think, didn't approve at first. Maybe she suspected something, but, under the pressure of her employer and the Major, she eventually agreed, and I signed up.

"Of course, it wasn't all strawberries and cream. It took me quite a while to accept that my superiors and their orders, beginning with my sergeant and horse-master, Corporal of Horse Allen, now controlled my life. Perhaps he'd been told by the Major to keep an eye on me, perhaps he wanted me for himself. He singled me out after the first week or so of basic training. I wasn't completely alone, as a couple of other lads also caught his attention in our unit.

"The first time he told me to report to his office one evening, I wondered what command I'd disobeyed. I marched smartly into the stables office, deserted at that hour of the day."

"All right, over here, Barstow. You know why the fuck you're here."

"No, Sergeant, I'm sorry if I've broken the rules. I don't know what I've done wrong."

"You're here, Barstow, because you're to undergo some special training, with another of your unit. Each fucking week, and maybe oftener, you're to report here at this time. Understood?"

"Yes, Corporal, Sergeant, whatever you say, Sir."

"Good, now pull your pants down."

"Sir?"

"Fucking hell, don't you understand the Queen's English? Pants down, and underwear, and lean over my desk. Now."

A light began to dawn. Corporal of Horse Allen was an arse man, too. My tight butt was getting me into trouble again. But, ever obedient and submissive, I did as I was told."

"Right, spread the legs, grip the desktop, and bend over, you stupid fucker. It's your tight butt I'm after. First, I'm going to give you six of the best with my swagger stick this week."

"It hurt. It fucking well hurt, but I could feel my lonely cock reviving at the ill-treatment. My body hadn't been made to suffer the effects of pain in over a month."

"Stay right there, Barstow. The other reason you're here tonight is to take this fucking butt-plug. Shove it up your hole every night and take it out each morning before you crap. Then stow it in this small box in your fucking locker. Let me demonstrate, soldier."

"He brought out what seemed to me to be an enormous black rubber plug, shaped like a penis. Some lubricant was added so that it glistened in the dim office lights. Then he rammed it straight home. My body jolted at the invasion, trying to expel the invader. Corporal Allen wasn't having that. He shoved and held it in place until my ass muscles accepted it.

"I can tell you, Sir, it was bloody hard work getting that plug in and out each night, although it did get easier towards the end of the week. My butt was bruised for a couple of days. Then gradually it started to harden, as Sarge had promised.

"The following two Tuesday evenings, I reported as ordered to receive heavier beatings and thicker plugs. Gradually I was being trained, stretched, and hardened. But Corporal didn't seem interested in fucking me, or perhaps he'd been ordered not to.

"The next Tuesday was different. I'd noticed that my mate, Pete Prentice, had been singled out by Corporal, especially in the riding lessons we'd just started. Pete was a big country boy from the hills of Derbyshire. As I soon discovered, he was also the owner of a couple of big melon-shaped arsecheeks.

"Okay, lads, you know the drill, but tonight is different. You'll flog each other—twelve blows with this leather strap. I get to fuck the one who puts the least fucking effort into it. It's also time to find out what size cock you can take fairly painlessly. So begin; pants down. You, Barstow, start beating Prentice."

"I didn't really care either way, since I enjoyed taking cock. Maybe the bloody Corporal knew that, 'cos it was Prentice who got the benefit of his handsome dick. I was told to watch, to wank myself off and to hold my cum in my hand. Maybe the Corporal was already feeling randy. It wasn't long before he was pounding Pete and seeding him generously in his rubber. Meantime, I just stood there like a prick and jerked myself off at the show. But there was more to come that evening."

"Here's our new toy, my fuckers. It's called a double dildo, and this is the medium size. I think you know where it's going. So, Barstow, take your cum and rub some of it into your shit hole. Now, spread the rest onto this end of the black monster. Good, now spread your asscheeks, and let's get it into you—three or four inches should be enough to start. Now that doesn't seem to have been too difficult so far.

"Next, Prentice, you've already received my cum up your fucking bum; I'll hold the other end and you can start taking your share. Back up, Barstow, in a straight line. Same three or four inches should get Prentice started.

'Well, look at the pair of you, properly mounted and ready for a trot round the ring. But there's a good fucking five or six inches still to go, so start easing backwards, lads. Shit, I can see from your stupid faces that you may have reached your limits for the moment. You see it gets thicker towards the middle. One way or another, you're both going to take it all in before I'm finished with you. You're going to walk up and down the corridor for five minutes, so you can start getting used to the weight and the feel of the bugger. Okay, Barstow, you're in the lead for the moment. Keep together. Don't lose it. Quick march."

"It was hell on wheels trying to keep together with one of us marching backwards. You really had to keep your ass muscles clenched, or you lost the dildo. I did once, and it was brutally shoved back up my bum.

"Five minutes was as much as we could take that first time. Then we were carefully dismounted. A quick look at the monster showed how it did, indeed, gradually thicken to what looked like an impossible size.

"That evening we were sent back to the barracks with an even bigger plug up our rears. But now, we were told it could only come out when we took a crap or worked out in the gym. The rest of both day and night it was to remain firmly in place. Most especially we 'wore' it during our riding lessons. It was agony for a few days. Still, the body is wonderful about making physical adjustments. We soon strengthened our ass muscles significantly.

"And by the third evening with the dildo, we were able to fully mount it and stood there, butt to butt, sweating and grinning. We were naked from the waist down to get a better purchase. The sergeant had bound our chests and waists together. The pressure was gradually increased until we could suck in the last inch or two. He strapped our legs and arms together, as well. So we were like one of those old mechanical dolls in a fairground, as we tried to walk.

"Horseshoe taps on booted feet echoed down the corridor."

"Bravo, well done, chaps. I congratulate you both, Barstow, Prentice. You've completed your special training for me in record time. I congratulate you, too, Corporal of Horse Allen, on opening them up so well. Let's see them march down the corridor."

"It was Major Trevor come to see the results of our efforts, and was well pleased. With every step, I felt as though I was being fully stuffed, poked, and penetrated. My fucking cock was loving it, leaking precum as we struggled to master a few steps."

"Excellent work all around. I'm going to exhibit them from time to time at some special private parties. All right, Allen, release them and dismount them. They're still to take the next size plugs back with them to the barracks tonight. Barstow, dress and come with me."

"I followed the sound of the Major's boots. I had to waddle along behind him like a pregnant duck; my arse had been so widely stretched by the dildo. I hesitated at the door of his office."

"Get in here, lad, close the door. Stand easy. You know why you're here?"

"No, Sir, I'm sorry, but I don't. Was it something I did wrong, Sir?"

"Damn it, man, you're brighter than this. All right, I'll spell it out for you. I like your style and I like your body—that why I got you into this regiment, why I've had you trained like this. Now you will learn to service me, not only with that bubble-butt of yours, but also with the rest of your body and mind. You will become my property.'"

"Begging your pardon, Sir, I thought I was the army's property, if I was anyone's."

"Don't get smart with me, Barstow, or I'll have you in the guardroom. I'll make it simpler. I'll want to fuck you from time to time. I'll need to use your body. I'll train you to suck my cock. I'll order you to lick my boots to a mirror-like shine like this. Now do you understand?"

"I think so, Sir. You want me to become your fancy boy, your male whore, Sir."

"Well, I wouldn't put it quite so bluntly. I can see you enjoy the Great Game. I think you can be fully trained over time. However, I insist on owning a proper man, a fine soldier, and not some pansy faggot. Understand?"

"I think so, Sir. You already know I like to be fucked, and hard, by a man like you. I suppose I can learn the rest. But what will the army think of such a thing, Sir?"

"The army—the regiment—will know nothing about it. You will never mention my name, outside of orders. You won't imply or snigger about any connection between us. Officially, you'll be posted to my division, when you 'pass out.' You will simply become the very best masculine soldier in your unit in public, and my boy or whore, if you prefer, in private.

"Now pull down your pants, lean over my desk, spread your cheeks. Let's see what you've learned so far. Hmmm, your anus is slightly swollen from the dildo. Otherwise you're unharmed and still well lubed. You'll have to give yourself an enema before you present yourself in the future. I'll show you what to do.

"For tonight, I want to find out whether you've been stretched enough to take my big dick comfortably, or whether I have to go to that lout Prentice. I'm going to roll this rubber on my prick, first. Spread wide and stand firm."

"I'd been stretched enough to take the Major's thick eight inches without too much of a struggle. We grappled hard as he fucked me; however, I also think we bonded together, at least a little.

"That's how it really started. At the time I didn't understand the mastery the Major began to exert over me, why I wanted to please him in any way I could. Now I think I've a much better idea of the dynamics involved, Master Tarquin. I know it's something I need in my life.

"As required by the Major, I passed out of basic and advanced training at the top of my class, Sir, with a special award for my marksmanship. Yes, I swaggered around in that fancy uniform with the heavy cavalry tall black boots, the breastplate and the helmet, all of which took hours to clean.

"At the same time, I worked my way up to corporal in the gunnery group. You do know the Household Cavalry is fully mechanized these days, Master Tarquin? We're not just ceremonial horsemen."

"Yes, I do. And the Major? What happened to him?"

"Yes, Sir, Major Trevor kept a discreet, but careful, eye on me from a distance. I think he was pleased with the way I worked hard to become a trooper he could be proud of. We never met in his office again. Gradually, and then more frequently, we'd spend a few hours in the flat he kept in town and there were a few weekends in the country.

"He taught me almost all I know about man-sex and a whole lot more. I never wanted a woman. I was kept for himself on a tight leash. I also wanted it that way. He scrubbed the lanky country boy out of me, went riding with me at his Sussex home. It was the Major who taught me how to dress and to speak properly. He bought me some decent clothes, even took me out to dinner as one of his fellow officers at an elegant restaurant in the country a couple of times. Of course, I fell in love with him, kept trying to prove myself to the Major. And him? I think he liked me well enough. He needed me, or someone like me, to satisfy his sexual needs and to keep him settled and content, if nothing more. I'll never really know.

"A couple of years after I passed out, or graduated, to you, Sir, we were deployed to Iraq—the southern part where the British forces were stationed. Of course, the Major was there. In fact, he was our Commander, so he saw to it that I was attached to his unit. We patrolled the cities and the wide-open desert spaces for well over a year and were coming to an end of our tour of duty. Then it happened.

"It was a humid afternoon and a routine patrol. Perhaps we were a little sloppy. The Major had stopped the small convoy to clear a gaggle of kids out of the way. He stepped out of his armored vehicle, while I followed automatically as one of his back-ups.

"The attack came suddenly out of nowhere. I heard a terrible thud as two bullets struck a bulletproof vest or body behind me. I stopped firing, swung around to see the Major sinking to his knees, blood pouring from his neck. I flung myself over his upper torso. I was too late.

"Another bullet struck him in the head; then I took one in the leg and started to blackout. The rest of the team returned fire and dragged us to safety. They told me I had to be peeled off the Major's body. Though I have no real memory of that. I never saw Major Trevor again. The remains were shipped back to Blighty while I was in the hospital."

"I'm truly sorry, Roger. It must have been a terrible experience to lose the first man you ever loved in such a violent way."

Roger suddenly broke down, burying his face in my leathered lap, clutching my boots, and sobbing bitterly. I held his head in my hands and let him gradually recover.

"I'm terribly sorry for my behavior, Master Tarquin. I haven't been able to let it out before, or even tell it all. I've needed to confide in somebody. Strangely, I already feel secure with you, Sir. Please excuse me, Sir."

"Nothing to forgive or excuse, slave. It does you credit that you risked your life to save him. What happened after?"

"Not much more to tell, Sir. It took longer for the leg to heal completely, what with the physical therapy and all. When I left the hospital back in Britain, I don't think the regiment was quite sure what to do with me. At that stage, I didn't care. Still, the colonel was proud enough of my actions to make me a clerk in his own office at headquarters, while I tried to get my head back together. Post-traumatic stress syndrome, I think they called it.

"I also learned how to be a valet to him, setting out and cleaning his uniforms, keeping his boots spit-shined and so on. When my enlistment was up just over a year ago, I decided not to re-sign. Even a machine as large as the British Army, and certainly the cavalry, seemed to have too many memories for me.

"I drifted around for a month or so, until one day, watching some ceremony with the Horse Guards on the telly, I realized that the Major had trained me to get on with life as best I could. Men don't mope around like fucking pansies, as he would say.

"So, I went out to enroll in the Cordon Bleu school, worked hard and passed the way the Major, and you, Sir, would have expected. Then I joined the hotel group, worked even harder, so that I ended up as a butler at the Rochester, as you know, Sir. I still wasn't satisfied. That's why I got my US visa, with some idea of hoping to find the discipline I needed over here.

"Sir, I knew I'd found my answer the evening I served dinner to you and Mr. Villier in your leather and boots in the hotel. I can't really explain why. I just felt some kind of power exchange pass between us then, and when we talked the following morning. That evening you'd looked so powerful, so secure, so demanding. I knew I wanted to serve you somehow, Sir.

"For the first time since the Major's death, I thought I might have found a new Master, that you were the man who'd continue my life training, my sex training, and my future, Sir.

"It took all of my courage to speak to you the following morning, Sir. I couldn't believe it when you said there might be an opportunity to become your slave, whatever that involved.

"Sir, I'd little time to prepare after you flew back to the USA. I knew very little about the Leather culture and communities, apart from what I'd seen in bars or online. Hell, I didn't own any leather gear or even a decent pair of boots. So I soaked up as much as I could from an older gentleman I met and played with. Sir, he told me he was 'Old Guard Leather' and that I should learn 'Trust, Honor, and Obedience', Sir.

"I don't fully understand what it all means or signifies, Sir. I'm here to learn, Master Tarquin, to learn what you want from me. If you would agree, I want you to train me, take me and make me into a true slave to you, Sir. I accept your terms without reservation—for six months, a year, or forever. Sir, I know I have to become your property, body and soul. Sir, I know I need that. I want that. That can only mean that I must have a Master like you, Sir."

I sat back, somewhat overwhelmed by his impassioned speech. The look of fire and determination in his eyes jolted me. Roger rocked back on his heels in front of me, once more going down, with his tongue licking my Dehners. I wasn't used to this much energy and vehemence in a potential slave. I did remember that Roger needed a job as soon as possible to remain in the country. Somehow, I didn't think that was his main concern. He wanted to serve a man, completely. I was the man he'd set his mind on. I decided that, with his enthusiasm, I really hoped and wanted him to please me.

His bootlicking skills seemed to be good, as I expected his other limited skills would be. Now I had to find out how suitable he might be for my form of slavery, how much training he would need.

"Thank you, oger, that's very thorough. Now I need to see the results of whatever training you may have had. So, finish off my boots. Come with me to the dungeon."

He scrambled to his feet and obediently followed behind me to the basement, like a large puppy. Clearly, our dungeon was something new to him. There was a moment of hesitation, as he looked around at the equipment and the toys in the dim light.

"Over here, slave, strip everything off. You can take a minute to check around, to familiarize yourself. This is to be your home for the next few days, while others and I evaluate you. Right, get your hands in front while I cuff them; then raise your arms to the pulley overhead."

He had obeyed immediately, while checking out his new quarters, alert, intelligent. I slapped his head twice.

"Focus now on me, slave. Always on me. For the moment, look at me. Normally you'll keep your eyes lowered in my presence, but I want you to follow me closely today."

I watched the range of expressions on his face as I caressed his body, running my hands, now in thin leather gloves, around his face, then over his shoulders and down his back, stopping at his anus. Nicely rounded, hard-muscled cheeks were on show. I slipped a finger into the hole; that surprised him so that he jerked in place. My other hand soothed his hairy chest. He settled down, as I added a second digit and explored his passage. I noticed that he seemed to have cleaned himself out, in preparation for an inspection.

"Sir, permission to speak, Sir."

"Yes, slave."

"Sir, if you wish to use me today, my hole hasn't really been used much over the last year or so. I think the passage has shrunk back down, Sir."

"Well, if your Major had a thick eight-inch dick, then it certainly has narrowed again. But, no problem, I like that. We'll soon have you opened up again."

"Sir, thank you, Sir. I'm partial to taking a hard fucking, if I may presume, Sir."

I smiled, drew my fingers out, and then continued past his perineum to the large cock and balls. I hadn't ordered them shaved, but he'd done a creditable job quite recently and closely trimmed his pubes. Much to my surprise, he sported a large PA, with a zero gauge by my reckoning, which glittered as I played along his lengthening cock.

"How long have you had your metal, slave?"

"Sir, the Major had me pierced right after I passed out of advanced training. After, he had it gradually enlarged. He said that a PA would show that I was owned. He added that it would prevent me from fucking around, Sir. I've kept it ever since, to remind myself that I'm 'a man's man' and not a slut. It can be removed immediately, Sir, if you don't want it, Sir. My body is now yours, Sir."

"No, no, I rather like it in you. No other piercings that I can see. What's the story on that little tall boot tat on your right arm?"

"Some of my mates took me to this tattoo shop one night when we were all pissed. We all had it done as the symbol of the regiment. I hope you don't mind it, Sir."

"You certainly carry your past with you, slave. I believe I approve for the moment. I may wish to add something personal if you 'graduate' with me." I was thinking of my record of branding or tattooing my own slaves.

Roger looked a little puzzled by my comment. However, by then I was checking his large but undeveloped nipples, which shifted his focus. He grunted as I gave them a good initial working and sweat broke out across the broad and hairy chest. So far, I was pleased with my new applicant. He obviously worked out and the musculature was well defined, with washboard abs.

His eyes grew wide as I selected one of my heavier floggers from the cabinet, trailing it over his torso. The sweating increased as I pulled his legs apart, roping the ankles to the floor rings. He looked appetizing, spread open under the single spotlight I'd left on. Just then, I realized this might be his first serious whipping, so shoved his discarded tee shirt into his mouth.

I was right. From the way his body twisted and tried to avoid my blows, I would say he'd only been mildly cropped in the stables before. Roger managed to stay balanced as I worked on his shoulders. Then he began to lose it as the red welts started to blossom across his fair skin. He was sweating, moaning, and trying to evade the stinging blows by the time I finished.

There was no pause. I untied his ankles and dragged him over to the fuck bench. Quickly, I released his wrists from the pulley and pushed him back down. The tee shirt was pulled out of his mouth in favor of a heavy black hood. Again, this was all something new to my probable slave. Roger didn't know how to mount the bench. He balked as I started to pull the leather over his head.

Three hard slaps across his face reminded him who the Master was. He subsided as I fitted the penis gag into place, checked the hood's nose hole and blindfold, before tightening the laces. Then finally came a thick leather collar with D-rings round it. He was locked in.

His naked body gleamed in the low light, as he tried to settle down for some new torment he could no longer see. I fingered the marks on his ass and spread the bruised cheeks. His pink hole twitched in anticipation and I ran my gloved hand round the puckering rosebud. His breathing grew more staccato and his body eager. He wanted to be fucked, but I seriously doubted he could take my large cock at present.

I made a selection of dildos from another shelf and lubed two or three of them. The first slid in too easily, to come back out immediately. The second required a harder push and set the body quivering. Still, I decided he could endure one size bigger and longer. It was more of a struggle, so I tried to take it slowly and carefully. My potential slave fought me at first. After a few more flogger blows, his muscles relaxed until finally he was able to take it all in. I slapped his rump and the hole a few times to make sure it was well seated.

"Right, slave, you keep that plug stretching you for an hour or two. Then I'll check back to see how far you've expanded. Relax as best you can. You've done well so far."

I rubbed his leathered head and left him, benched in the darkness, checking him on the remote camera as I did some work in my study. Rufusboy had called to say he would be home later in the day, so I suggested to Paul that we might put the two boys together and see what happened. He smiled at the possibilities.

When I got back to the basement, Roger was slumped over the bench, already exhausted from the strain, his large body tightly secured, dildo still in place, reeking of sweat. The hooded head reared up as I deliberately banged the door, but I'd changed my mind about an immediate fuck.

"Good, I'm glad to see you're surviving, Roger. I'm going to release you for the moment. Now, I'll lead you to the corner of the dungeon that's going to be your home. You'll feel your way and check out the space. There's a sinkhole for you to piss and crap into. There's a chain and irons on one wall that will be attached to your wrists and ankles. You'll be hooded and fettered for the next few days. No gag for the moment. Your meals will be slave chow and water in bowls on the floor. You will be sluiced off with a hose once a day. Your holes will be used by whichever Master is on duty. Yes, one of my team will keep an eye on you 24/7 until we break you down into a slave animal."

Roger's naked torso and his thickening dick were quivering; I could see his hairs standing on end. I fettered him in a crouching position, with a chain just long enough for him to reach the sink hole and the food bowl. It was designed to be as uncomfortable as possible. He could lie down on the bare rubber flooring to sleep, but was free to move only a foot or so in each direction.

"I'm going to push a larger plug into your asshole. The penis gag will be removed from your pussy hole at the same time. I'm leaving you again to think of the best ways to serve me in the future. If you survive my form of 'basic training'."

That phrase seemed to rouse him from his dazed state. His head swiveled in his chained and crouched position. He blindly sought my boot and then reached down to lick it fiercely.

"*Yes,*" I thought, "*This one definitely has potential.*"

Then I left Roger alone, fettered, hooded, and blind, listening to the taps on my boots receding as I left the basement. I wanted that sound associated with me as Master in my new slave's mind, as soon as possible.

When Rufusboy turned up that evening, Paul took him upstairs to play, so I didn't see the two of them together until the following morning. I hoped they were trying to rebuild their relationship. The actor/boy was told to get naked. Then, hooded and blindfolded by his Master, he was led into the basement. At the last moment Paul added a leather bit gag, stretching Rufusboy's lips and mouth to receive it, rendering him voiceless for all intents and purposes.

Meantime, I'd had time to prepare Roger that morning. I'd unlocked several of his heavy fetters. This time, he was attached upright to the wall of his cell by a metal belt around his waist. His wrists were enclosed in a long chain attached to his collar; also, his ankles were stretched wide and anchored to the wall. He seemed dazed and uncertain of place or time. Still he tried to smarten up as he heard the tap of my boots.

Paul clipped Rufusboy's collar to a chain and pulley before he massaged his boy's ever-active dick to full strength. His Master manacled his wrists in front of him, finally maneuvering him a foot in front of Roger. Both young men were of a similar weight, both could hear breathing around them, both could hear chains rattling, both could sense another man in front of them, but neither could see anything.

"All right you two, check each other out. Lean in and kiss one another."

It was Paul's voice as he shoved Rufusboy into Roger. The two faces collided and slid round the leather covering their heads. Paul used a small flogger on both their groins. They bucked, eager to obey. Roger's tongue came out and found Rufusboy's mouth, slobbering over the leather gag that covered it. Paul rubbed their heads together, as Rufusboy moaned in frustration. However, I noticed that both their cocks had begun to enjoy the action.

"Use your hands; Roger first," commanded Paul. "Feel each other out, or you'll feel my flogger again."

At first, Roger's fettered wrists could only reach round Rufusboy's leathered head, exploring the bit gag, grunting his surprise and pleasure, patting his companion's face. I gave him more chain, so he could explore below to check Rufusboy's big nipples and tentatively pull on them. The actor gurgled through his gag, raising his hands to join in. They explored one another's bodies greedily, checking the buffed pecs and moving down to their cocks and balls. Both boys had impressive packages. These showed well, especially now they were both excited and leaking plenty of precum. They squeezed and massaged one another with delight.

"Get Rufusboy up on the step stool and let Roger suck him off," I suggested.

It was a complicated maneuver, since I wasn't certain of Roger's experience in giving blowjobs. Neither boy seemed to mind. Rufusboy obviously remembered the layout of the dungeon. After all, he had been chained to the wall, himself, from time to time. With help, he blindly climbed the steps. Then, with one hand on the wall, he fed his thrusting dick into Roger's questing mouth with his other. Roger was willing but uncertain, but Rufusboy pushed firmly in. For our entertainment, they continued to play with one another's torsos as best they could. All too soon, Rufusboy began to moan, snarling round his gag. Then he shot as Roger tried to swallow the large load that overflowed his mouth.

It was an unusual hook-up that had Paul and me excited, too. We released both boys, pulling them to the floor. Then we Masters worked our weapons and sprayed them both with our joint creamy cum. I chuckled at the sight of all four hunky men with slowly subsiding penises. It was a good morning's work. It ended with me using the hose to spray cold water all over the hot and panting bodies.

Rufusboy was taken off by Paul to clean up for lunch before driving back to Valencia to prepare to shoot the last episode of his series. At least that relationship seemed to have quieted down.

Meantime, I settled my potential slave back in his corner, locking him back in his binding and heavy fetters. I let the water dry on his clean torso before feeding him extra rations. Somehow, he managed to lower his damp leathered head and nuzzle my boot. My imprint was beginning to take hold. So, I rubbed him all over before I left him alone in the dark again.

That was the pattern for the following days and nights. Paul alternated with me in watching and using him. Dr. Lance came over to check him out medically. Even Tim the Horse Master lent a hand. James, I deliberately kept away at this stage. I had my old slave and houseman Virgil over several mornings to 'help out' and to help himself to a good cock sucking.

We would wake Roger in the middle of the night, so that Paul or I could fuck him gently or fiercely as we felt. Then the asshole was stoppered with increasingly large plugs. Sometimes his mouth was forced open with the larger O-ringed gag. Later, he would be fed someone's boned muscle to practice one of his new services.

Although he was getting increasingly dirty and stank, I thought it important to complete this stage of his preliminary training. He had learned to eat his food on the floor, to piss and crap like an animal, after drenching himself a few times. Finally, he blindly accepted the different sized cocks that were fed into him at both ends.

He was now ready for his 'initiation' by his new Master. He'd learned to recognize my footsteps. As a result, he always tried to assume a properly respectful position, not easy when fettered to the ground. That morning I sprayed him long and hard with soapy warm water, dried him with a rough towel, slid a stool under his stomach to get him in position for a proper fucking.

He began to tremble when he realized what I intended, so I slapped his hooded head to settle him down. The butt plug was slowly pulled out and his chains adjusted to get his ass high in the air. I suspected that he desperately wanted to please me. So, I talked quietly to him as I prepared my willing prick for action.

"You know you're ready, slave. Your anus has been stretched over and over again this past week. It should now be well able to accept your Master's pole-ax. You know you want it, want it badly, want it buried deep in you, so that you can please me. By now you know that's going to be your mission in life—to serve and service me in whatever way I wish.

"I'm not wearing a rubber today, because your Master is going to breed you, to make you his owned property. I can tell you've been well lubed all week, as I slide up and down these firm cheeks of yours. Now I'm reaching under to check the state of your dick. Good, it's fully alert, even dripping a few drops of precum.

"Now get ready for a frontal attack. My pile-driver is in position and banging at your gate. Open up, to let me take possession of the fort. Stop trembling and start working. Yes, I've a heavy weapon, still you only have to relax and let it do its job.

"I'm going to take you, I'll brand you as mine. I will mark you as my slave-in-training. This is what your time in the dungeon has been leading to. This fuck will bind us today. This fuck transfers your body to me, your new Master. My piston will plough up your passage, seeking the very depth of your being."

I was snarling and breathing heavily. Roger was quivering now with excitement. He started to anticipate my demands by humping back onto my prick and fiercely squeezing with his hard ass muscles. Sweat skidded over his heated torso as it strained in its chains. He ground his chest into the stool, matching my thrusts in and out as best he could. I leaned over to take his leathered head, forcing my fingers into his mouth. He responded by first slobbering over them, then delicately nipping at my skin. He seemed to be an instinctive and natural slave. These were not learned techniques to please a Master.

Roger was trying to follow my rhythms as I picked up speed. In reply, he was gurgling over my fingers. Blind and panting in the black leather hood, he was shaking as he began to accommodate my large pole skewering him. Then he relaxed as power dynamics pleasure spread between us. His tight hole was open for me to plough. My thick dick was now giving him more pleasure than pain.

We sweated, both working harder. My cock reached farther into him. My demanding strokes began to force the pace. I wanted him conquered, but still spirited. He wanted me as his new Master, not his destroyer. We became white-hot and one. Suddenly, I reared up for that final total fuck thrust. My seed blasted into him. He whimpered, in need himself.

"Yes, my slave, cum now!"

He did as ordered, not once, but twice, spilling over the stool and onto the floor. This was the Rapture as I remembered it from long ago.

For a good five minutes, we rested with my cock firmly and fully inside him, kept there by Roger's muscles contracting around it. Then I tapped his head. He sighed and released. I stood up, moved around him, fed him my penis to clean off my juices. That was also something new to him; still he tried hard, with his head still laced into the hood and fetters encumbering his every movement.

Slaveroger had done well at his initiation. I told him so as I unlocked the chains and undid the hood.

"You can stand up now, Slaveroger, slowly. Take your time. You have been on your knees all week. You can now see again, so I want you to move into the corner under that showerhead. Yes, you can turn it on. Start to lather yourself up with the soap there. Work from head to toe. Give your rectum and cock a thorough going-over. Hmm, you're beginning to look better already, although you are going to need a shave and a hair trim."

I left him to complete his ablutions, a slave-in-training arising from the animal I'd broken down. My normal working outfit of harness, chaps and boots was damp from the heated exercise. I felt I needed to shower.

"Slaveroger, follow me up into the house. It's time for you to learn how to wash me in the master bathroom."

I happened to look back at his face as I said this. The sudden realization of his new slave-in-training status was a beaming smile, a pleasure to watch. Instantly he was back on his knees, kissing my boots, kissing my hand, and, daringly, kissing my cock, too.

Yes, he'd made a good beginning. However, now the regular training had to start. We began with my showering routine. I told him what he should do. Very carefully, but with vigor and power, he followed my instructions, peeling off my gear. His first lathering and washing of my body followed, with Slaveroger kissing whatever part he was working on. It took quite a while to complete the shower that first time. His rubdown was a little too enthusiastic. Nevertheless, we both felt much better for it, since I allowed him to shower again, in warm water, and to use my damp towel to dry himself, too.

After he'd helped me dress in leather jeans and a sweat shirt, I dressed him in a proper leather slave collar, locked in place. Then I pushed his package and PA into a black CB-3000. Clearly, he had never worn a chastity device before.

"Please Sir, I won't be able to erect for you, Sir."

"For the moment, that's the idea; you cannot get hard for anyone. It is part of your training. Later, you will learn to make yourself stiff and hard on a voice command."

"But, Sir, how do I piss, sir?"

"Through the hole at the bottom, idiot. Stop complaining or I will send you back to the fetters in the dungeon."

"Sir, yes, Sir."

"For the next hour or so, you are free to make you way around the house. Find out where food and supplies are kept. Familiarize yourself with the kitchen."

Once the question of his status had been resolved, Slaveroger settled down remarkably quickly. I allowed him more freedom in the house than I normally did for a slave at this stage of his training. We needed someone to deal with the cooking and cleaning. My new slave took over his tasks enthusiastically and competently. It would take longer to make him a competent sex slave suitable for my pleasure. Still, we were making steady progress.

Other problems reared their heads, instead. A couple of days later, at my office, I received a phone call from a frantic-sounding Rufusboy.

"Master Tarquin, I need your help urgently. I've fallen at the condo. I think I've broken my right ankle; it's already swelling rapidly. The production office is closed this week. I can't raise Paul on his mobile. I know it's a lot to ask, but could you possibly come out and help me?"

There was a tremble and a note of hysteria in the voice that was unlike Rufusboy.

"Well, it seems to be a quiet morning, so, yes, I think I can break away. Try to find out where the nearest hospital emergency room might be. And leave your front door open."

Perhaps I should have checked more carefully, I thought as I drove out towards Valencia. Perhaps I should have suggested that Rufusboy call the paramedics. But he was a relative stranger in a relatively strange land and needed a reassuring hand to help. Since he and I were not on the best of terms, perhaps I should have insisted he keep calling Paul. However, I was well on my way by then.

The front door to the condo was indeed open, although it was gloomy inside with the curtains drawn. Rufusboy's voice called from the bedroom.

"Is that you, Tarquin? Thank God. I'm in here. Come on in."

Without really thinking, I walked into the spider's web. Rufusboy was lying on the bed, completely naked. Naked, apart from wrist and ankle restraints, tit clamps and chain, together with a cock ring. There was no sign of a broken ankle, only an oiled and slippery torso. I couldn't believe my eyes in the gloom until I was alongside the bed. An arm snaked out and seized my belt, unzipping my fly and grabbing for my cock all in one swift movement.

"Thank God you're here. I knew you'd come. I knew you wanted me. You've waited patiently for months. I didn't realize how much I need you. I need your strong cock up my ass or in my mouth."

Despite my efforts, he'd succeeded in undoing my belt, ripping open my pants and seizing my surprised dick. He pulled me onto the bed, flipped me over and started massaging my penis into erection.

"Yes, you've come to take me the hard way, to make me your slave. I want it, want it now."

"Stop right now…."

The door crashed open behind us, and suddenly Paul was in the room, storming across to the bed. Where the fuck had he come from?

"See, I told you, Paul. I told you Tarquin wanted me. Now he's here to prove he's the real Master. You're just his former slave, who doesn't have the balls to win for himself."

"Stop lying, Rufusboy, to Paul, to me, to yourself. This is all a crock of shit. Stop right now. Where is this broken ankle? What is Paul doing here? Just stop your childish actor games."

"Oh, come on, Tarquin, you know you're just waiting for me to suck you off, to give you a taste of my skills."

I realized what it must look like to Paul. Besides, Rufusboy's barbed remarks cut too close to the bone. I was sprawled across the bed, pants undone, cock blowing in the wind, with a near naked Rufusboy hovering over me, mouth at the ready. Paul hadn't said a word. I sat up.

"Lie back, Sir. Let me show you what you've been missing."

"Cut the crap, Rufusboy, this is not some new show you are auditioning for. How did he get you out here, Paul?"

"He told me you were threatening him with bodily harm. He said he needed protection. That's hardly what this looks like."

Paul started to giggle.

"Rufusboy told me he had broken his ankle; he needed help immediately and you were not available."

"Balls and fucking rubbish."

Rufusboy flung himself down on the bed. Paul looked at my torn trousers and began to laugh. I sneaked a look in the mirror on the wall. I scarcely looked the part of a mature senior executive, let alone a Leather Master. I gave in and laughed, too.

"Oh Tarquin, I know you too well. I can't imagine a less likely scene involving you. It's no use, Rufusboy, you went too far. You won't get either of us this way. You'll lose me completely."

Rufusboy flounced, yes, flounced off the bed.

"Screw you. You both think you're so high and mighty. If I can't have you one way, Tarquin, I'll get you another way. Sod off, the pair of you."

He ran into the bathroom. With the aid of my belt, Paul and I got my pants more or less back together amidst further laughter. Then we went home and made love together.

Still, I was worried. I had heard that Rufusboy was going back to Britain for Christmas, but what would happen after? Without the TV series to keep him anchored, was Rufusboy going to fall completely apart, or just pull some more dirty tricks?

CHAPTER NINE - PAUL

That morning in Valencia was the last I wanted to see of Rufusboy, at least for the time being. Clearly his priorities had changed. I'd been the means for his entry into this country. I did think he'd also enjoyed the sex. There had been a spark between us that summer in Britain. But he needed something more to keep his career moving ahead. Certainly, Tarquin wasn't willing to provide that. I heard Rufusboy had gone back to England for Christmas to see his parents and his Butt Master Bart, who maybe could knock some sense into him.

Besides, I had other things on my mind. Escrow had closed on the new house in Palm Springs. I was delighted and horrified to realize I had the first real home of my own, the first piece of property I'd ever owned. I was settling into becoming the typical householder. Would middle-age spread be next? I suggested to Tarquin that we move in early in the New Year. Few improvements were needed, apart from resurfacing the pool. Two thousand eight was only a couple of weeks away.

Before that, I needed to complete my individual initiations with the other Masters in the Circle of Six. I had three votes I could count on, but I still had to win over Vittorio and James.

It was Vito I heard from, first. He wanted me to meet him after work at his office downtown in two days' time. The week before Christmas wasn't the best time. Still I wanted it over, so agreed.

It was already dark when I went to find my car in the small underground garage we used. A dark-haired man in suit and tie stepped out from alongside the Escalade as I came up.

"Mr. Everest? Mr. Paul Everest?

"Yes."

"I've a message for you about this evening's meeting."

I never heard the second man approaching me, never felt the sudden jab in my left arm, only the sudden blackness as I slumped into his arms.

When I came to, I was still in darkness; when I tried to move my arms and legs, I was being held tightly.

"So, you're coming to, kiddo? I wanted to get you quietly to my warehouse, which is fitted up both as an office and a dungeon. Guess which one you're in? Here you are all ready to be 'ripped and stripped.' I had you hooded first, so it'll all be a surprise for you."

"Fuck you, Vito. Let me loose. Who's got my arms?" I shouted through the leather.

"Don't try struggling too hard, as my guys manhandle you. That would be extremely unwise. They both carry very sharp knives, all the better to strip you with."

Vito's voice was jovial. Still I felt the prick of cold metal on my throat and stopped jerking around. Tarquin had warned me about the knives. They'd already stripped off my jacket. Now I felt hands on my belt and pants. The temptation to kick out with my booted feet was enormous.

However, a new steel jab close to my dick persuaded me otherwise. A knife slid down the seams around my genitals. It cut easily through the material, until it was hanging in shreds around me. Then the belt was loosened, and the trousers fell in tatters.

"Lift your feet up, big boy, while we get rid of the pants. Now, let's see that great cock I've heard about. Yes, it's struggling out of its nest."

"Stop it, you motherfuckers. You've got me hooded; you don't need to start tying me up."

The answers to that were one pair of hands ripping my shirt open with buttons flying in all directions. Another pair of hands followed, slitting the fabric in the front of my briefs, allowing my excited prick to fall out. Knives cut along the shirt seams and the panels fell away front and back. A few additional snips. The short sleeves slid off my now outstretched and held arms. I began to struggle again as the hands reached down and started to shave my pubes.

"I told you, kid, I wouldn't do that, unless you're into castration. Okay, boys, it's easier to drag him over to the table, cinch him down, lather him up for a close shave. Then he's ready for the big event."

Vito's thugs were certainly efficient. They soon had me on my back on a hard table, tightly bound, especially between the waist and the knees. The two of them had obviously performed a close shave before. Soon, I could feel the air conditioning blowing round my now denuded groin. Finally, they moved up to remove the heavy mat of hair from my chest.

"Great smooth job, guys, one of your best. Really makes the large dick and those heavy tit rings stand out. Don't you think so, kiddo? Oh, fuck, I forgot you couldn't see through the leather hood. Well, I'm taking it off, altar boy, and giving you a pillow for your little head. I'd keep very still, if I were you, or your skin will feel sorry."

I opened my bleary eyes to look down on myself; Vito leaned over to kiss me hard on the mouth, forcing his tongue inside. The smell was old cigar smoke. As he withdrew, I saw that his boys had been busy placing small lighted votive candles all over my body. Two were installed on my tit rings, well-lit with the molten wax beginning to spill over. My shaved cock and balls had been forced into a thick Gates of Hell metal device and fastened down, as more candles surrounded them.

Vito came back into view with a larger colored candle, starting to drip hot wax onto my imprisoned cock head and metal PA. Inevitably, my body jerked with the pain. Wax spilled over my nipples and tit rings. I jumped again, and a pool of wax started to run over my balls.

It was endless torture. Whenever I managed to steady myself, Vito would add a few drops from his multi-colored weapon, so that I would flinch again. Gradually, my tits and my naked cock were encased in molten wax, while I could only lie there and groan loudly.

It wasn't each individual drip so much as the cumulative effect of hot wax on skin only recently made bare. My body tried to shrink away from the increasing pain. My slightly raised head had to watch every tilt of the candles.

At last, Vito seemed to be satisfied.

"Okay, kiddo, you've made it. You survived as Vito's altarpiece. Now, let's get you out of here. Candles out, guys. We'll let the wax harden for a few, and then peel it off you."

Of course, it was my tits with their steel rings and my dick in its metal closure that hurt the most, as the wax was eventually removed slowly and painfully. Vito gave me a pair of expensive-looking sweats to wear, as well as the remnants of my own clothing. He embraced me in a great bear hug, which caused more flickers of pain in my abused nipples.

"Okay, big boy, you've got my vote. I wasn't sure you had it in you. And you look even better now you've been shaved, in my opinion. Keep the sweats; I'm happy to have you as a Master in the Circle."

I staggered out into the night and found my car parked safely in his garage nearby. My chest felt cold without its rug, while I missed the brush round my package, still I'd gained one more vote.

This now left only James's inspection to endure. I hoped Tarquin, in his turn as Chairman or whatever of The Circle, would be easier on me. James wanted me for an evening between Christmas and the New Year. I resisted ruining the Christmas spirit until Tarquin recommended going ahead, promising me an 'unusual' New Year's Eve as a reward.

Christmas Day, itself, was a quiet celebration as we exchanged gifts. The new slave was given his first pair of chaps, while he and Tarquin bonded closer together in the dungeon. They even dragged me in for a robust threesome, using both of roger's holes. The slave also cooked an excellent Christmas turkey, with all the trimmings, including a couple of extra British side dishes. Slaveroger was settling in well.

James had ordered me to present myself in full leather at his house the next night. Expecting the worst, I dressed down in my third best outfit of old tight leather jeans, black muscle shirt, short tight gloves and my old Wescoes. I thought it showed off my still impressive musculature, as I drove up to the Bel Air mansion. It was a house I'd visited so many times in my career as slave and Master. That evening I had to convince a doubting James that, as a Master, I could be a worthy addition to the Circle of Six.

His two household slaves, tim and tom, greeted me with an initial customary warmth. Then, remembering the purpose of the evening, they added a thick leather collar to my outfit. They pulled me by the attached leash down into the dungeon. There, James sat enthroned, the dim light reflecting on a shiny new latex uniform of black shirt and breeches, with his traditional red stripe.

"So, the sl…slave comes begging for favors, does he? The sl… slave better get down on his knees and st…start cleaning my boots. Pull him down, boys."

I was tumbled to the floor in front of the always-shined Wescoes, with my leash handed over. I put my gloved hands out to balance myself as my face came down to the boots. James promptly lifted up his Wescoes, then ground them down into my fingers. I groaned, moved my mouth into the required position on his boots, went to work as ordered. This promised to be a long, hard night.

He allowed me about five minutes on each boot before he told me to stand up. As I did so, another tall figure in a black latex catsuit and hood glided out of the shadows. This new man silently began to undress me. tim and tom worked off my boots and sox. Soon, I was left in nothing but my collar and cock ring.

"Boys, I want that bi…big cock fluffed up—not too hard, as yet. Then pull it down and under. Let's see whether the sl…slave's dick reaches his asscheeks. Impressive—it does. Hold it tight back there. Bring out the hu…humbler."

I shuddered. The two halves of the wooden torture device were fitted over my stretched penis and balls, squeezing them hard. The two curved arms held it painfully in place behind my ass. A thick leather strap was attached to my collar at one end, while at the other were two cuff bracelets into which my hands were fitted. The whole restraint was tightened by pulling my wrists up my back, well clear of the humbler.

This thrust my chest out, as the silent man in black came towards me with a rubber blindfold and a set of 'tit tuggers.' I'd only experienced these torments once before as a beginning slave. This time my ringed nipples were pulled as I grunted indignantly. When they had been extended far enough, the clamps were forced on them and tightened. The metal arch was erected then above my chest, causing the pain to tingle through my body. The black blindfold was snapped into place. Almost immediately a mouth closed over mine and a tongue slid past my teeth, filling the space momentarily before withdrawing. Somehow, it seemed familiar.

"Stop fu...fucking about, boy. Get the sl...slave over to the fucking bench. St...strap him down as he is. Yes, cr...crush the tit tumblers into his chest. Next, I want rubber plugs in both his holes. Make sure the rubber gag is properly ti...tight, as he's not going to enjoy this next part. Maneuver that rubber di...dildo around the humbler. All of that should keep his ass occupied, to judge from his mu...muttered groans. Oh, tighten the humbler a notch and really sq...squeeze those genitals. Here, boy, you take my riding wh...whip and crop him well from sh...shoulders to ass. I want to see real we... welts on that bu...bubble-butt."

I knew James was intent on humiliating me, reducing me to an animal, a faceless slave. I was determined to resist him at all costs. Still, it promised to be a long, drawn-out battle. The humbler, the tit tumblers, the dildos all tormented and stretched the most vulnerable parts of my body and the straps kept me firmly anchored to the bench.

The crop blows started slowly and easily. However, after three or four across my shoulders, the mystery boy in black latex began to hit his stride. A series of well-placed blows livened up my asscheeks around the humbler and my butt felt on fire. He moved back to my shoulders with six vertical strokes that spread the blaze further. I yelled round the gag, writhing as best I could on the fuck bench. The pain was overwhelming me.

"That's enough, boys. That ass is heated up enough to merit fu...

fucking. The slave's about to feel a big latex co…cock up there. Get the humbler off him and pull the dildo out. I want to give him his first ride of the night."

There is something demeaning about having a prick covered in ribbed latex, even well-lubed latex, shoving its way past your sphincter. At the same time, latex-covered hands worked the tit tumblers, squeezing down on my nipples. I was panting and heaving, but James was well in the saddle, pounding my sore ass, occasionally using his crop again. The pungent smell of the latex outfit rose around me.

He felt like a machine, a first-class fucking machine. I got little pleasure from his expert movements that evening. It didn't matter, as James certainly did. Soon I could feel his balls churning, followed by the final fuck thrust of the latex penis in my innards. There must have been a piss slit in the latex as his cum still flowed into me. He sighed with satisfaction, to pull out almost immediately.

"Right, st…stopper that asshole. I want my cr…cream to stay in him for the next round. That dildo back in him should wo… work well again. Now get him up off the be… bench. Walk him around for a minute or two to loosen him back up. Take off the ti… tit tumblers; just put on a pair of butterfly clamps with long ch… chains. Yes, you don't care for them, do you, sl…slave boy? Well, you'll have to endure them for this evening, at le…least for the next minute or two.

"Now get him into the red latex ca…catsuit, the sp…special one with the all-round zipper and the tit panel. Pa…pat him down first with a towel to absorb some of this sw…sweat. Then make sure there's pl…plenty of powder on the suit. Yesss, it's de…definitely a great fit.

"I hadn't realized how well muscled you've become, sl…slave, although I did enjoy working that well-known bu…bubble-butt. Reattach the tit clamps. Be sure to run the lo… long chain inside the suit to the cr…crotch hole. Keep his gag in place, but ro…roll the latex ho…hood over his head, the one with eyeholes. Sp…splendid. Now let him see himself in the mi… mirror."

For once James was right; even I was impressed by the figure in the mirror. The catsuit fit like a second skin, showing my body to best advantage. I was glowing red in the dim light, with my tit rings and clamps adding a metallic sheen. My cock was also impressed, struggling to get loose, until the man in black unzipped my crotch all the way. My package fell out, also my ass was bare, ready for action. A quick cut by James's crop quieted that down.

The long tit chain was soon attached to my cock ring, forcing me forward as it pulled on my tit rings. Finally, my wrists were manacled behind me before I was led back to the throne. I vaguely noticed that the arms had been removed.

This time, it wasn't James who was sitting there; it was the other silent man, whose cock stood up straight in front of him, sheathed in black latex like the rest of him. James was watching to one side, still giving the orders.

"Right, sl...slave, you know what happens next. You're going to fu...fuck yourself on my boy's upright ro...rod. You can st... struggle all you want for the moment. You have no option except to obey. We will st...string your arms up to the beam overhead and blindfold you. The dildo will be pulled out. Then gradually you will be lo...lowered down onto his prick. It's been we...well-lubed and your asshole is fu...ull of my cum, so your entry will be well greased. Begin."

I tried to get away, but I was already restrained. Soon I was dangling from the beam, gradually forced downward by James and his two houseboys. I felt the tip of the prick at my naked ass entrance. I twisted and cried out, but James was too quick and also remorseless. He positioned me perfectly. I was sinking down on the latex rod, my legs pushed out in front of me. The penetration felt deeper than a normal fuck. Still, my greased hole was taking it all. I slid smoothly down until I could feel his balls at my asscheeks.

I was mounted; a Master on a boy's prick. I was filled; a Master fucked by a boy's weapon. I was flying; a Master seduced by his own sexual desires. It was like nothing I'd experienced before. I began to move up and down on that black latex cock because I wanted to. I had to. Perversely, I was enjoying it, as James had intended. I made my moves more rapid. Excited, I was breathing noisily through the gag. The movement tugged my tits mercilessly, still I couldn't stop. Latex slid over latex. My back was on fire from my previous beating. Fresh blows from the crop only encouraged my frenzy.

Suddenly I rose and plunged frantically, jism spurting out of my slit in a white rainbow. The cock-man reached over to kiss me hard, as, for the first time, I looked into his eyes.

It was Rufusboy.

It was Rufusboy fucking me. It was Rufusboy for whom I'd cum in a perverse fantasy. It was Rufusboy humiliating and demeaning me. He knew immediately. He laughed, driving his dick hard back up my passage, until I felt his cream invade my private parts. He and James were both chuckling as I was pulled off him.

This was intended to be the ultimate degradation, but I wouldn't give in. I was feeling groggy, still I struggled upright, as tall and proud as I could manage, manacled, gagged and clamped as I was. My arms were lowered. I blazed in that red latex suit. As Rufusboy rose lazily to stroll towards me, I head-butted him hard. We both rolled over on the floor. With my arms still twisted behind me, I was more than limited. Still, my head and body pummeled him in my rage. I'd be damned if my former boy thought he could win this round with James's help. We both grunted and growled, right through the gag in my case.

James was furious, began kicking me with his steel-capped boots. Rufusboy was trying to fight back. Still I held my own for several minutes. Then, sheer weight of numbers overpowered me. Finally, panting and exhausted, I was hauled back on my feet by tim and tom.

"Get that fucker over on the cr…cross," hissed James. "Clamp his wrists and ankles hard to the wood. Unzip the ca…catsuit at the back. Get out my po…police baton. I'll teach this sl…slave cunt how to behave."

His slaves were experts in restraining a struggling man, though I was determined not to go easily, tired as I was. When the manacles came off, I lashed out with my arms, before they were quickly seized. I was pulled across the wooden cross and clamped in place. I felt a thick police nightstick being forced into my now sloppy hole. It was shoved well up there, with still more of the baton sticking out of me. The handle was off to one side, waiting to deliver further torment. Then I heard Rufusboy's voice.

"Sir, I've got a novel idea for a special punishment. You remember that roll of barbed wire you ordered for the perimeter fence? How about wrapping some of those barbs tightly round him, reattaching him to the cross and then flogging him?"

The idea was devilish, but also kinky. My fucking cock started to rise at the thought of feeling such savage torture, well beyond the norm of the Circle's initiations. I saw that James smiled in delight at Rufusboy and nodded. Tim and tom were soon back with the roll of wire and began to wind lengths of it around each of my legs. The barbs easily penetrated the latex. They started cutting into my flesh as the slaves wove higher, carefully avoiding my genitals, before twice tightly crossing over my bruised asscheeks.

I shuddered, as any move seemed to force the small spikes into another part of my torso. The catsuit had already been unzipped from my lacerated back. The wire scraped painfully across my wounded skin. I wriggled to avoid my nipples being impaled, but the clamps and tit rings proved a good surface around which to weave the barbs. My arms were sheathed in two separate sleeves of wire and finally the slaves wove a collar of spikes around my neck.

It was total agony for my battered body as I was hung back on the cross, but there was worse to come.

"I don't allow ba…badly behaved slaves," snarled James, "and normally you'd get a pr…proper whipping for fighting with my guest. Better, a well-placed ca…caning will have the same effect on you in your barbed wire prison. So you'll get ten of my be…best across your back and ass. Your boy Rufusboy will administer them."

That was enough for me. As my now former boy delivered an excruciating punishment, as the blows from the cane drove the barbs further into my body, I refused to give way. Through a red haze of pain, I bit down hard on the gag and even bloodied my lips to keep silent. Whatever happened, I was going to stay proud and tall.

I think even James was impressed by my discipline. He ran his gloved hand over my bleeding back, ruffled my short hair, twisted the long baton almost half-heartedly, before ordering the slaves to release me. That proved to be a delicate operation, even with wire cutters. Still eventually I stood, swaying but upright, in the remains of the latex suit. I had survived.

"Zip up the back of the suit again so he's covered. Then give him his clothes and send him on his way. Fuck you, Paul and that damned Tarquin of yours, you made it through it all—even the wire. I still don't agree with slaves becoming Master, but you're a powerful argument in its favor. I won't oppose your new membership in the Circle."

I don't know how I made the drive home. Tarquin was horrified when he saw my bloody and bruised body, threatening to rip the balls off James and Rufusboy until I dissuaded him. His new slave, Roger, got me out of the remnants of latex by simply cutting it off me, making it a total waste of money. They soaked me gently in a warm bath, then carefully applied ointment and nursed me continuously over the next few days.

We were getting stuff together for the new Palm Springs house while I recovered. Since it was now mine, we planned a short vacation there early in the New Year. With good, suitable furniture already in place, there wasn't going to be much work needed, except for the pool and parts of the garden that had to be restored.

On New Year's Eve, Tarquin in his good leathers took me down to the dungeon, laid sheepskin on the bench, so that he could very carefully and very thoroughly fuck me. It was an act of love, a physical celebration of the powerful relationship that bound us so tightly. It was also the tribute of the Chairman of the Circle of Six. As he withdrew from inside me, he kissed the brand he had burnt into my flesh years ago. In turn, as another memory of days long gone, I licked his big cock clean before feeding it back into his black leather breeches.

He took my eager prick in his mouth in turn, sucking and tonguing my hard muscle. I held his head tightly until I exploded in him. Tarquin swallowed it all. I had my final vote for the Circle.

We had filled one another once more and we were content, or so we thought.

CHAPTER TEN - TARQUIN

Like a big boy with a big new toy, Paul was keen to move into the new house in Palm Springs as soon as practical. The existing furniture in warm desert colors meant we didn't have to redecorate, only to add our own personal touches. The second weekend in January, I left the house in Hancock Park early on Saturday morning to check the new pool in the desert. It had been recently surfaced with *PebbleTech*. We had been promised that it would be refilled early that morning. Slaveroger was preparing some food for the weekend and would come out with Paul an hour or so later.

Dull grey clouds covered the stormy sky as I left LA. But, as I reached the Banning Pass, the entrance to the Coachella Valley, they were parting and drifting away over the San Jacinto Mountains. The sun was shining when I got to the house. However, I wanted to make certain it still looked as good now that we, or rather Paul, owned it.

The house had been closed up for a few weeks, so I started airing it, leaving doors open as I wandered through the quiet rooms. Then I opened the wall of glass that overlooked the pool. The water was splashing in and it was over half way full. I admired the way the *PebbleTech* colors seemed to change. The deep end of ten feet had a floor of a dark blue, while the shallow was closer to an earth tone, which blended into the decking and the renovated garden. I knew Paul would be pleased with the way his ideas had worked.

A noise behind me in the house itself made me look up. Rufusboy, of all people, was standing there, looking nonchalant and sexy.

"Good Morning Tarquin. This is quite a place you've got here."

"Rufusboy. How the hell did you get here?"

"I followed you from Los Angeles. I've been shadowing your movements for the last few days. You've paid no attention to my tracking you."

"Why on earth would you do that? Although, after your disgraceful treatment of your former Master at James's place, I think you know that neither of us has any particular interest in talking to you ever again."

"Yes, I was afraid of that. That's why I came back so soon from Britain. But Paul looked so hunky and masculine that night with blood oozing out of the barbed wire cuts. I just felt I couldn't let either of you go."

"That is enough, Rufusboy. You need not come out any further. Fuck off. Get out of this house and get out of our lives."

"Oh, come now, Tarquin, it's fine to play the noble partner when he's around, while you know fucking well that we want one another. I'm here to give you another chance to screw me."

"Once and for all, Rufusboy, understand me clearly: I do not want to fuck you. I do not want to have you sexually in any way. What I do want is you out of our lives—right now."

"If I can't have you, then that fucker Paul won't have you, either."

Rufusboy had been slowly walking toward me, without my noticing it. Out of his pocket he calmly produced a revolver and a cloth.

"Put that toy away. Get off our property, Rufusboy."

"You think you're so goddam high and mighty by making me suffer and beg and then constantly refusing me. Well, now it's your turn to suffer and beg, and that pig partner of yours."

I thought Rufusboy was playing games—reenacting a scene from his television series. Then he pulled the trigger, and I felt a blinding pain in my right leg.

The little bastard shot me, I thought as I slid to the ground on the pool decking, blood starting to trickle through my pants. Rufusboy crouched over me, shaking some liquid into the cloth in his hand. I blacked out as he covered my nose and mouth.

I came back, slowly and painfully. I could not move my arms or legs and I had a terrible headache. My body felt cold. As my vision cleared, I found I was actually in the new swimming pool. It began to feel like a living nightmare. Not only was I in the pool, but I was naked. My torso was bound hand and foot to what felt like a plank of 4x4 wood to my limited exploring fingers. My legs were roped apart; I was wearing some kind of heavy chastity device on my cock and balls. It was like an extreme scene in our dungeon, with roles reversed.

My wrists were loosely tied behind me. The rope continued up and round my neck and then my forehead. I was not moving anywhere. And the cold water was already almost chest height. I was gagged effectively with a leather penis in my mouth. This was one hell of a fix, with my blood still seeping out of the leg wound.

Then I became aware of Rufusboy treading water in the pool in front of me. He was also naked and sporting a huge erection. In one hand he was waving a small wire flogger and his eyes glittered when he spoke.

"Welcome back, Tarquin, how do you like being all tied up in your fancy new pool? Not too uncomfortable, I hope. I'm going to use this nasty little stinger on your chest and tits. I want to keep you warm and stirred up while the water rises. Let's see how you react."

The steel-tipped wires dug into the tender flesh of my nipples. Almost immediately, welts began appearing on my cold, matted chest. This was extreme torture in my circles. Rufusboy seemed to have slid over the edge. My guess was that he wanted me to suffer physically for whatever pain he had experienced mentally. I thought I had done nothing to suggest I would take over from Paul as his Master. Still, that scarcely mattered now. I tried shouting; with the rubber penis in my mouth, it came out as incoherent guttural shouts.

"Oh dear, Tarquin, am I hurting you? Well, it won't last much longer as the water's covering your chest, already. I was hoping the drowning process would take longer. It's an unpleasant way to die,

I'm sure. You'll slowly be submerged in your own pool. It's not a bad revenge for me, considering I've had to improvise. Fucking hard to get you and the four-by-four into the pool upright, but there you are.

"I told you if I can't have you for myself, then nobody gets you. Certainly not that pig partner, my dear former Master, or that new cockney slave you've acquired.

"I've called Paul on his cell to tell him he'd better get a move on if he wants to say his last farewells to you. He's already on his way out here. Whether he'll make it or not depends on how fast he can drive. The water's already too high to use this wire flogger. I might just as well climb out of your new pool. Pity you can't join me. First, I need that one last kiss."

I lay back on the plank. But my racing mind was unable to come up with any plan that would stop the crazed Rufusboy as he swam up to me and slobbered over my gagged mouth.

This was a ridiculous way to die. Of the thousand thoughts that flitted through my mind, only one seemed important. I wanted so much to say goodbye to my lover and partner, Paul.

CHAPTER ELEVEN - PAUL

Driving along the freeway from LA with Slaveroger beside me, I couldn't believe what I was hearing. Rufusboy's voice sounded high-pitched and strained, though clear enough in my earphone.

"Good morning Paul, I'll bet you didn't expect to hear from me again. I wanted to let you know that I'm about to drown Tarquin in the nice, new pool at your nice, new house."

"Is that you, Rufusboy? What the fuck are you talking about?"

"Of course, it's me. I told you before, if I can't convince Tarquin to take me as his slave, then nobody gets him—least of all you."

"But…but…what are you doing in Palm Springs? How do you know where the new house is?"

"Elementary, my dear Watson, I just followed Tarquin this morning. He didn't expect to be stalked, so it was really quite easy. He didn't suspect anything. When I saw the pool filling so quickly, I knew what I wanted to do."

"This is ridiculous, Rufusboy, Tarquin's a big powerful man."

"Well, I did have to shoot him in the leg. He looked so surprised. Then I had to tie him up before I pushed him into the pool. He's roped to a piece of four-by-four. He looks gorgeous naked and bound, really sexy. Of course, he won't be for much longer as the water's rising."

"Stop it, Rufusboy. Turn the water off. At least wait until I can get there."

"Well, you'll have to hurry up, slave trash. I don't know how to turn the water off. Bye, Paul."

"Rufusboy, Rufus, wait."

But he was gone and didn't answer his cell.

"Sir, what's happened, Sir? Is it my Master, Sir?"

"Yes, Roger. I'm going to drive like a bat out of hell to try to save him from a madman. Hold tight."

I reckoned we were about half an hour from the house at regular speeds in normal traffic conditions. So I pressed my pedal to the metal, praying for no road hazards or accidents to slow us down. Roger's eyes widened in shock as I filled him in on Rufusboy's phone call. I shot off the main 10 Freeway onto the 111, the Palm Springs bypass.

"That fucking bastard, wait 'til I get my hands on him."

"I get first shot, slave. The problem is that I don't know whether any of it is true. Still, we can't take a chance."

The twists and turns along the 111 seemed endless. Then there was a delay from a group of mobile homes moving slowly along in search of fresh winter quarters. Finally, I got past them and sped down Palm Canyon, past the Tramway turnoff.

"Sir, you need to watch the speed limit, Sir."

"Okay, slave, I know. There isn't much time left. It's already fifteen minutes since the call. I don't know how fast that pool fills."

At last we reached our turn. The house was just down the road.

"Give me five to ten minutes with the bastard, Roger. If you haven't heard from me by then, then come in, with both guns blazing, so to speak."

"Sir, yes, Sir. If you're sure you'll be okay?"

"I know Rufusboy as well as anyone—unless he plans to shoot me, too."

I left the keys in the ignition as we stopped in front of the house and sprinted to the front door, which was still ajar. I hesitated for a moment, listening for sounds, then pushed it open quietly and walked through the house.

I couldn't process what I was seeing. A naked Rufusboy with a full erection was prowling round the decking with what looked like a 9mm revolver in his hand. Roped upright in the middle of the long side of the pool was my lover, a thin stream of blood oozing from his leg. He was naked, cock and balls in chastity, severely gagged and bound. The water was lapping at his shoulders. It was like a scene from a 'snuff film.' Tarquin's head turned as he saw me, and that triggered a reaction from Rufusboy.

"Well, Paul, that was fast. You must have broken the speed records. As you see, I've really done what I told you on the phone. This stupid bugger turned down my offer to become his slave—again. So, I told him, and I mean it, no man gets him if I don't. Certainly not you. Oh, where's that new nancy slave boy from London?"

"I left Roger behind in LA. This is supposed to be a quiet first weekend for both of us in the new home."

"It doesn't seem to be working out that way, Paul. You've just got time to say your goodbyes. Unfortunately, Tarquin can't say anything, but that's just as well."

"Stop it, Rufus, you don't realize what you're doing. You don't want a dead Tarquin. What good is that?"

"I keep telling you, no one can have him except me. You, in particular. You've enjoyed him far too long."

"Then take me instead, Rufus, take me and drown me. Then you can have Tarquin all to yourself. After this experience, I'm sure he'll come willingly."

It was a challenge I had to offer, but it stopped Rufusboy pacing and waving his gun. I moved down into the pool area.

"You'd change places with him? You'd give your life for his? Die a slow death so that he'd be spared for me?"

"If it was the devil himself who was asking me, yes. I love him. If it's the only way to save him, I'll take his place."

I thought for a moment. Time stopped. A thousand images flashed through my mind of Tarquin and myself. A young naked slave clutching his boots. The branding iron searing my butt. Tarquin spoon-feeding me as I tossed in a fever. The contented slave being fucked in the dungeon. Two men struggling to define their real relationship. The empty years apart in lonely places. Two Masters joyously sucking each other off in the big bed. Tarquin's dark eyes laughing at me, his lover, my partner.

As I looked at the big man drowning in the pool, I knew he'd do the same for me, if ever it was needed.

"Yes, Rufus, take me instead. Then you can have Tarquin and the houses all to yourself. But we better be quick."

His feverish eyes looked at me. I finally realized that the sexy young British actor I'd met a year ago had left Rufusboy's body. Some sadistic madman had taken possession.

"Right, Paul, you stupid fool, help me drag another of those planks over to the pool side. Slide the four-by-four into the water. Steady, we nearly drowned him. Let's get you ready. Off with the shoes, the clothes. Fluff up that dick that I've endured up my hole so many times. Hands by your sides as I rope you tightly. Hmmm, I can still see some of the welts from the thrashing I gave you at James's."

"Wait, I have to kiss him goodbye. You have to wait."

"I need to improvise a gag for you, too—can't have too much noise. Stick out your tongue and I'll make a slipknot with this thin cord. Round your tongue it goes tightly and then around your head."

So I couldn't talk, couldn't speak my farewell to my lover? I'd see about that. No time was left. I jumped into the pool, bound and gagged with more rope dangling behind me to bind me to the plank. It was only a foot of distance over to Tarquin. Still the displaced water from my splash was seeping round his gag into his mouth. I moved very slowly, trying to settle the water. My partner's eyes had never left me. He was shaking his head as my roped tongue reached out to lick his leather gag. It wasn't a real kiss, as my body swayed in, trying to slither over his, but it was the best I could do. I crushed my mouth and dripping tongue over his and tried to suck his love out of him. Rufusboy started tugging on the ropes.

"Goodbye. I've loved only you and I thank you for all of it," I managed to lisp round the rope gag.

I looked up. There were tears in his eyes, as he tried to stretch up tall and proud for me. I did the same for him and smiled before my eyes misted over. Then I was half pulled, half stumbled over to my punishment plank. Rufusboy had slid back into the pool to quickly rope me in place as best he could with the rising water. I could still turn my head. I needed one last look at the proud, buffed and blooded body of my life-love as the water rose above his chin.

"Now, Rufusboy, now, let him go. You promised."

"You're a fool, Paul, as always. You really thought I would release him? No, I'm going to climb out of the pool. I'm going to watch you two perverts drown in front of me. That way you both lose your most cherished possession and I can go off and find my new Daddy."

"You bastard. You rotten filthy bastard." I snarled something through the gag.

"Goodbye, Paul. Yes, I did enjoy the fucking and the games. I'm sorry, Tarquin, I never got your big dick up my ass. However, I'm going to have an excellent view of your sad deaths from over here."

Two shots rang out in rapid succession. Rufusboy screamed an unearthly, high-pitched noise as he clutched his groin. The water hose split, so that the water started pouring into the garden, not the pool.

Roger was standing there, firing Rufusboy's gun, with a savage expression on his face. He yanked off his shoes before jumping into the pool, a kitchen carving knife in his other hand.

"Hold tight, my Masters, try to just breathe through your noses."

He dived beneath the water. I watched him slicing through Tarquin's ropes, rising back up, lifting the almost inert body. My partner is no lightweight. His slave was cradling him in his arms as he staggered up the pool's steps. Then he was right back, cutting through my bonds, helping me carefully out of the water, as I struggled to undo the gag.

I collapsed on the side of the pool, resting for a while. Then I walked over to where Rufusboy was writhing on the ground; blood was seeping out of his groin as his hands covered his wounded genitals. He was making loud mewing noises. Unfortunately, I thought he was going to live.

My partner also lay on the decking, with Slaveroger carefully removing the chastity device and gag and checking his leg wound. I called Dr. Lance in LA on his emergency line. He promised immediate local help. Tarquin was as pale as death, shivering with cold, going into shock. I lay down beside him, beckoned Slaveroger to join on the other side. We held him between us, trying to restore warmth and energy into his well-loved body. Finally, he groaned, opened his eyes, looked around, and then smiled at me. Then he slowly reached over his other side to squeeze his slave's arm, hard. Gradually as his body warmed, his cock started to harden. After a few more minutes, he reached around until he was holding both our dicks firmly in his hands. Thankfully, Tarquin was definitely going to live.

It took quite a while to sort out the mess. Tarquin, being Tarquin, had contacts in Palm Springs to help with it all. A discreet doctor appeared, summoned by Dr. Lance. Both wounded men were taken away to his private surgery. While we waited, Roger and I had found the turnoff for the pool hose, washed away the blood off the deck. Finally, exhausted, I collapsed in Roger's arms. He had to revive me, too, before tucking me into one of the beds in the new house for several hours. Roger was proving a total tower of strength. He also then made coffee in a new house from the supplies he'd brought from LA.

Tarquin asked to see us both that evening. He was propped up in a hospital bed with his wounded leg elevated. He was pale, but looked happy to be alive. He hugged, kissed, and held each of us in turn. Slaveroger sank down on the floor to hold his Master's hand. I sat on the bed to hold my lover's other hand.

"How do I ever thank you two for your gifts today—offering to exchange your life for mine and then literally saving me? No man could ask for a more loving partner or a more faithful slave. I know that I am truly blessed. Once we get over this mess, I must do something serious about it. I think it is about time you and I got married, Paul. We've done everything else. It's legal here in California right now. Marriage might even settle us down."

"If that's what you really want, Tarquin, then that's what I want, too."

"You know it is, love, and we will get on with it as soon as I am out of here. And you, Slaveroger, how did you do it? I had given us up for lost."

"Well, Sirs, Master Paul has told me to wait ten minutes or so by the car, while he took on Rufusboy. I decided to equip myself with the carving knife I'd brought for the prime rib dinner tomorrow, Sirs. When I sneaked through the front door, I couldn't believe what I saw, Sirs. My Master was being murdered in the swimming pool. His partner was tied up, naked, too. My Sirs were being threatened by a crazy man with a hard-on. I crept closer to the pool, not too difficult with the noise of the pool filling and plenty of large furniture to hide me in your new living room, Sirs.

"I didn't care for what happened next. Master Paul was being manhandled and tied up by that crazy naked bastard—pardon me, Sirs."

"Not a problem, roger. Please go on."

"Sirs, Rufusboy had put down his gun to rope Master Paul, then turned away to argue with him about you. I had to wait until you, Sir Paul, jumped into the water to save my Master at the cost of your own life." The slave swallowed and blinked. "Then I understood what being part of a Leather Family really meant. It got me really, really stirred up. Sorry, Masters, back to my report.

"Sirs, I used the noise and the distraction of your activities in the pool to slither out, grab the gun. Then hide in the bushes there by the pool, sticking the carving knife in my belt. When I heard Rufusboy shouting that he would allow both of you to drown, Sirs. As he climbed out of the pool with his penis on full alert, I knew exactly what I had to do, Sirs. I took a moment to get a clear line of sight. Then I shot the guy in the balls. I hope he'll never be able to fuck with his tool again, Sirs."

"You're an amazing marksman, roger. You just needed a single shot?"

"Yes, Sir, as I said, I was really pumped. It wasn't a difficult shot, not after my Army training, just so as he stayed still for a moment. I had a few seconds to check the magazine and then squeezed off the shots. I guess I was lucky or God was on our side, Sirs"

"I think some Higher Power must have guided you. I doubt I could have lasted another five minutes." Tarquin smiled as I nodded.

"Well, Sirs, I didn't know where the water turned off either, so I put a bullet in the hose where the flow would move away from the pool. Sirs."

"Whatever you did, I will be eternally grateful. It seems odd for me to say it, but my life is yours, slave. What do you want in return?"

Slaveroger blushed, squeezed Tarquin's hand and covered it with kisses.

"Thank you, Master. This all I want—to complete my training with you, to become the best slave you ever had, Sir, begging your pardon, Master Paul."

We two Masters smiled at one another. I knew that Slaveroger was going to be 'the keeper' for Tarquin and that pleased me, too.

"You get your wish, Slaveroger, but do not imagine this means I will be gentle with you. Come up here. Let me kiss you properly. And now you, my love. Tonight, I think you better let me rest, but, after that, I'm going to need both of you—always."

CHAPTER TWELVE - TARQUIN

It was almost a week before the surgeon released me into the care of Dr. Lance in Los Angeles. We had managed to keep the shooting out of the media, explaining to the police that the gun was fired accidentally. Then I was allowed a regimen of supervised exercise and 'light' office work to satisfy my restless spirit. I persuaded Paul to go back to his job. Slaveroger was more than competent to look after my daily needs. As he had already passed his California driver's test, we were not housebound.

"You certainly seem to have acquired a variety of unusual skills in the British Army, slave. I am certain you never thought you would use them in a situation like this recent one." Slaveroger was driving me in my Jag to my office.

"Sir, no, Sir, I did take some additional training, like basic medic. I was determined to be the best soldier I could in every way, for the Major, God rest his soul. It really paid off, didn't it, Sir?"

"Indeed, it did. However, you also showed considerable initiative that morning. You made decisions and took action—no messing around, no waiting for someone else to give the orders."

"No, Sir, because it was you, Master Tarquin, you who was going to be killed. There wasn't any option. I wanted you to continue to be my Master and me to be your slave, Sir."

For Slaveroger, it was all quite simple.

I wasn't sure I agreed completely. "For some men there might have been several options, and I might not be here. I have thought a great deal about you over the last few days. I believe not only are you a 'natural' slave, but you are also a monogamous slave, if there is such a being, devoted to one man, one Master."

"Sir, Yes, Sir. If I may presume to say so, Sir, I've done some thinking, too. Now I'm more certain than before that my entire future lies in service to you, learning how to pleasure you more and to make you proud of me, Sir."

"Yes, it is definitely time we did something to show off your progress. I am going to have your nipples pierced and get your PA changed. I will have you permanently 'collared' at the same time."

Slaveroger steered the car to a handy nearby parking spot. He turned off the engine, leaning over to kiss my hand, before placing it on his head.

"Thank you, my Master, if that would please you, Sir."

"Yes, it does. Bert, whom you know as my regular barber, also does my piercings. He has been doing an excellent job over the years. I will arrange it for next week."

The following Monday morning, after both our regular hair trims, I checked whether Bert was ready.

"Oh, yes, Mr. Charlton, I've brought everything with me. White gold will look very nice against the youngster's fair skin. Besides, it should not present any problems with airport security checks. Do you want to do the piercings down in the basement, as usual, Sir? It should only take me a few minutes to get set up.

"Since you told me you wanted something large on him to make something of a show, I'll start his tits with an eight gauge. It will be uncomfortable for a few days, but this Roger's a big lad and can take it, I'm sure."

We got Slaveroger down in the dungeon, suitably restrained on the bondage table. I sat down beside him while Bert fussed around before swabbing the large brown nipples. The slave was pale and sweating lightly. He had a low pain threshold, I knew, so I took his big hand in mine.

"Relax, Slaveroger, this will be no worse than any other pain you have already experienced. I have thought again about your PA. It is already a zero gauge, so, for the moment, I am merely going to have your existing metal one exchanged for one in white gold with a bigger ball. We will get to collars in a few minutes. Then, you will really look like my slave."

My slave's hand squeezed mine hard, as Bert carefully pushed his sterilized needle through the flesh. There was a gasp from Slaveroger, then I heard him gritting his teeth. Another groan followed as the needle was followed by the gleaming ring, itself. This, the piercer carefully made into a circle and closed with a ball. My hand was almost crushed when the process was repeated with the right nipple. He was panting hard for the next few minutes before he calmed down. Slaveroger did seem genuinely pleased when Bert showed him the finished result in a mirror, particularly after the existing metal PA had been replaced by one in gleaming gold.

Slaveroger's eyes sparkled as he turned on the table to look at me. I smiled back at him. "Looking good, slave, and definitely more like my property. Now, Bert, what have you got to show me by way of collars?"

I chose a simple, yet supple and thick gold band for his collar. Using a thick pad to protect the neck and an electric acetylene torch, Bert welded it round Slaveroger's neck. Again, the slave was allowed to look at himself in the mirror, He was a big guy who was now permanently marked as another man's possession. These markings now brought him into accepting his full slave mode, even in his manner of speech.

"Sir, it needs to thank you for your new gifts. it knows that fucking your slave is still too painful, with your leg and all. Sir, may it have the privilege of sucking you off? Will you allow your slave to do the same to Master Bert, too? it hasn't had any cum in its stomach for the past ten days. it misses the taste, Sirs."

Both of us chuckled. I took my place again in the barber's chair, unzipping my pants in the process. Slaveroger was on his knees instantly, using his fingers to free my cock. Then he clutched his hands together behind his back. My prick eagerly scented the air, while my slave just as eagerly took the tip between his lips to start licking and savoring my cockhead.

I growled, settling back to enjoy myself. His mouth was warm and wet. He closed around my muscle expertly, so I began to thrust back into his throat. We had worked hard to overcome Slaveroger's gag reflex. I was pleased when he was able to swallow all of me with just a sharp intake of breath. Immediately, he started working on me in earnest, using a steady rhythm of 'push and pull,' coating my prong with saliva to ensure a smoother passage, while licking hard to increase the excitement.

I had not been able to have much sexual activity myself recently, so my growls became typically louder as my passion increased. I grabbed his ears to pull myself fully into his throat. He gurgled with delight. My balls tightened so that I could release a large load down his throat, pulling out quickly so he could savor my final drops on his tongue as he milked me. We ended up both panting with satisfaction. In turn, I tongued him hard, tasting the last of my cream as, in turn, I explored his mouth.

Then, I gestured to Bert to take my place in the chair. He had been flattered by the offer, already had his cock out, massaged to full erection. I had never noticed that my barber had a dragon tattooed on his penis; actually, I could not remember ever seeing his dick before. Slaveroger swallowed the prick whole, giving him a good ride to glory from Bert's moans. I could tell he was thoroughly enjoying the service. He groaned long and low as he ravaged Slaveroger's mouth and added his cum to mine in my slave's stomach.

When he finished, he insisted that the slave was entitled to similar treatment.

"After what he did for you ten days ago, Mr. Charlton, I'd like to show my gratitude. He's quietly leaking over there. I'll bet he's had no relief in quite a while, either."

"Is it permitted, Sir?"

Smiling, I agreed and somewhat nervously my slave took his place in the barbering chair. It was true, pre-cum had been oozing round his new PA. He was now quivering with excitement and his thick pole was standing upright. Bert had obviously done this before, as gently he hefted the slave's weapon, massaging the shaft before taking it slowly into his mouth. Slaveroger sighed quietly with satisfaction, winced once as the new PA reached to the back of Bert's throat, and lay back in the chair while his penis slid backward and forward with increasing friction. It was over quickly. My slave had been obliged to store up his seed and was very ready to spill it. Bert swallowed and sampled the flavor, pronouncing it "bloody satisfactory."

So ended a most "satisfactory" morning. The slave went back to his domestic duties, the new jewelry gleaming brightly against his bare skin. That evening, Slaveroger proudly showed it off to my partner as soon as he got the opportunity.

A few weeks later, when I had sufficiently recovered, Paul was formally initiated as a Master into the Circle of Six. It was a deliberately low-key affair, a simple dinner which I, as President, held at the house. Only the six Masters and their personal slaves were present at the formal meeting. All six of us wore our best leathers and boots. I elected to use black candles as illumination. The tall tapers reflected onto the gleaming black leather and shining boots to give a properly dramatic effect as we lined up in our traditional circle. I presented Paul with his cap badge of a silver circle with a red and silver flame at its center. Each Master embraced him in turn, and even James joined in with good spirit. Something about the 'incident' with Rufusboy had circulated, so James was on his best behavior. As soon as he arrived, he enquired solicitously about my own recovery, as well he might since he'd encouraged so much of Rufusboy's schizoid behavior.

Slaveroger had been very nervous beforehand, as it was the first major event at the house since he had joined us. The food had largely been catered, still he was concerned about observing the correct slave etiquette, quizzing Paul about the protocols.

"Master Paul, how will it know which Master is which? it has never met most of them."

"Don't worry so much, Slaveroger. You don't have to know who they are when they arrive; just kiss their boots and their hand, if that is offered. Then you take their caps and put them on the shelf over there. Their slaves will help you, so it's a great chance to meet some of your opposite numbers."

Slaveroger's part in the 'Rufusboy incident' had been widely gossiped about. Both Masters and slaves were curious about the deadly marksman from London. I was going to have to be careful it didn't go to his head, though the slave was far too busy trying to remember the correct behavior to be distracted that evening. His concern then, and after, was to be a credit to me, his Master, rather than to himself. That evening and his behavior in the house, as well as in the dungeon, showed his determination—and his success. An ongoing strict regimen of exercise, discipline and sexual education continued to be an excellent way of honing his body, as well as his full slave potential.

§ § § § §

As the days warmed into spring that year, our attention became more focused on arrangements for our upcoming wedding. Dr. Lance, who was probably our oldest friend, and who certainly knew the most about our lives together, had insisted that the wedding be held at his estate in the rolling hills of Calabasas. The other three Masters in the Circle were to co-host the reception in the same spot. All seemed to be thrilled that two of their numbers were to be joined in marriage. A friendly judge was to perform the ceremony; our local Episcopal Rector agreed to give a blessing. We tried to limit the numbers. That was a useless exercise. With friends, family, and clients, the invitation list kept growing.

We were determined that since this was to be a formal occasion, both Paul and I would wear morning suits with the traditional black cutaway jackets, grey vests and pin-striped trousers. But to honor our Leather lifestyle, we had black leather cravats made, the buttonholes were black carnations. Over his pants each of us wore his best Dehners, which had been lovingly spit-shined to perfection by Slaveroger. We also decided that my slave's role should be as ring-bearer, dressed in a black suit with a similar leather cravat designed to also show off his white gold slave collar.

On a breezy Saturday afternoon in April, our little motorcade left Hancock Park with the principals in James's Rolls Royce, complete with chauffeur. Vito had been concerned about our safety, although

Rufusboy, himself, seemed to have disappeared. So, he had arranged to hire a couple of off-duty CHP motor officers to ride along with us for extra protection.

I was surprisingly nervous—and excited. It had been a long, sometimes convoluted, sometimes exhilarating road that Paul and I had traveled over the previous eight years. Few gay men we knew had successfully evolved from Master and slave to loving Masters bound together in body and soul. We had been physically joined in the most intimate forms of such sexual activities as fucking and fisting, although that had been in private. Now, we were publicly proclaiming a permanent relationship.

I know Paul was feeling the same mix of emotions as we prepared to stand in front of our friends and acquaintances. By reciting a few simple phrases and exchanging plain black and gold identical rings, we would find ourselves married—husband and husband.

So much had happened in recent months to crystallize our feelings for one another. The previous eight years had been like a long prelude. They had been a series of opportunities to meet and explore each other's minds, as well as our buffed torsos. We had to be tempered in the fires of rejection and separation, and to be given a second chance, to realize that labels and names were unnecessary. Now, we could just be our true selves.

The 'near-death' experience had made us both realize that nothing is certain in this world, that our lives could be destroyed in a brief hour. This marriage, then, was our public declaration of who and what we were—two now mature, gay men who loved and needed one another. Now, we were members of more than one community. We were business professionals, homeowners, Leathermen, lovers, married people.

The setting was a beautifully-tended garden, bright with the spring flowers of Southern California. Framed within a black archway, on a high table stood two tall vases of white calla lilies, bound with a black leather cord [what else!]. We both spoke our vows loudly and clearly, without benefit of microphone, although I confess to being misty-eyed. We kissed each other tenderly and determinedly, as freshly-minted members of this new world.

Then, we turned and mingled with our guests. There were four beaming Masters of the Circle, resplendent in black leather, boots, and badged caps, including James, waiting to greet us first.

Paul's sister Ellen with the almost brand-new baby and husband John in tow, a sprinkling of my celebrity clients being gracious and unassuming, partners and associates from Paul's design company, and my law practice, friends like Tim Bronson, our horse master, and Walt, the owner of Paul's favorite leather bar and early sanctuary. There were Masters, boys, and even slaves from both our previous lives. Everyone seemed delighted to be part of a less conventional commitment ceremony.

I looked out and, standing uncertainly on the sidelines, was my handsome Slaveroger. I beckoned. He loped over, sliding gracefully down on one knee to kiss my boots and then my hand in public. I pulled him back to his feet and gave him a full-throated kiss. Then he went over to do the same to Paul.

This made me pause for a moment, letting the festivities wash around me. I needed Paul as my partner and lover, yet I also wanted a slave like Roger, a submissive man whom I could train slowly and painfully to respond to my needs, sexual and domestic. Yes, I could hire someone to clean the house and cook our meals, yet it was much more than that. I required a man whom I could control and dominate in ways different from my relationship with my partner. There had to be a slave regularly in the training process for my pleasures, hard and demanding as they may be. That was part of my core, my essence, my very being, if you will. I knew that I was not complete without a slave to service me or on my boots. Roger was that man-slave.

Paul had some of the same needs, though he did not seem to require the 24/7 attentions that I craved. He could be happy with a weekend boy, a trained sub who was regularly available. That afternoon I remembered that no such person was presently part of his existence. Rufusboy was gone with no regrets. I was happy with Slaveroger, but Paul was on his own in this regard, and had to be needing.

As the celebration wore down, we noticed the CHP officers sitting near their bikes in the shade. So we both walked over to thank them and to invite them to have some food and champagne. The drink was politely refused, but they were pleased to try the wedding cake. I led the way to the food tables with the younger officer while Paul came behind with the sergeant.

Only later did I find out what they talked about.

"We do appreciate your help and service this afternoon, sergeant. Sergeant Fitzgerald, I gather from your name tag?"

"Yes, Sir, it's our pleasure. I think this is the first gay wedding I've attended, at least in a professional capacity."

"Well, it's the first I've attended, too, and it was my own."

Both Paul and Fitzgerald chuckled and that broke the ice. They checked each other out casually and liked what they saw. The sergeant was tall and well-built, dark-haired, and probably of Irish ancestry. He filled out his well-tailored CHP uniform very nicely with a tight bubble-butt and highly spit-shined boots. Paul thought they were both about the same age and decided to take a gamble.

"So, you take an active part in gay life, sergeant?"

"Yes, Sir, I'm out, and proud of it. And I admire what you've just done, Sir."

"Thank you. It can't be easy in law enforcement, even these days?"

"Can't complain, Sir. Though I don't mix my pleasure with my job. So the guys don't really bother me, once they get the message I can fucking well look after myself."

"I'm sure you can with those muscles, Fitzgerald. Let's talk again, soon."

And Paul quietly reached out to grope the package in those tight khaki breeches.

"Hell, Sir, you just got married!"

Paul laughed, "And Tarquin will always be my partner. However, I also need to train and enjoy a boy, as well. I have a healthy libido. Well, we better catch up with the others."

The sergeant looked startled for a moment, and then slowly

smiled.

"Sir, yes, Sir. I'd like to get to know you better, Sir."

So, Paul was doubly content; he was officially married to the man he loved, and he had made a fresh boy connection.

Our honeymoon was a few days in Paul's Palm Springs house. We hadn't been back since January and were determined to overcome the specter of death that hung over it in our minds. That was not easy, still we worked at removing the shadow of Rufusboy. We fucked in the pool, sucked each other off on the surrounding decking, and then lay on the master bed, playing with one another's bodies. We refused to answer cell phones, pagers, or emails so we could spend the time getting thoroughly reacquainted, each with the other man who was so important in his life. Then feeling refreshed and renewed, we set off to return to everyday life in LA.

The freeway traffic was unusually busy. Sure enough, we encountered the inevitable driver who thought the road was made for him, alone, as we got close to Los Angeles. A white Hummer3 danced back and forth round Paul's Escalade. Then, the driver darted into what he apparently thought was an empty space and smashed into the rear of a smaller Honda Accord. Almost instantly, there were another couple of fender-benders as cars screeched to a stop. Paul managed to get to the shoulder without any damage other than a bruised wrist on me.

He turned the engine off and climbed out of the car to see if he could help. I felt dizzy, but got out my cell to call for assistance. I was amazed at how quickly two CHP motor officers arrived, soon followed by a patrol car, all with lights flashing.

They rapidly took charge of the incident, helping the Honda driver out of her car, then checking the Hummer driver who was pacing up and down, shouting into his cell. I saw Paul talking to one of the booted officers, who was asking questions and making notes. Then they got the traffic flow started again. Paul was back in the car, clutching a business card.

"I've just met Sergeant Fitzgerald again; you remember the hunky gay motor cop from our wedding? Tarquin, he remembered me. We didn't really have much time to talk, so he's given me his card and I've invited him over to the house for a drink in a couple of days, when he's off duty. Fuck, maybe I'll get lucky enough to find me a new, mature, sane, and reliable boy to train."

He bubbled over with excitement most of the way home, and fortunately there were no more traffic accidents. That decided me that this was the moment to ask about Rufusboy.

"I honestly don't know what's happened to the bastard, Tarquin. I don't care very much either. He seems to have disappeared after his 'accident.' I actually talked to James about him and even he's not certain.

"It looks as though he's gone back to Britain for good. After the surgery to try to repair his testicles, which James paid for incidentally, the network wanted him to do publicity for the *Spycatcher* series. He claimed he was still wounded, and too ill to work on "such minor things." That pissed them off. So the show opened without much attention to the leading man. Anyway, it doesn't seem to be getting much of an audience and hasn't been renewed."

"Well, he will be no great loss to this entertainment industry. I doubt he will get invited back here any time soon."

We finished the drive back home with one boy eliminated and the possibility of a welcome replacement for Paul.

It was now almost six months since Slaveroger had appeared on our doorstep. Much more than slave training had happened during his probation period. Indeed. Slaveroger's probation had not followed the pattern of his predecessors, still I knew he was getting anxious about his future. He worked out long and hard in our home gym so that his buffed body was now in almost perfect physical condition. From my point of view, there was no doubt that I would keep him, although he still needed further training in the arts of pleasing me. However, for him, there was uncertainty. He had said several times that his life now was to be devoted to servicing me, and we both believed that. Still there was always the initial threat that, after six months, I could throw him out into the street. That, for him, would mean out of the country and the probability of never seeing me again.

I decided to end his misery.

"This is almost the end of your probation period, Slaveroger. Put your mind at rest. I am going to keep you for further training. How could I do otherwise with the man who saved my life? Now you get to say whether you want to stay on."

"With all its heart, Sir. it feels it has so much more to learn from you, Sir, to practice giving you proper service and to satisfy your needs."

"Very well, we are agreed. I will make you my property and take you as my permanent slave. You know there is a ceremony of submission and what that involves?"

"Sir, Yes, Sir. Master Paul kindly answered its questions about his brand, and it hopes that you will mark it too, permanently as property."

"Tonight, in the dungeon, you will be thoroughly fucked and then branded as mine on your right asscheek. Paul has agreed to take part. Make certain you clean yourself thoroughly, inside and out."

It was to be a solemn occasion for all three of us. Paul was the only other man who proudly wore my emblem burnt into his body; other slaves had failed to make that final grade. My new slave was naturally concerned since that was a high ideal to live up to.

Both Masters wore chaps, harness, gloves, and tall boots in honor of the ceremony. We assembled in the dungeon; Slaveroger had come down earlier to prepare himself and the equipment. He was kneeling, naked and quivering, alongside the fucking bench.

"Now, slave, hoist up your equipment and get over to the bench where you will be properly restrained for a good fucking. Also, I'm going to properly hood and gag you for later."

He obeyed promptly enough, though the sweat broke out when he straddled the bench. As I fastened him down tightly, I looked at my slave carefully to see what we had accomplished during his probation. His pecs and abs had become better defined with daily exercise; his nipples now stood out proudly with their gold rings.

The white gold flashed on his thick collar and the full-strength PA on an excited penis which seemed to have grown and strengthened. Weights had helped to bulk up his arms and shoulders, while cardio work had strengthened his legs. All in all, he truly was a handsome, desirable, tanned piece of man-meat lying there waiting. My cock jumped in anticipation.

I rolled the rubber over it, since I didn't want any cum or shit in the area I was going to mark shortly. Then I told Slaveroger to raise his head for the hood and gag. I heard a small sigh of satisfaction, I hoped, as I spread the leather over his face and pushed the leather penis into his mouth. Then, I tightened the laces and zipped the outer layer closed. After I had checked his breathing, his head bowed down submissively to his Master.

My man-pike was now more than ready, as I spread some lube over the condom. His rosebud hole was twitching expectantly. I could see that he had greased himself well ahead of time. So, I shoved in my cockhead. We both grunted with satisfaction. By this time, I had widened his passage, though not too much. It was more enjoyable to penetrate him slowly, to enjoy the sensation of his muscles working to receive me. I pushed further, forcing his channel to accept my cock as it slithered along.

He began to pant as well as perspire heavily, while I could feel his ass muscles expanding and contracting around my pole. I snarled as I rammed home the rest of my eight inches. A snort came from beneath the hood as we began to work together, with the steady movement of muscles and slick shining sweat. He began to hump back to keep me firmly inside him. Equally determined, I would slide down to his entrance and then back up again.

Sweat began to drip off me onto his back as I leaned over him. My gloved hands reached round to tug on his tit rings. He tried to rear up, demanding cock. I forced him back down to dance to my tune. We were both growling and panting, two men in heavy man-sex battle-heat. My butt muscles propelled me further in, as he eagerly devoured every inch.

I could feel the orgasm building, so I gave that wonderful full-fuck thrust. Even with rubber on, I could feel my seed spurting into the tip. Slaveroger hunched and humped. He then rose to spurt his own cum over his stomach.

I stayed in him for a few minutes, both of us coming down with endorphins flying, while I calmed the slave beneath me. He was now ready, pumped up for the ultimate ceremony.

Paul had turned on the electric branding iron. Now, he helped me to bind a squirming Slaveroger very firmly in place, especially round the waist and upper right leg. I talked quietly and soothingly into the leather-hooded head that was shaking with fear, excitement, as well as exhaustion from the fierce fuck he had endured. I had stoppered his hole with a butt plug momentarily, and then swabbed the right asscheek and allowed the alcohol to dry.

Then, Paul handed me the glowing iron before going to take hold of one of the slave's big, sweaty paws. I ran my thickly-gloved hand over the trembling torso. I pulled his asscheek fully open.

The branding took less than two minutes. I pressed the iron down firmly into the space I wanted. Flesh sizzled as I pushed further. A scream came around the gag and hood; I waited a further ten seconds and then pulled the iron straight up, turning it off at the same moment.

The mark was excellent, crisp and deep—a solid circle with a Roman T at its center. I was pleased with my efforts; this was not something I did exactly every day. Then the burn was rapidly covered with calming ointment. Paul was loosening the hood and the ropes, but not yet allowing Slaveroger to move off the bench. I stood over him, muttering soothing comments on his bravery and courage for half an hour. Then I added some more burn liniment and a soft gauze pad before I encouraged my slave to slowly stand up. I put Slaveroger's arms round my neck and held him close against me. His heart was still beating rapidly, and sweat was streaking down his body. He was whimpering from the pain, so I murmured more words of praise and endearment into his ears. Slowly he came back to me. The whimpering gradually changed to whispers of "Master, it thanks you, my true Master."

Slaveroger was now mine, my property with my brand burning

his butt, my slave with my thick gold chain collar, the heaviest PA and gold tit rings, mine to train, to cherish, to keep and, above all, to protect. A man could not ask for more.

I turned and smiled at Paul, as the doorbell rang upstairs.

"That will be my CHP sergeant, as ordered, and in uniform, I hope. Will you need the dungeon much longer tonight, Tarquin? I've some lessons to give this evening, too."

We looked at one another and laughed. There was so much more of life awaiting us and we wanted to experience it, all of us together.

ABOUT THE AUTHOR

OBSESSION — LEATHER MASTERS and slaves — is the eagerly awaited conclusion [for the present] to Alex Ironrod's highly successful trilogy of BDSM novels about Tarquin and Paul, their slaves and boys, their friends and their enemies, beginning with SUBMISSION - LEATHER MASTERS and slaves and then DOMINATION – LEATHER MASTERS and slaves in new, substantially revised editions.

He also has another series – about two LAPD detectives and their relationship – Mark and Dan, beginning with LEATHER NIGHTS and LEATHER DAYS. The two heroes then moved to Palm Springs as Private Investigators in DECEPTION-PALM SPRINGS and CAGES- CATHEDRAL CITY. Next will come POSSESSION-PALM DESERT, Part 1 – SLAVE JOURNEY later this year.

Alex has also written two gay BDSM historical stories – RED KNIGHT RISING, set in the time of the Crusades and the new THE MAN & THE MASK, which starts in the bawdy England of the 1750s before moving to the "American Colonies" of the 1760s.

He has had his two collections of Leather short stories published — THE IRONROD CHRONICLES PART I and PART II and, most recently, a novella, THE TRAINER. He welcomes all comments on the results to date at alexironrod@aol.com. Details of all his books can also be found on his web site www.alexironrod.com and are available from Amazon.com, Barnes & Noble.com and gay book stores everywhere.

Alex is the pen and play name of a mature Leatherman, who grew up in the north of England and has lived for many years in Southern California.

His boots and leather fetishes go back to his teenage years, but only recently has he started to use them as a spur for stories.

Now semi-retired, he relishes life as an author, a working theatre actor/director, a researcher and a member of several charitable boards. He's more or less given up horseback riding, although he still enjoys working out at the gym.

Most importantly, Alex values his relationship with his wonderful husband Michael, while enjoying the camaraderie and support of LGBTQ and straight friends across the world. He's still working on improving his Leather topping skills with the active support of a number of generous bottoms.

Next Alex will be editing a collaborative autobiography with a well-known male porn star, COLE TUCKER. He hopes readers and friends will stick around for these and many more.

He plans to catch up with you all at the next MAL, CLAW, IML, Dore Alley or Palm Springs Leather Weekend in full Leather and tall boots.